GW00391608

Citrus Blossom

Sarah Pond

Citrus Blossom
Copyright Sarah Pond 2016

Paperback edition November 2017

This is a work of fiction. All of the characters and
events described in this novel are products of the
author's imagination. Any resemblance to actual events
or persons, living or dead, is purely coincidental.

This book may not be reproduced or used in whole
or part without written permission of the author.

Cover design by Janet Nethercott-Cable

~~~~~

For the girl who didn't think she could, and never
dreamed she would

~~~~~

PROLOGUE

She didn't know when it started, when things had changed. Had there been signs, and she had been too caught up in other things to see them... Maybe it was just a phase, or was she starting to lose it? Or maybe she was beginning to find herself. Perhaps she could just give in to it, let herself go...

ONE

Not so long ago things were different, they seemed more straightforward. As a child, Olivia loved to read. Her parents would often find her curled up on her bed or the sofa, with her nose in a book. Her green eyes would occasionally look over the top, she would smile at them, then carry on reading, her long brown hair falling over her face. She loved to get lost in stories of other people and far away places, and the adventures that they would have. Olivia had been a good student, and did well at school and college. She decided not to go to university in favour of getting into the 'real world' of work and earning a living. She had been working in her friend Becky's art gallery in St Ives, Cornwall for nearly four years. Olivia had loved working there, but now she was ready to spread her wings. She had always had a yearning to go to London. Olivia and her boyfriend Liam had broken up a few months ago, mutually deciding that although they really cared about each other, that something extra wasn't there anymore. Olivia would often talk about moving to London. Liam thought that it was quite amusing, usually you would hear about people wanting to do it the other way around, like her parents had done, moving away from London for a quieter life.

Olivia had applied for three jobs, and the one that really attracted her was at the small publishing company in Cavendish Square, not far from Oxford Circus. She didn't want to work for a big faceless company, but somewhere smaller where things were more hands on. The company were looking for an assistant for one of the partners. If Olivia got the job, she would begin by doing general office duties, taking on more responsibility as she gained experience.

At twenty two years old, Olivia was really ready to begin living a more independent life. She knew that moving to London from Cornwall would be a real change of culture, and although it was rather daunting, it was also one of the things that excited her about it. When Olivia was a child, she used to dream of working in London, the buzz and excitement. Her family had originally lived in Middlesex, and her Dad had worked in central London, travelling by tube from Pinner every day. Once she and her brother Ben were born, her parents had wanted a change of pace, and moved the family down to Cornwall when she was two years old, and her brother was four. Olivia had very fond memories of growing up in Cornwall, with what seemed like endless summers on the beach. Living in St Ives, Olivia and Ben had grown up with a familiar community of people around them, and it seemed that everyone knew everyone else.

Olivia turned up ten minutes before her interview with Jason Albright and Jasmine Carter, who ran JJ Publishing. She had decided to wear a black trouser suit for her interview, hoping that she looked smart and professional enough. Olivia was welcomed in by a lady who introduced herself as Laura, Jason's assistant. Olivia thought that she was probably in her early thirties at a guess. Laura had short, dark brown hair, and grey eyes. She seemed very friendly, and Olivia found herself wondering how long she had worked there. Laura asked, 'Would you like a drink? We have tea, coffee, water or juice.'

'No thank you, I'm fine.'

Olivia had remembered some advice that she was given when she was at college. If you accept a drink, with a bag or case in one hand, and holding a drink in the other, you wouldn't be able to shake hands with anyone. Also, she was still feeling nervous, and she couldn't trust her hands not to shake whilst she tried to drink it. She would treat herself to a coffee at this lovely cafe she had recently found, just around the corner from the office, if the interview went well. Or if it didn't.

Olivia had tied her hair back in a ponytail, and when some loose strands slipped down, she nervously tucked them behind her ear. Laura offered her a seat, and she sat down and waited in the reception area, taking in her surroundings. The office was a large open plan area, with a blue sofa, the one that she was sitting on, in front of which was a large wooden coffee table, with magazines strewn across it. There were bookcases on the opposite wall, crammed full. Then there was Laura's desk, and next to it, an empty desk, which would hopefully be hers if all went well. Opposite the desks were two offices, presumably one for each of the partners. Laura chatted to Olivia, asking about her journey, and how far she had travelled. Olivia liked Laura, and immediately felt comfortable with her.

The door to the office on the left opened, and a friendly face appeared. The man was probably in his late twenties, and clean-shaven. He was slim, and wearing jeans, with a blue open neck shirt and a tweed jacket. He had soft wavy light auburn hair, and a twinkle in his pale blue eyes. Olivia liked him immediately. He walked over to the sofa, hand outstretched towards Olivia, and she stood up. 'Hi, you must be Olivia. I'm Jason, thank you for coming, and being so prompt. Come through to my office.'

Olivia rose, and shook his hand, glad she hadn't accepted a drink. 'Yes, thank you,' and followed Jason into the office.

'Do take a seat.' Jason gestured to the comfy looking chair opposite his desk. His office had a cosy feel about it, with books and papers everywhere. It was lived-in rather than untidy, and had an old-book smell to it, reminding Olivia of a second hand book shop.

'Jasmine will be here in a moment, we're joint business partners, as I think you already know. Laura has been working for both of us, and we have had temporary help in as and when we needed to. We really need someone full time now to work with Jasmine, although we all muck in together when we have a lot of work on.'

'I like the fact that it's a small office. I've been used to just two of us working at the gallery,' Olivia said as she sat down.

The chair was very comfortable, and Olivia was beginning to relax a little. She became aware of a movement behind her, and turned to see a striking woman walking into the office. She was quite tall and slim, with long dark wavy hair and dark brown eyes. Her skin had a sun kissed glow about it. Wearing a tailored navy trouser suit and white blouse, she exuded class and beauty as she walked gracefully across the office. The woman was probably a similar age to Jason, maybe a bit older. Olivia began to feel nervous again, and stood up as the woman walked towards her.

'Hello, I'm Jasmine, you must be Olivia.' As she shook Olivia's hand, Olivia was aware of Jasmine's hand feeling soft and warm, and she flushed, aware that her hands were sweaty from nerves. 'Please, do sit down again. Sorry I'm a bit late, I got caught up reading a manuscript.' She smiled warmly, and Olivia began to relax again.

They asked Olivia about college, working at the art gallery in Cornwall, and why she wanted to move to London. Jason asked why she particularly wanted to work for JJ Publishing.

Olivia explained that as much as she loved Cornwall, she was ready for some new experiences, and how as a child she had wanted to come to London. She talked about how she loved working with her friend Becky, and how much experience she had gained working there. She got to meet artists, and help them promote their work. For some time now, though, she had had a calling to move away, and it was London that she was drawn to. Voicing this dream, Olivia hoped that Jason and Jasmine wouldn't think that she was chasing a childish dream. On the contrary, they saw her determination and dedication, and appreciated her honesty. Jasmine noticed that Olivia was nervous, her hands fidgeting in her lap, until she talked about her friend, and moving to London. Then, the nervousness gave way to passion about her ambitions, and she emanated a different kind of energy, her face lighting up as she spoke.

Olivia went on to explain that she would love to work with a publisher, as she loved books. 'I love the idea of creating something that starts out as an author's idea, and develops into a book, which can be read and shared by an infinite amount of people.' She paused for a moment, before continuing, her eyes shining, 'It's a bit like artists bringing their work into the gallery.

Something that started out as a thought in the artist's mind, taking a physical form that can be appreciated by others. '

As Olivia spoke, Jason and Jasmine exchanged a look, and smiled. Olivia noticed their exchanged glance, and guessed that they were good friends. The whole office had a comfortable feel about it. This is somewhere I'd really love to work, thought Olivia.

When the interview came to an end, they all stood, and Jason shook her hand, thanking her for coming along. Then Jasmine shook Olivia's hand, and with her left hand touched Olivia's arm, saying, 'It was such a pleasure to meet you. We'll have a chat and let you know very soon. Thank you.'

Laura showed Olivia to the door, and she stepped outside into the fresh air. The June sunshine felt warm on her face, and was perfectly offset by a gentle breeze. Looking at her watch, Olivia was delighted to see that well over an hour had gone by, although it hadn't felt like it. She knew this to be a good sign, unlike a previous interview which had finished after just over twenty minutes. She knew that she wasn't going to get that job.

After Olivia had left, Jasmine sat back in her chair. She knew immediately that Olivia was the person for the job. She was so passionate, so fresh. The way that she had spoken about books and paintings starting as a thought had really touched her. Jason called Laura into the office so that they could all have a chat. Jasmine asked Laura what she thought of Olivia. Laura said that she liked her, and thought that she would fit in well. Jason agreed, Olivia was by far the best person who had applied for the job. There had been a couple of people with experience in publishing, but they didn't have the passion that Olivia had. So it was decided, Olivia would be offered the job.

As she had promised herself, Olivia walked along the road and headed towards Joe's Cafe. In addition to a large latte, Olivia thought a chocolate brownie would be a lovely treat. Having collected her coffee, she found a little table where she could sit and go over the interview. On the whole, she thought it had gone well, although she had been rather nervous. She was sure that they would take that into consideration, though. She really liked everyone there, which was obviously a big bonus. As this was the third and final interview for the time being, she was going back home in a couple of days. This week she had been staying at her friend's flat. Emma had a great place, not far from Bond Street tube station. Emma's last roommate was a journalist who had moved out to go travelling, which was perfect timing. It had been fun catching up with Emma. Having moved to London straight from college, Emma said that she would be able to help Olivia settle in.

Emma and Olivia had met at college. They had become firm friends when they both realised that they loved the same kind of music, particularly Pink. They would play her albums at full blast, singing along at the top of their voices, then roll around in fits of giggles. At college, Emma had a succession of boyfriends, and Olivia found it hard to keep up with her and who she was dating. As soon as Emma had left college, she had applied for jobs in London. Then she got a job at an advertising agency, just as she'd always said she that she would. In the four years that she had been there, she had progressed swiftly. She was intelligent, full of great ideas and very outgoing. She was popular with her colleagues and worked hard. Emma found her job fun, but it could also be quite pressured, and she found physical exercise a great way of letting off steam, which kept her fit as well. The gym was good for meeting people too, and there were plenty of guys who liked to keep in good shape. With her blond wavy hair, beautiful blue eyes and lovely figure, not to mention her outgoing personality, she was always getting attention from guys. Her current boyfriend was a really nice guy called Matt, who she had met at the gym a few weeks ago.

It was now Thursday, and tomorrow Olivia would be heading back to St Ives. She couldn't stop thinking about the publishing job, though. Olivia wanted it so much, the thought of it gave her butterflies. As she and Emma were walking through Covent Garden, arms linked together, she heard her phone ringing. 'Hello, Olivia speaking.'

'Hi, it's Jasmine, from JJ Publishing,' Olivia's stomach began twisting with anxiety, now was the moment of truth. 'We would like to offer you the job. Would you like to think about it?'

'No. Yes. I mean yes, please, I'd love to take the job, thank you, this is wonderful,' Olivia said excitedly, her face beaming.

'That's wonderful,' said Jasmine warmly, 'In that case, we just need to go through some details, and sort out your start date. Are you are able to pop into the office, so we can go through everything in person?'

'Yes, of course. I was going to be travelling home tomorrow afternoon, but I can change that.'

'Well, how about tomorrow at ten?'

'That would be perfect. Thank you, thank you so much.'

'Until tomorrow, then. Goodbye, Olivia.' Olivia put her phone back in her bag, practically jumping for joy. Emma hugged her, Olivia laughing, thinking that this was one of the best moments in her life.

Emma said, 'Right, time to celebrate! I'm treating you to dinner, there's a great Mexican restaurant just around the corner. They do the best fajitas ever!'

Jasmine put the phone down, smiling to herself. Olivia was so natural and free, no pretence. She was an honest and genuine person, that had come through clearly at the interview, as had her sincerity and passion. Yes, it was going to be great working with Olivia, Jasmine was really looking forward to it.

The Mexican restaurant was a really cosy and vibrant place, painted in warm, bright colours, with a wonderful atmosphere. The bar was on the right as you walked in, with the restaurant at the back. The aroma emanating from the open kitchen was warm and wonderful, and made Olivia's mouth water. There was a painting of a mermaid on the whole of one wall, and pictures everywhere. There were not many dining tables, but fortunately Emma and Olivia were able to get one. They both ordered chicken fajitas, on Emma's recommendation. Emma said, 'I think we should have cocktails. What do you fancy?'

Emma chose a margarita, and Olivia plumped for a pina colada. When the drinks arrived, Emma raised her glass, 'A toast, to your new job and a new life in London.'

'Thank you.' They clinked glasses, and Olivia took a sip of her cocktail. 'Um, delicious. I hope everything here tastes this good!'

'So, what's your new boss like, then?'

'Well there are two, Jason and Jasmine are partners. Laura works for Jason, and she will be teaching me the job. She seems really nice, very friendly. I think she's been there quite a long time, they all seem to get on very well together. I liked Jason the moment I met him. He's got twinkly eyes, I think it will be fun working with him. His office is very messy, with books and manuscripts all over the place. I felt like I'd walked into one of the teachers' rooms at Hogwarts! He's probably in his late twenties too, but he has a mix of maturity and boyishness. I'll be working for Jasmine, once I know what I'm doing. She seems really nice too, and very pretty. She really looks at you when she's talking to you, she makes you feel important.'

Emma smiled, 'That sounds brilliant. It also sounds like you've got a bit of a crush on Jason!'

'No, don't be silly. He just really nice, that's all.' Olivia blushed.

Emma laughed. 'Anyway, I'm so pleased you've got this job. It's going to be brilliant fun having you as a flat mate.'

They had a great evening, Emma telling Olivia about the clubs and bars they could go to, although that wasn't really Olivia's scene. Still, she wanted to have some new experiences, so she could give it a go. Olivia was looking forward to going to films and concerts, as there would be a lot more choice here in London than she was used to back home. 'Thank you so much Emma. You've been amazing, putting me up, helping me get around.'

'It's a pleasure. It's been great spending time with you again. I'll have to ask Matt if he has any friends we can set you up with, just in case Jason isn't available!'

It was ten to ten on Friday morning, and Olivia was just approaching the office of JJ Publishing. She was so excited, and also rather nervous. Laura greeted her when she arrived, and showed her to Jasmine's office.

She offered Olivia a drink, and this time she accepted, asking for a coffee. Jasmine's office was quite different to Jason's cosy office. It was tidy and had a light wooden desk, with cream chairs on either side, and a cream sofa at the side, in front of a bookcase. It smelt fresh, with an almost indiscernible fragrance of citrus and flowers. Jasmine stood as Olivia entered, and they shook hands. 'Thank you for coming in this morning, I do appreciate it.'

Olivia was beaming, 'The pleasure is mine, I was thrilled when you offered me the job. I'm so excited, out of the interviews I had, this was the job that I really wanted.'

Jasmine smiled back, 'You are certainly the most enthusiastic applicant we had! To be honest, we knew there and then at the interview that we wanted you. Please, take a seat.'

Jasmine explained that the purpose of the visit was to arrange a start date, sign her contract, and get Olivia's bank details to pay her salary. They sat across the desk from one another, then Laura brought the drinks in. She gave Olivia her coffee, and a cup of tea to Jasmine. Jasmine and Olivia both thanked Laura, and she smiled as she left the office. Jasmine and Olivia went through the paperwork and arranged a start date of fifteenth of June. Olivia was thinking that this would give her a week to go home, pack up what she needed, and get back to London again. She wouldn't need many things as the room in Emma's flat was fully furnished. It would mostly be clothes, really. She looked up to see Jasmine looking at her, and blushed. 'Sorry, I was just thinking about all the things I've got to do in the next week.'

Jasmine smiled kindly, 'Yes, it's going to be quite a change for you. If you want any help at all getting settled in, you will just ask, won't you?'

'Thank you, that's very kind of you. Emma, my old college friend, has been great, helping me get around. Our flat is nice and close for work, too.'

'Well, I think that's everything for now. Do you have any questions, Olivia?'

'I don't think so at the moment.' Her mind was still buzzing with excitement.

'Well, if you think of anything, just give us a call. I hope your trip back to Cornwall goes well. I'm so looking forward to having you here, you're going to fit in perfectly.' She looked Olivia in the eye as she smiled, shaking hands with her.

Jasmine walked Olivia to the door and as they were saying their goodbyes, Jason appeared at his office door. 'Olivia, wonderful. I'm so pleased you've accepted the job. Welcome on board!'

'Thank you, I'm really looking forward to it.' Olivia smiled at Jason.

With his twinkling eyes and ruffled hair, he had the air of a mischievous schoolboy. Yes, Olivia was going to enjoy working here.

TWO

From the office, Olivia set off to catch the train to Cornwall. It wasn't far to walk to Oxford Circus tube station, and it was only a few stops on the Bakerloo line to Paddington. The long part was the train journey to St Erth, which took nearly five hours, before the short train ride from there to St Ives. Olivia had books to read and music to listen to, to pass the time. She also enjoyed looking out of the window and watching the world go by. Arriving at Paddington, she found her train and sat down next to the window. The train was due to leave soon, so Olivia put her bag on the overhead rack, keeping her book and train ticket handy. She had bought some lunch from a sandwich bar on the concourse to eat on the journey. The train jolted slightly as it pulled away from the station, heading home. Well, what was home for the last twenty years. Soon her home would be in London, and this exciting thought gave her butterflies in her stomach.

Whilst the train made its way out of Paddington, Olivia began to think about the people she would be leaving behind when she moved to London. Her best friend, Becky, was still running her own gallery. Olivia and Becky had been friends since they were very young children, and they lived just a few doors away from one another. It had been fabulous working together at the gallery. Olivia got to meet lots of artists and really interesting people. But as much as she enjoyed it, Olivia knew that it was time to move on. It would be very easy to stay in St Ives, which she did love dearly, but she had been getting itchy feet for a while now. Becky said there would always be a job for her at the gallery if she wanted it. Olivia liked knowing that she could come back if she wanted to. Knowing that Olivia would soon be leaving, Becky had reluctantly started looking for someone to take over Olivia's job, although she was hoping that going to London would be a short term thing. There was a woman called Lucy who would often pop by the gallery, and when she heard that Becky might be looking for someone to take over from Olivia, asked if she could be considered.

Olivia's thoughts turned to Liam. They had met when they were sixteen. She and Becky had gone to the cinema to see Harry Potter and the Half Blood Prince. They came out of the cinema, eagerly talking about the film. They noticed a couple of boys hanging around, then saw them coming over to talk to them. 'Hi, what did you think of the film?' asked Liam, looking at Olivia. He was blond, quite well built, and had a very boyish face.

'I really enjoyed it. Who would have thought that about Professor Snape. The films are getting pretty dark now,' Olivia replied, feeling self conscious, as Liam looked at her.

Liam and his friend Dan introduced themselves to the girls, and invited them to go for a milkshake at a nearby cafe. The girls were excited, and Liam and Dan, trying not to show it, felt really nervous. They made their way to the cafe, ordered their drinks and sat down. They chatted a lot about films to start with. Dan worked at the cinema at weekends, so got to see nearly all of the new films. He knew a lot of film trivia, and before they knew it, they had been at the cafe for over two hours. Olivia thought that Liam had a gentle way about him which she really liked. Dan was more outgoing, and he and Becky seemed to really hit it off. Olivia could see Becky's eyes shining whilst she looked at him, hanging on his every word, and he looked equally smitten with her.

Within a few weeks, the four of them had become firm friends, and hung out together after college and at weekends as much as they could. Becky was at art school now, and Olivia was doing A levels in English language, literature and art. Olivia, Liam and Becky would go to the cinema, and Dan would meet them after work. Becky and Dan were getting pretty serious now, they had really fallen for each other. Liam and Olivia were good friends, although Liam desperately wanted to be Olivia's boyfriend. He just wasn't sure how to ask her, and he didn't want to risk messing up their friendship. One day on their way home from the cinema, they stopped off at the beach, and sat down side by side. Olivia watched the sea rippling, listening to the gentle sound it made as it washed over the sand. Being by the water always relaxed her. They chatted about the film, and were laughing and playfully nudging each other. Then Liam, his heart beating so fast, bent down and kissed Olivia. To his relief, she kissed him back. Liam was over the moon, he had wanted to kiss Olivia for such a long time, and they had been friends for nearly two years. Olivia's lips felt so soft to Liam, he couldn't believe that this was finally happening. Olivia felt so comfortable with Liam, she wondered why they hadn't kissed before. They pulled away from each other, giggling. Ever since then, they had been pretty inseparable, along with Becky and Dan.

Over time though, as much as Olivia loved Liam, she had been talking about moving to London, it was something that she just knew that she had to do. Liam could see that she was getting restless, and didn't want her to stay because of him, and regret it later. He loved being in Cornwall, and Olivia knew that if she did go to London, it would be the end of their relationship. Liam was settled here, and it was too long a distance for a relationship to really work. It was because of this that she waited as long as she did to take the plunge and start applying for jobs in London. In the end it was Liam who suggested that they just be friends.

As the train pulled into the station, Olivia picked up her bag and looked out of the window. She could see her mum waiting for her on the platform. Getting off of the train, Olivia walked over to her mum, and they embraced warmly. 'Hi, Mum, it's great to see you. Thanks for picking me up.'

Ella smiled at her daughter, 'Hello darling, did you have a good journey here?'

'Yes, very good. I've been thinking on the way here about how different things are going to be, friends I'll be leaving behind. I'm going to miss everyone, but I know this is something I have to do.'

Her mum gave her another hug, 'You'll be fine, darling. And you know you can come back anytime you want to. So, tell me all about your new job.'

They made their way out of the station, Olivia chatting about the job, staying with Emma, and how excited she was about it all. Opening the front door, Ella called out, 'Steve, we're back!'

Olivia's dad walked into the hall, arms outstretched, 'Hello pumpkin,' and gave her a big warm hug. As long as Olivia could remember, her dad had nicknamed her 'pumpkin', and she loved this term of endearment.

'Hi Dad,' Olivia said as she hugged him back.

She had a close relationship with both of her parents, and knew that although they were very supportive of her, they would miss her once she moved to London. She probably would have moved out soon anyway, but to leave home and move to London at the same time was a pretty big step for her. Olivia took in the familiar feel of home, realising that this would be the last time that she would be here for a while. This cottage had always been home to her, as she was too young to remember the house in Pinner. The front door opened straight into the lounge, where there was a fireplace to the left. Although it was June, and the fire was not being used, there was still a faint and familiar smell of woodsmoke in the air. Around the large coffee table, there were two beige sofas opposite each other and a pale blue armchair facing the fireplace. The colours were all soft and washed out, giving the whole cottage an air of tranquility. There were stairs leading from the lounge up to the first floor, and straight ahead was the large kitchen diner, with a pine table in the middle where they ate their family meals, excitedly chattering about their day. Olivia took it all in, remembering many happy times here.

After the long journey, it was already early evening, and they sat down for dinner. Olivia's brother Ben had arrived, with his girlfriend Tina. 'Hi, Sis, how are you? Congratulations on the new job.'

'Thanks Ben, I'm so excited about it. I'm home for a week, then I'm getting the train back on Saturday.'

The family sat around the table together, asking Olivia about her few days in London, the job and her new colleagues. Olivia spoke animatedly about everything, and her parents were thrilled to see her so happy. After dinner, they decided on a game of Monopoly, happily chatting and laughing whilst they played. The family loved playing board games together. After this week, they probably wouldn't be getting together for a few months, so they all wanted to make the most of it.

On Saturday morning, Olivia was tucking into a cooked breakfast that her dad had made for her. She was going to be catching up with Becky, Dan and Liam today. They arranged to meet at the same cafe where they had gone for their first drink together. As Olivia walked in, she couldn't believe it had been nearly six years ago. Then, she was just beginning a friendship with Liam, now it had gone full circle, and they were back to being friends again. Olivia could see the others sitting at a table laughing away together, Becky and Dan snuggled up tightly next to each other. They were as head over heels in love as they had been since the beginning. Olivia smiled, feeling so happy seeing her friends together. And there was Liam, lovely, gentle Liam. The others looked up, and as they saw Olivia walking towards them, they jumped up to greet her, hugging her tightly. Becky wanted to know every last detail about Olivia's trip to London. When they got together like this, it was as if time had stood still, and they were teenagers again. Becky started teasing Liam, telling Olivia that Lucy, who would be taking over Olivia's job at the gallery, was often asking after Liam. 'I think she's got a bit of a thing for him,' she laughed. 'They did meet briefly at an event at the gallery one time.'

Liam replied, 'At the moment, I'm quite happy as I am, thank you.'

In truth, Liam wasn't ready to meet someone else yet, he was still getting over not being with Olivia. He hadn't really wanted to be the one who suggested just friendship, but could see it was inevitable. He knew Olivia was desperate to go to London, and as much as he wanted her to stay, he could see that she wasn't truly happy. Olivia hoped he would meet someone, he was a really sweet guy.

The friends spent the whole weekend together, going to the cinema, listening to music, and hanging out at the beach, just like old times. Olivia had a wonderful time. Although a part of her knew that she would be leaving behind something very special, she was really excited about the next part of her journey.

Over the next few days, Olivia sorted through her room. She decided to get rid of quite a few things, including some old clothes and toys, which she took to the local charity shop. Then she packed up two large suitcases to take to London. If she needed anything else, she could get it on her next visit.

It seemed that in no time at all, Saturday had arrived, and it was time to head back to London. Olivia said goodbye to her mum, dad, Ben and Tina at home. Ella said, 'Make sure you call us as soon as you've arrived safely.'

Olivia looked lovingly at her mum, 'Of course, Mum.'

They hugged and kissed in the hallway, then there was a knock at the door. Becky, Dan and Liam were driving Olivia to St Erth, so she wouldn't have to change trains with her luggage. They packed up the car, and headed off to the station. Olivia waved out of the car window until she couldn't see her parents any more. At the station, her friends helped Olivia onto the train with her bags. Olivia said, 'I'm really going to miss you guys.'

'Go get 'em,' said Dan, giving her a hug.

Liam pulled her into a big hug, saying, 'See you soon, special girl,' and kissed her.

Olivia looked at Becky, suddenly feeling very emotional. They hugged one another tightly. Becky, with a catch in her voice, said, 'Call me when you get home, okay?'

Olivia nodded, she couldn't speak for a moment. Then regaining herself, she boarded the train. 'I love you guys. See you soon.'

She waved through the window, and Becky, Dan and Liam waved and smiled back. Olivia sat down, pleased that the train wasn't busy. As she sat there, tears started rolling down her cheeks.

THREE

The train pulled into Paddington station. Whilst she waited for Emma, who was meeting her to help her with her cases, Olivia rang both her mum and Becky to let them know that she had arrived safely, and that Emma was meeting her there. 'I'll call you tomorrow, Mum. Love you.'

'I love you too, darling, bye,' and they hung up.

She looked up to see Emma and Matt walking towards her, waving and smiling. 'Hey, city girl! This is where your new life starts!' Emma laughed as she hugged Olivia.

What Olivia had no idea of, was just how much her life was going to change.

They made their way back to Emma's, and put Olivia's cases in her room. 'Matt is going to pop out and get a takeaway tonight. After your long journey, I thought you probably wouldn't fancy going out.'

Olivia said, 'That sounds perfect, thank you. I am really tired, it's been quite an emotional week, actually.'

Whilst Matt went out for the food, Emma started getting out plates and prepared some drinks, leaving Olivia to begin unpacking. Matt arrived back with the curry, and its fragrant smell was delicious. Olivia's rumbling stomach reminded her how hungry she was, and she decided that she had done enough for today. She would finish unpacking tomorrow, as she had all day. Emma asked, 'So how was your week back at home?'

'It was lovely, but it's really dawned on me that I'm actually doing this. Saying goodbye to my friends and family was hard. I know it's not like I won't see them anymore, it's just that now I've made the move, it all feels a bit real.'

Emma smiled. 'I know what you mean, it took me a bit of time to adjust when I first moved here. Before you know it, this will feel like home.'

Emma took Olivia's hand and squeezed it. Olivia smiled back at her friend, 'Thank you, you've been so great, letting me stay here, helping me to get settled.'

The three of them talked about the coming week and their plans, then Olivia said that she was going to go to bed, as she was exhausted. Matt started clearing up, and they said their good nights. Having got ready for bed, Olivia snuggled in under the covers. She was so tired, that sleep came almost immediately.

Waking up on Sunday morning, Olivia felt refreshed. She looked at the clock, and realised that she had slept until nearly eleven. Well, I obviously really needed that, she thought to herself. She got out of bed and wandered into the kitchen. Matt and Emma were in the lounge reading magazines, and as Olivia appeared, Matt looked up, 'Morning sleepyhead! Did you sleep well?'

Olivia stretched and smiled, 'As a matter of fact, I slept like the proverbial log! I feel much better today. Sorry, I probably wasn't much company last night. Thank you for the curry.'

Emma said, 'I'm glad you slept well. If you want any help unpacking today, just let me know.'

'Thank you, I think I'll be fine. It's mostly clothes, really.'

Olivia made herself some breakfast, and sat down to eat. She spent the day pottering around, unpacking and settling in properly. She put up some framed photographs. One of her favourite ones was of her and Becky on the beach at St Ives, which Becky had taken of them, arm outstretched with the camera turned towards them, laughing. Olivia smiled fondly at the memory. She decided to phone Becky, and let her know that she'd settled in. Then she rang her mum. So, this is it, Olivia thought to herself. Tomorrow, she would be starting her new job, and she was really looking forward to it.

Olivia set off to work on Monday morning, with butterflies in her stomach. She set out in plenty of time, and arrived at the office fifteen minutes early. Laura was already there, and greeted her warmly, 'Good morning, how are you?'

'Morning, I'm fine thanks. Well, a bit nervous to tell you the truth.'

Laura smiled, 'No need to be, I'll help you get settled right in.' Laura liked how honest Olivia was, she was sure that they would get along well. Olivia really appreciated Laura being so nice, and began to relax. 'First things first, would you like a drink?'

'Not at the moment, thank you.'

'Okay, well we have a little fridge here with juice and milk in it. We can make tea and coffee here, but it's only instant. When we fancy something a bit nicer, one of us will pop to the cafe around the corner,' explained Laura.

Laura showed Olivia the basics of the job to get started, saying that she would pick up a lot as she went along. The door opened, and Olivia looked up to see Jasmine, followed by Jason, walking into the office. 'Good morning, ladies,' said Jason.

Jasmine smiled, 'Hi, did you have a good weekend?'

Laura replied, 'Lovely, thank you, did you?'

'Yes I did, thank you. How was your week back home, Olivia?' Jasmine asked.

'It was lovely. It still hasn't quite sunk in that I've made the move. I feel like it's just temporary, it's a strange feeling.'

Jasmine said, 'If you need to talk any time, or need some time to yourself whilst you adjust, come and talk to me.'

Jason smiled at Olivia, 'If there's anything you need, we'll do what we can to help you feel at home.'

Olivia suddenly felt very emotional. She really appreciated how nice they were all being. 'Thank you, you're all so kind,' she said, clearing her throat.

Jasmine and Jason went into their offices, leaving Laura to continue showing Olivia what to do. The time flew by, and at eleven o'clock, Laura declared it was time for a break. 'Let's pop to the coffee shop for a drink. I'll let the guys know that we're popping out. Also, you'll know where the cafe is when you fancy something different or want some lunch,' explained Laura.

They walked along the road, then Olivia saw the cafe that they were heading for. 'Oh, I know this place, it's Joe's cafe. I came here after my interview, it's lovely.'

Laura laughed, 'Well, that was a good sign then! As it's your first day, we'll have a drink inside. Usually, I take the drinks back to the office. I told Jason and Jasmine that we'd take something back for them.'

They ordered their drinks, and went and sat at a corner table. Olivia asked how long Laura had worked at JJ Publishing. 'Since they started it up, four years ago. It used to be just me, and over the years it has got busier. We have had some help here and there, and now we thought it would be good to have another person full time. It's great for me, having someone to work with, as well as to share the workload!'

Olivia said, 'It's such a lovely atmosphere in the office, you all seem to be good friends.'

'Yes, we do get along well. Of course, we've all been together since the beginning. The only time there was any issue was when we had some of our temporary help. That's why it was important to get the right kind of person, and that all of us made the decision of who to hire,' Laura smiled at Olivia.

Olivia asked, 'I know this might sound a bit nosy, but are Jason and Jasmine an item? I noticed that they came in together today.'

'No, they're not. They are friends, and get on very well together though. They met at university, and that's where they had the idea to start up a business together. Jason has had a few girlfriends, but I think he's single at the moment. Jasmine is so involved with her work, I don't think she has time for dating.'

As they finished their drinks, it was time to get back to the office. Laura picked up a caramel latte for Jason and a tea for Jasmine, and they headed back.

Olivia's first week flew by, and before she knew it, it was Friday. She had found it very busy, but had really enjoyed it. Each evening she had been tired, as there was such a lot to take in. She had constantly had to check things with Laura, who was very patient and helpful. That morning, Jasmine walked over to Olivia's desk with some letters to type up. She noticed the photo of Olivia and Becky laughing together on the beach. 'That's a great photo, it looks like you two are having a lot of fun!'

'That's Becky, who owns the gallery I worked at. I've known her practically my whole life,' Olivia smiled fondly.

Jasmine smiled at Olivia, 'Well, I'll leave these letters with you. There's no rush for them,' and headed back to her office.

A little later, Jason came into the outer office, and asked, 'Olivia, are you free after work this evening?'

Olivia looked up, surprised. She suddenly felt nervous, was Jason going to ask her out? 'Jasmine and I would like to treat you to dinner, to celebrate your first week. Laura is invited too, of course.'

Olivia felt embarrassed. What was she thinking, Jason wouldn't ask her out, she had only been there a week, and he was her boss, she chided herself. Olivia pulled herself together, 'That would be lovely, thank you.'

'Excellent! Catch you later,' and Jason disappeared into his office.

Friday afternoon soon came around, and Jason appeared in the outer office. 'Okay ladies, are you ready to go? Jasmine is going to meet us at the restaurant, straight from her meeting. I wasn't sure what you like to eat, Olivia, but they have a really good selection, so I'm sure you'll find something you like.'

Jason had booked a taxi to take them to Covent Garden, to one of his favourite restaurants. 'This is so lovely, thank you,' said Olivia.

When they arrived at the restaurant, they took their seats and began looking through the menu. The restaurant was spacious, with beautiful bare wood floors, and pale green walls. It had a funky retro feel to it. The bare wooden tables each had a small vase in the centre, with a single brightly coloured flower. Jasmine approached the table, looking stunning in a fitted, off the shoulder deep burgundy dress. 'Hello everyone, sorry I'm a bit late. As my meeting finished quite early, I thought I'd get changed before dinner.'

Olivia looked up at Jasmine, 'Your dress is gorgeous, you look beautiful.'

Jasmine beamed at Olivia, 'Thank you so much,' and she sat down on the seat that Jason had pulled back for her.

Olivia could see by the look on his face, that Jason also thought that she looked stunning.

'Are you going out after dinner?' asked Laura.

'No, I just thought as we're celebrating tonight, I wanted to wear something nice!'

Olivia wondered whether Jasmine had dressed up for Jason. The thought gave her a little pang of jealousy, which she knew was crazy. Laura said, 'I feel rather underdressed now!' Jasmine replied, 'Don't be silly, you look lovely.'

The four of them chatted easily, firstly about work, then about themselves. They were keen to hear more about Cornwall, and why Olivia had wanted to move to London. Olivia talked about how she and Becky had been friends since forever, and how when Becky had set up her gallery, she had asked Olivia to work with her. 'Becky and I get on so well together, I don't think that we've ever had a cross word between us, we're really on the same wavelength. I helped her choose paintings and artists, even though I don't have any qualifications in that area. It's great to be given that artistic freedom.'

Jasmine smiled, 'You obviously have a natural instinct for art, which is wonderful. I'd love to go to Cornwall sometime, it sounds so beautiful.'

'Oh, yes it is. Well, if you ever do visit, I can always show you around.'

Jasmine looked at Olivia and smiled, 'Really? That would be wonderful.'

Olivia was so happy that she had had the good fortune to get this job, with these lovely people. At the end of the evening, Jason proposed a toast. 'Olivia, to your first week with JJ Publishing, may it be the first of many. Cheers!'

Jason looked at Olivia, his twinkly blue eyes creasing at the edges as he smiled. Olivia looked back for just a bit too long. They all raised their glasses. Olivia was feeling a bit embarrassed by the attention, but was also very touched. 'Thank you, I've had a great first week. You've all made me feel so welcome, I can't imagine working with nicer people.'

Emma had suggested that she and Olivia spend Saturday together. They got up late, and chatted over breakfast. After a busy first week at work, with so much to take in, a lazy day was definitely in order. They spent the day looking at magazines, chatting, and watching the music channel on television. In the evening they watched Bridget Jones' Diary, with a big bowl of popcorn and some wine. It was getting late, and after a few glasses of wine, Emma said, 'It's really good having you here. My previous flat mate was a journalist, and he was hardly here. It's good to have someone to have girly chats with!'

'Talking of girly chats, how did you meet Matt? He seems really nice.'

A cheeky look came over Emma's face, and she went into storyteller mode, 'Well, it's quite a story, actually. I was at the gym on the cross-trainer, and on one of the machines opposite was a very attractive guy in grey sweatpants and a white training vest. As he trained, I was watching him, and I hadn't realised that I'd been staring, until I suddenly noticed that he had stopped and was just looking at me, smiling. I felt really embarrassed, quickly smiled back, then picked up the pace on the cross-trainer. He stood, ran a hand through his ruffled brown hair, and said, Hi. I'm Matt. I slowed down on the cross-trainer, panting slightly. I said, Hi, sorry, was I staring? I got a bit lost in my thoughts. I'm Emma. He gives me the most sexy, crooked smile, and says perhaps we can work out together sometime, and sauntered off. I thought yes, I'd work out with him any time!' and they both giggled.

Olivia was thinking that nothing like that would ever happen to her. She thought she was pretty ordinary looking and didn't have Emma's outgoing personality. Emma just seemed to attract guys, Olivia had noticed. She must give off some kind of energy or something. Olivia was waiting for the next part of the story. Emma continued, 'A few days later, I saw Matt at the gym again. We do some workouts together, then he leaves. Then, as I'm leaving to have a shower, I bump into Matt outside. I said, Oh, I'm so sorry, Matt looks deep into my eyes, says, Don't be, and bends down and kisses me. There we are in the hallway, sweaty, all over each other. I said I needed a shower, and with that, Matt takes my hand, and leads me into the shower room. Fortunately there's no-one else there at this point, he grabs some shower gel and pulls me into the shower with him. We strip off, and boy does Matt have a great physique. So we're making out, hands all over one another, under the hot shower. Things get very steamy, in more ways than one!' Emma smiled as she remembered what happened next. 'That was the best shower I've ever had!' she laughed.

Olivia said, 'Oh my god, it could only happen to you! What happened next, did anyone come in?'

'Matt went and got a towel, wrapped me up and smuggled me out! Then I went and got changed. We met outside and went for a drink, and the rest is history, as they say!' Emma laughed. 'So, how about you? Do you still have a crush on your boss, Jason, is it?'

Olivia's face flushed, 'No, don't be silly. I'm not about to get involved with my boss. He's really nice though, very sweet.'

Emma thought there was a bit more to that story, and Olivia reluctantly told her about Jason inviting her for dinner, and how for a moment she had thought it might be a date.

'Oh, you poor thing! So what's the deal with Liam? You guys were together a really long time.'

Olivia explained, 'Yes, I've really grown up with him. I do love him, but as a friend, not in the same way as I did. We did get to know each other slowly, which was great. We had a good physical relationship, too, but when you talk about some of your relationships, they sound much more passionate and exciting.'

'Yes, some of them have been. But I've never had a relationship last like you have. I think the longest of mine was a year. To be honest, I'd switch some of that passion for a deep relationship.'

'How about Matt, then?' Olivia noticed a soppy expression pass over Emma's face, 'I think that look on your face answers that!' she laughed.

Emma giggled, 'Oh, he really is so gorgeous, and sweet. I have to admit, I think I'm really falling for him.'

Olivia smiled at her, raising her glass, 'To Emma, may this be the deep and meaningful one you've been waiting for!'

Emma laughed back, raising her glass too, 'Here's hoping!'

Monday soon came around, and Olivia was back at work. The days went quickly, as there was so much to learn. Still, Olivia was absolutely loving it. She got on really well with Laura, and they had started having lunch together most weeks. Olivia found out that Laura was thirty four, and had been married to Peter, an accountant, for ten years. Olivia asked whether they had any children. Laura said, 'Yes, Felicity is six, and Harry is eight. They are great, although they do like a lot of attention! They do after school clubs, and then Pete usually picks them up from work as he starts quite early. Weekends are our real family time. Do you have a partner?'

'Not at the moment. I had a long term boyfriend, Liam, back home. We broke up before I came to London. With all this change at the moment, I'm not in a rush to date anyone, although my roommate says she's going to see if her boyfriend has a friend for me!' They both laughed.

Over the next few weeks, work was getting busier, and Jasmine was spending more and more time in the office. One morning, Jasmine called Olivia in. 'Take a seat, Olivia. Firstly, I wanted to say that I'm really pleased with how you're getting on. Laura said that you pick things up quickly and you work very hard.' Olivia was chuffed to bits. Jasmine continued, 'I was thinking that it would be good to get you more involved with what we do. I'd like you to take a look through this manuscript. The author is called Caroline Oakley, and this is her first book, it's called First Flight. Please would you read it and write a report for me.'

Olivia was thrilled, 'Really? I'd love to, thank you.'

Jasmine smiled, 'That's great, I've got so much to do at the moment, so it will be a big help. It looks very interesting.'

Olivia took the manuscript back to her desk, and began reading. She found the story really interesting, and had never read anything like it before. It was a beautiful story of a girl's journey of self-discovery, realising that she was a spiritual being, and in turn, how she helped other people to find their own spirituality, and follow their own path. Olivia was enchanted by the story. A couple of days later, Olivia had typed up a report, and took it into Jasmine's office. Jasmine looked up from her desk as Olivia walked in, and smiled. 'Hi, I've finished the report for you about First Flight.'

'Great, do you think it's worth me having a look at?'

'Oh yes, it's a wonderful story, very powerful. It's given me a lot of food for thought, actually. The author takes you on a wonderful journey, and it made me feel like I was taking the journey with her. Although, it's really about following your own path and listening to your inner voice.'

Jasmine sat back in her chair, watching Olivia as she spoke animatedly about the manuscript. She loved seeing the passion in Olivia's eyes whilst she spoke, and could see how the story had affected her. Jasmine asked Olivia to take a seat, and tell her more about it. Olivia excitedly explained her favourite things about it. 'I suppose I can relate to the story, because I feel like that's what I'm doing now. I followed my instincts by coming to London, even though staying at home would have been easier.' She paused for a moment, lost in thought. 'I don't think my friends really get why I had to do this.'

Jasmine watched Olivia for a moment, thinking how beautiful she looked. Eventually, when she spoke, her voice was so soft, it was almost a whisper, 'I agree that you have to follow your heart.' Jasmine held eye contact with Olivia, and Olivia wondered whether she should say something. Just then, Jasmine seemed to come to, 'Well, after that enthusiastic description, I probably don't really need to read your report now! Please can you contact Caroline and invite her in for a meeting, and I'd like you to be there too.'

'Really? That's wonderful, thank you,' Olivia said excitedly.

Jasmine looked at her fondly, she loved it when people were as passionate about their work as she was.

At home that evening, Olivia rang her parents to tell them about the opportunity at work with the manuscript, and how Jasmine wanted to meet the author as a result of how much Olivia had loved it. Steve was thrilled, 'That's fantastic, pumpkin! You're obviously doing a great job, and your boss sounds great, giving you that responsibility.'

He asked her about how the job was going generally, and Olivia told him how much she was loving it. Also, she was getting more used to being in London, and was really enjoying the experience.

Back at work, Olivia arranged with Caroline, the author of First Flight, to come in for a meeting. Caroline was thrilled to get the chance to talk about her manuscript. When she arrived, Olivia showed her in to Jasmine's office, and introduced her. Jasmine stood up to shake Caroline's hand. She thanked her for coming in, and explained how Olivia had been so excited about her manuscript, that she had dropped everything else to read it. Caroline was thrilled to have this opportunity. Jasmine invited Caroline and Olivia to sit down, and they discussed the possibilities for the book. They started putting things in motion to get the book published. There was proof reading to do, artwork to design for the book jacket, and an author biography to be written. Jasmine found that she could leave a lot of the work with Olivia, with a bit of help, as she was so enthusiastic and wanted to get it moving.

Over the next few weeks, Olivia and Jasmine spent more and more time working on First Flight. They had both been working long hours, often staying until late in the evening. Olivia really enjoyed working so closely with Jasmine on the launch, she was learning so much, and she really felt that she was properly a part of the team now. This was what she had envisioned when she applied for the job, and Jasmine was such a great boss, always having time for Olivia.

One lunchtime, Laura mentioned to Olivia that it was going to be Jasmine's birthday the following week. Jason had said that he would take them all out for a meal, and asked Laura to book the table. It was booked for the evening, so there would be time to get changed after work. Jasmine was touched that they all wanted to celebrate her birthday with her. She did have some arrangements with friends, but that wasn't until the weekend.

Jasmine arrived at the restaurant to see the others already there. 'Happy birthday!' they said in unison as she arrived. 'Thank you all, so much,' and she kissed each of them on the cheek, coming to Olivia last. Feeling Olivia's lips on her cheek, Jasmine's heart started beating faster.

Jasmine looked stunning in a tailored black trouser suit and a deep red lacy top with spaghetti straps.

Olivia thought that Jasmine always looked so sophisticated. Jason said, 'So, it's a big one this year then! Thirty years old.'

Jasmine looked at him, with a raised eyebrow, 'Thanks, then, for broadcasting that!'

Olivia said, 'Well, you look fabulous, and younger, too.'

Jasmine smiled at her, 'Thank you, Olivia.'

They had a lovely evening, and asked Jasmine whether she was doing anything special to celebrate. Jason was trying to find out whether she might be seeing someone. Although they had known each other a long time, he knew nothing of her relationships, as she was very private about her personal life. All she said was that she had some plans with friends, then she changed the subject.

That weekend, Jasmine's friends Phoebe and Fran were throwing her a birthday dinner party. They lived in a town house in Islington, with steps leading up to a large black front door. It was going to be a fairly small affair, with about fifteen to twenty people going. Phoebe invited Jasmine in. 'Happy birthday! Chris and Ali are already here, so are Sam and Susan,' and she hugged her friend.

Jasmine followed Phoebe through to the kitchen, where she greeted Fran, who poured her a drink. Fran asked her how things were, and Jasmine told them about going out for dinner with Jason, Laura and Olivia. They asked how Olivia was settling in. 'She is a wonder. She works hard, and is so good at the job. In fact, we're working together on the launch of a new book. She was so excited about it, I asked her to invite the author in for a meeting. It's so great working with someone who is so passionate.'

Phoebe gave Jasmine a look, which she ignored, raising her glass, 'Cheers!'

Fran said, 'Come on, get your dancing shoes on, we've got some music going.'

Back at work after the weekend, Jasmine and Olivia were preparing for the book launch. Emma had started joking with Olivia, asking whether she now lived in the office. Olivia had replied that after the book launch, things would go back to normal. She couldn't believe that she had already been in London for over three months, it didn't seem that long at all.

One evening, as Olivia was going through a check list for the book launch, Jasmine said, 'I really appreciate all this extra time you're putting in. When we've had the launch, you can take a few days off if you'd like to, or work some half days.'

Olivia replied, 'I'm happy to do it. I didn't think I would get to be so hands on this early on, I love being involved, it's so exciting. Not to mention, I've got this really nice boss!'

Jasmine looked at Olivia, and smiled, 'As long as you're happy.'

Olivia smiled back, 'Oh, yes, I'm very happy.'

FOUR

It was now the end of September, and Friday was the day of the book launch, which was due to start at two o'clock. They were all going to meet at the venue, just around the corner from Trafalgar Square. Olivia was so excited, and arrived quite early, meeting Caroline at the entrance. Caroline was feeling really nervous, so Olivia took her off to get a coffee and have a chat with her. Looking after Caroline helped to take Olivia's mind off of the fact she was nervous, too. Soon, Laura arrived, followed by Jason. Olivia thought, Wow. She had never seen Jason in a suit before. He was wearing a tailored blue grey suit, with an open necked white fitted shirt, which showed off his great physique. He looked gorgeous. Laura noticed Olivia looking at him, saw a look in her eyes, and raised her eyebrows at her. Immediately, Olivia blushed, and looked away. 'Hi ladies, you're all looking lovely.' Jason smiled at them.

'Why thank you, you look very handsome, Jason,' said Laura, then looked at Olivia, who had gone very red.

Then Jasmine arrived, wearing a long midnight blue halter neck dress, with her dark hair loose on her bare shoulders. Olivia gazed at her, thinking how elegant she looked, 'You look really beautiful.'

As Jasmine looked at Olivia, time seemed momentarily suspended. She then realised that she hadn't replied, and softly said, 'Thank you, Olivia.'

The guests and press were arriving now, and it was time to introduce Caroline and her book. Jasmine gave special mention to Olivia, which she found really touching.

The launch went really well. Caroline was quite emotional, thanking Olivia and Jasmine profusely. In turn, Olivia thanked her for the opportunity of reading it, saying how helpful she had found it, and that it had given her the confidence that she was doing the right thing in her own life. Caroline was thrilled and touched that her book meant so much to Olivia. Olivia asked Caroline to sign a copy for her, and she wrote, 'For Olivia, Enjoy the view on your first flight, knowing that you have helped me on mine, With love, Caroline.' Olivia read the inscription, and felt tears well up in her eyes. She hugged Caroline, and said, 'Thank you so much.'

Jasmine noticed the exchange between them, and smiled. Most people had left now, and Laura was just packing up and about to leave. Olivia said, 'Have a great weekend Laura, see you Monday.'

'Yes, you too. Don't do anything I wouldn't do!' Laura laughed as she left.

Olivia began packing up. She had had a great week, but with all of the work leading up to the book launch, she was glad that it was the weekend, and she would be able to relax. Jasmine walked over to her, looking relaxed and happy. Olivia had never seen Jasmine get flustered, she always seemed so calm and in control. Other people seemed to be frazzled by Friday evening, but not her. Jasmine smiled at Olivia, 'I just wanted to say thank you for all your hard work this week, well over the last few weeks really, your work on this book and the launch. It's in large part due to you that this all happened. I knew we'd made the right choice hiring you, you've been amazing,' and she touched Olivia's hand gently.

Olivia flushed, feeling very pleased, and at the same time, a bit embarrassed. It made such a difference being appreciated for your work. She knew people who hated their jobs, and never received praise or recognition, and this made her extra thankful. Olivia said, 'Thank you for the opportunity, it's been wonderful working with you so closely, I've learned such a lot. We've been working together so much, my flatmate thought that I live in the office now...' and she trailed off as she looked up and saw the look in Jasmine's eyes.

'I knew. The moment I saw you, I knew I wanted you.' Her dark eyes were intense, her pupils dilated, and behind the intensity was a longing. Olivia was completed floored by this revelation. 'I was never going to act on it, but these last few weeks, working so closely with you, seeing your passion... you are so natural and free, so beautiful, and when you spoke of following your heart, I think that's when I started to fall for you.'

Fuck. Olivia's head whirled, she couldn't comprehend what Jasmine was saying, although she certainly had a stronger understanding of the expression 'head-fuck'. Jasmine leaned towards Olivia, 'I really want to kiss you,' slowly moving towards Olivia, closer, closer still, until her lips were almost touching Olivia's. 'You can just say, and I'll stop...' she whispered.

Olivia could smell the sweet and exotic scent of Jasmine's perfume, saw her lips full and slightly parted. Olivia felt light headed, and for a moment she couldn't move. 'Um. I don't know... I, I...' Olivia flushed, feeling giddy, and then Jasmine's mouth was on hers, so soft and gentle, seeking permission.

Olivia felt Jasmine's hands gently touching her hips. At first Olivia didn't respond, her head still swimming, trying to make some sense of what was happening. It was like an out of body experience, it wasn't really happening to her. As Jasmine moved her hands up Olivia's back and into her hair, a thought flashed through her mind, to just give in to it, let herself go...

A feeling of electricity shot through her body, and Olivia suddenly began kissing back. Jasmine deepened the kiss, holding her body closer, her soft kisses becoming urgent and passionate, and Olivia responded by running her hands through Jasmine's long silky hair. Olivia was aware of her skin being so sensitive to Jasmine's touch, as she ran her hands along Olivia's arms, across her back, and back through her hair. Jasmine relished the feel of Olivia's skin, she had wanted so desperately to kiss Olivia, to touch her like this, she could hardly believe that it was actually happening. Every part of her being was so highly sensitised, she was drawn to Olivia in a way that she had never been drawn to anyone before. Olivia felt a strange sensation, unlike anything she had ever experienced. It felt so unusual, and also familiar and safe. The kiss seemed to go on forever, then Olivia started to pull back. What the hell am I doing? It was like she was awakening from a dream, that weird sensation when you don't know what's real and what isn't. Olivia pulled back, breathing heavily. She leaned against the wall, trying to get her bearings. 'I, I have to go. Sorry.' Olivia grabbed her bag, and bolted towards the door, leaving Jasmine looking bewildered.

'Shit.' Jasmine was usually good at reading people, she must have really got it wrong. What was I thinking, I'm her boss, for fucks sake. But she had felt a connection on numerous occasions, she was sure that Olivia had looked at her with something more... Fuck. What should she do now, go after her? Probably not. She picked her phone up and rang Olivia's number. It went straight to voicemail. That was hardly surprising. Jasmine was pacing up and down, chastising herself. She decided that she had to go and see her, she couldn't leave things like this. She looked up Olivia's address. It wasn't that far from here, and Jasmine remembered that Olivia said she was staying with a friend whilst she got settled. If she walked, it would give her time to clear her head a bit, and think what she was going to say to Olivia. What on earth had come over her? Boy, she might have really blown it. Still, for a moment Olivia had responded, had kissed her back... Shit, how was she going to handle this.

Olivia rushed along the road, her cheeks hot and flustered. After a few minutes she slowed, then stopped and looked behind her. At least Jasmine hadn't followed her, which was a relief. She needed some time. What the fuck had just happened? Thank goodness it was Friday, and she had the weekend ahead of her. It was a cool evening, and Olivia now slowed her pace. She decided to call Emma and see if she wanted to meet up for dinner, as she didn't want to go home yet. She needed something to take her mind off of what had just happened. Thankfully, Emma had just finished work. She usually managed to get away about five o'clock on a Friday, but the rest of the week it could be six or seven depending on the work load. They arranged to meet at the Mexican restaurant, and Covent Garden was nearby. Making her way there, it was crowded with people. Couples and friends were chatting and heading off for meals before going to the theatre, or for a night out clubbing. Arriving at the restaurant, there were a couple of empty tables, as it was still relatively early. She knew that by six o'clock the place would be packed. Once shown to her table, Olivia sat down heavily, relieved to take the weight off her legs, which were feeling rather wobbly. She ordered cocktails for herself and Emma, then sat back in her chair. There were already quite a few people at the bar, and the noise levels were beginning to rise. Emma arrived, giving Olivia a quick hug before sitting down. Noticing the drinks, she said, 'You've started sharp this evening!' then saw Olivia's face. 'Hey, what's happened with you? You have a very strange look on your face.'

Olivia felt her face flush. Shit, was it that obvious that something had happened. 'It's just been a hectic week, today in particular with the book launch. Let's relax and forget about work.'

Being glad that it was Friday, Emma was happy to go along with this request. They ordered fajitas and another cocktail each, and Olivia started talking about films to take her mind off of what had happened. Over the course of the evening, Olivia began to feel more normal, to the point of wondering whether she had dreamed what had happened earlier. It had been very busy recently, and she had been doing long hours, and was very tired. She tried to talk herself into believing that she had fallen asleep after the launch, and had a strange dream. Olivia was feeling exhausted, and as the evening wore on, she became muzzy headed. Perhaps I've had enough cocktails for this evening, she thought. The bar area was getting very busy and noisy, so they paid the bill and decided to head home. Out of habit, Olivia glanced at her phone, and saw that she had multiple missed calls from Jasmine, and a couple of voicemails. She felt the colour drain from her face as everything came flooding back. Hopefully Emma wouldn't notice. What surprised and shocked Olivia, was that at the remembrance of the kiss, she felt a twist of excitement in her stomach and heat between her legs. Fuck.

'Livvy, are you okay? You look really weird.'

'No, I... I'm fine. Just maybe one too many cocktails, and I'm really tired. Let's go home.' Hopefully that would cover it, Olivia thought, she really needed some time to process this.

They walked back to Emma's place, and Olivia was glad of the fresh air, maybe it would cool off some of the heat that she was feeling. Arriving home, Olivia said she was going straight to bed as she was wiped out. As soon as she was in her room, she closed the door and sat on the bed, her phone in her hand. She pressed the voicemail button, her heart pounding furiously in her chest. The first message was a simple, 'Hi, it's Jasmine. Give me a call.' The next one said, 'Hi, it's me. We really need to talk. I'm so sorry about what happened. Please call me back.' Olivia flopped back onto the bed, staring up at the ceiling. What was she going to do?

Jasmine was going mad with worry. She had tried Olivia's number a few times with no reply. When she arrived at the flat, she pressed the buzzer. No reply. Shit. She rang Olivia's mobile number again, this time leaving a message. Please, please, please pick up or call back. She decided to make her way home in the meantime. Arriving at her front door, she took her keys out of her handbag and let herself in. Discarding her bag on the table, she went to the fridge. Taking out a bottle of wine, the condensation on the smooth bottle felt cold against the warmth of her hand. Having poured out a large glass, she moved to the sofa. The cushions squished beneath her as she sat down, and she sighed heavily. Now what? She checked her phone again, although she knew that no one had called, her phone had been in her hand the whole way home. She rang Olivia's number again, and again it went straight to voicemail. Jasmine left a second message, then put her phone down on the sofa next to her. She took a sip from her cool wine, before setting it down on the coffee table. She leaned back into the sofa, and a tear ran down the side of her face.

Olivia woke from a fitful sleep on Saturday morning. Automatically, she checked her phone which was on the dresser. Thankfully there were no new messages. She decided that a day to herself was what she needed, and was pleased that she hadn't made any arrangements with anyone today. She walked into the lounge, and through to the kitchen. It seemed that Emma wasn't up yet, which was good. Olivia didn't feel like talking this morning. She felt disconnected, as though she was watching someone else's life, not living her own.

Although Olivia wasn't very hungry, she thought that she ought to eat something, so decided on a muffin and some orange juice. Then she caught the scent of Jasmine's perfume on her skin.

Waking with a fuzzy head, Jasmine sat up, realising that she was still on the sofa. This is crazy, I've got to pull myself together. She replayed that moment the previous evening, walking over to Olivia slowly, thinking she had never seen anyone so beautiful. It was more than a physical attraction, something Olivia exuded, something intangible. She had never before got involved with anyone she worked with. She had always kept her romantic life very much separate, never talking about her relationships. In fact, Jason and Laura assumed she wasn't interested. She loved her career, and they had never heard her talk of partners, only the occasional friend. Shit, she really had messed up. But when she thought about that lingering kiss, the feel of Olivia's skin beneath her fingertips, and how Olivia had kissed her back, her lips so soft, she had a feeling of longing, and felt bereft.

Olivia took a shower, washing off Jasmine's scent, and started to feel better under the hot, soothing water. She decided that she would go to the Natural History Museum, which she had loved when she was a kid. It was years since she had been there. The anonymity amongst all the tourists would be good. The thought of taking the underground really wasn't appealing, what with the volume of people and everyone rushing around. The bus would be much better, and she could people watch along the way. She liked to make up stories about the people and their imaginary lives. Olivia dried herself off, dressed quickly, and left the flat without seeing Emma. She walked along the road to the bus stop, catching the bus to South Kensington. When she could see the museum in the distance, she got off and walked along Cromwell Road to the museum. It was a very busy Saturday, as usual in London. Standing in the grounds of the Natural History Museum, Olivia looked up at the magnificent building. It really was beautiful. She walked up the steps, remembering how excited she was to visit here when she was a child. Walking into the main hall, with the imposing Diplodocus holding court, it was just as she remembered it. She still had that feeling of awe.

Olivia wanted to see the blue whale. She remembered as a child looking up in amazement at the massive whale, finding it hard to believe that there was really a creature that big in the world. Now twelve years later, it was more than another lifetime away, which seemed a strange thought to Olivia. Having checked the map, she turned left off the main hall, though the mammal area, towards the blue whale. Olivia approached the whale, then stood still. Standing here, Olivia felt reassured that she was a small part of something much bigger than herself. It helped her to put a perspective on things. She felt safe here, as though things hadn't changed, and she was that ten year old girl again. Olivia walked up the stairs to the viewing balcony, and stood at the tail of the blue whale, looking at the sheer size of it. After a while, she moved to a bench to sit down, still looking at the whale. It dwarfed everything else, even the elephants looked small in comparison. Olivia looked up, above her head, to see whales and dolphins suspended above her, and it gave her a feeling of being underwater. Her thoughts began to drift, and she began to idly people watching. Out of the corner of her eye, she caught sight of a tall woman with long dark wavy hair. Jasmine. Her heart began thumping hard in her chest, like an over-tightened drum. No, the chances of that were very unlikely. As the woman turned around and looked up to where Olivia was sitting, she could see it was someone she had never seen before. Boy, get it together, she thought. Olivia realised that rather than trying to process what had happened, she was trying to shut it out. She stood up and stretched, and was aware that she was feeling hungry. She hadn't eaten much that morning, so decided it was time for some lunch. Olivia made her way to the cafe to get some coffee and a sandwich. She found an empty seat at one of the tables in the middle of the cafe area, and as she idly ate her lunch, she took in the architecture and stained glass windows around her. The cafe was bustling with families and excited children. There was so much life here.

Once she had eaten, Olivia felt a bit better. She decided to have a wander around the dinosaurs, another favourite of hers when she was a child. It was packed, with parents trying to keep up with their children, exclaiming over the size of the dinosaurs. Olivia followed the exhibition around to the animatronic Tyrannosaurus rex. It was a great showpiece, and although it didn't roar very loudly, some of the younger children were scared, and were being comforted by their parents, whilst others were taking photographs. As the time went by, Olivia became tired, deciding it was time to head home.

Jasmine spent the day at home, trying to relax by reading magazines, and watching a bit of television, as she couldn't concentrate on reading a book at the moment. Nothing would take her mind off of Olivia and the monumental mistake that she had made. The kiss had been amazing, but she dearly hoped that it wouldn't drive Olivia away. It would be so much better if she could at least talk to her, and sort things out. She hoped and prayed that Olivia would be understanding, and wouldn't quit her job. Apart from loving having her around, she was damn good at her job. She would accept that her feelings were not reciprocated, and remain professional. Jasmine realised how out of the blue it must have seemed to Olivia. For Jasmine, she had been attracted to Olivia from the day that she had met her, and she thought about her a lot. She hadn't meant to just come out with how she felt like that. Something had just come over her, and she couldn't stop herself. Jasmine sighed. She tried Olivia's home number, and Emma picked up. No, Olivia wasn't in, in fact she didn't know what her plans were this weekend. Jasmine decided to leave another voicemail message, dearly hoping she would get a call back this time.

Olivia opened the door to the flat, and was greeted by Emma, who was in the lounge. 'Hi, did you have a good day? A woman rang for you not long ago, I said I didn't know when you would be back.'

'Oh, do you know who it was?' Olivia asked, hopefully innocently, knowing full well who it must have been.

'No, she said it wasn't urgent, she would try again another time.'

Olivia then remembered that she had turned her phone off at the museum, and hadn't turned it back on again. 'Okay, thanks,' she said as she turned and walked into her room.

Turning her phone on, Olivia sat on the bed. Sure enough, there was a message from Jasmine. Pressing the voicemail button, she waited for the message to start. 'Hi, it's me again. Look, we really should talk. I've been so worried and feel really bad about what happened. Please give me a call so we can talk and clear the air.'

Olivia knew she couldn't just keep ignoring Jasmine, but she also wasn't ready to talk to her yet. What on earth would she say? If she sent a text, maybe Jasmine would let it be for now. *'Sorry I haven't returned your calls. I'm not sure what to say or even think at the moment. Just give me some time please*.' There, that should do it for now. Almost immediately, her phone pinged with a response.

'Of course. I think it would be good to talk in person, though.'

Now that she had time to sit and think, Olivia replayed what had happened on Friday. Had she really had no idea? She got on really well with Jasmine, and thought that they had a great working relationship. Occasionally, Jasmine would touch her arm, or smile warmly at her. But she was like that with everyone, wasn't she? Had she lead Jasmine on in some way, given off some signals that she hadn't been aware of. Olivia had no point of reference, what should she do. Could she pretend it hadn't happened. Jasmine certainly seemed very sorry and seemed to want to sort it out.

But something was worrying Olivia, at the back of her mind. The kiss had really turned her on. This was a shocking realisation. Fuck. It was the sexiest thing that had ever happened to her. When she had just let go, the feeling was sensational. She had never known that a kiss could convey so much, and the way that Jasmine had held her body close, she felt connected in a way she hadn't known was possible. This is crazy, Olivia told herself. Maybe it was just the attention, the complete surprise, and she was just caught in the moment. Olivia told herself that it was the spontaneity that she had responded to. But why couldn't it have happened with Jason, or some other guy.

Jasmine was relieved that she'd had a response from Olivia. She had been worried sick. Well, best to leave things for tonight. She would decide in the morning what to do. Now she was feeling a bit easier, she decided to lose herself in a book, curled up on the sofa. Rocky, her beautiful black cat, came padding over and curled up next to her. Rocky looked up at her owner with sparkling green eyes, and purred. It reminded Jasmine of Olivia's beautiful green eyes, and the thought filled her with sadness, as though she was losing something which had never been hers in the first place.

Sunday morning was beautiful. Jasmine got out of bed and opened the curtains, being greeted by sunshine and a clear blue sky. After showering and having breakfast, she fed Rocky and decided to go for a walk. One of her favourite places was Regent's Park. Even after all these years, she would forget just how green and spacious London was in some areas. It really felt like she was somewhere else, and gave her the space to breathe. After wandering around for a while, she headed to the cafe and ordered a pot of tea. She decided to try calling Olivia again. To her surprise, Olivia picked up. 'Hi, how are you?' Jasmine asked, and heard some hesitation before the reply.

'I'm fine, thank you. Sorry I couldn't talk before. I just needed a bit of time to myself.'

'Of course. I just wanted to say how sorry I am. I've never done anything like that before, I don't know what came over me. I feel awful. I really hope that you'll stay on working with me, but I do understand you may not want to. I would obviously give you an outstanding reference. Believe me, I would have never made a move if I'd realised... If I'd known...' Her voice trailed away.

Olivia could hear the worry and concern in Jasmine's voice. 'Look, it's fine. You caught me off guard, that's all. I've never had anything like that happen before, not even with a guy,' Olivia hesitated, then before she could stop herself, she said, 'Actually, it was kind of romantic.'

At those words, Jasmine felt a rush of relief. 'I'm glad you're okay. All I can do is apologise again. I promise I will be completely professional from now on. If there's anything you want me to do, just say.'

'It's fine. See you at work tomorrow, bye.'

And Olivia was gone. Jasmine was relieved, although she also felt sad, knowing that it wasn't to be. Of course, nothing changed the way that Jasmine felt, she thought Olivia was gorgeous and she loved being with her. She would just have to shelve those feelings away. She had years of experience, putting a front on things. But Olivia had said she thought it was romantic, and that thought gave Jasmine a kick of longing and excitement.

Olivia decided to stay in on Sunday, and have a quiet day. Emma was at Matt's, so she had the place to herself. She could read, watch a film, laze around. Olivia was glad that she had spoken to Jasmine, and she thought that things would be okay now. It had just been a mistake. Jasmine was very apologetic, so that was that. She still wondered why Jasmine would risk making a move like that, maybe she knew something that Olivia didn't. Despite everything, Olivia couldn't deny that it was the most romantic and sexy thing that had ever happened to her. Still, at the thought of it, she felt that tingle, the excitement, the wonderful feeling of getting swept up in the moment, being lost in something much bigger than she was...

FIVE

On Monday morning, Jasmine was feeling nervous. She walked into the outer office, greeted Laura, and headed straight for her office, closing the door behind her. She sat at her desk, trying to think about what she had to do today. She didn't have any meetings, as she and Jason usually kept their Mondays clear to catch up with work after the weekend. Also, after the book launch, it would be good to slow things down a little bit. There was a tap on the door, and Jasmine said, 'Come in.' She looked up to see Laura standing there.

'Just to let you know, Olivia is going to be in a bit later today, she said that you mentioned that it would be okay if she did a half day. I expect she's exhausted after all that work for the book launch, she put in so much time and energy. Anyway, I can cover anything you need today.'

'Thank you, Laura. I don't have too much to do, mostly I'm going to be reading manuscripts today.'

Laura looked concerned, 'Um, are you alright, Jasmine? You don't seem your usual self, if you don't mind me saying.'

'I'm fine, thank you. I'm just a bit tired,' and she smiled weakly.

Laura went back to her desk, closing the door behind her. Jasmine slumped back in her chair, sighing heavily.

Olivia came in after lunch. Laura thought that she seemed a bit quiet, and put it down to tiredness. Jasmine came out of her office mid-afternoon, and stopped in her tracks when she saw Olivia. Jasmine was overcome with feelings of longing, and seeing Olivia made her both happy and incredibly sad. Despite how she felt inside, Jasmine kept her voice calm, 'Hi. How are you?'

Olivia's face flushed, then she recovered herself, 'I'm fine, thanks.' She looked down again, avoiding eye contact.

Jasmine walked slowly over to Olivia's desk. 'I just wanted to check my appointments for tomorrow.' Standing so close to Olivia, Jasmine was careful not to touch her, and leaned forward, resting her hand on the desk. She tried to search Olivia's face for a clue as to how she really was, but Olivia kept her gaze downwards. 'Okay, thank you.' Jasmine disappeared into her office, closing the door behind her.

Olivia exhaled slowly, and could feel her cheeks beginning to cool down. She was pleased that there wasn't much to do today. She found it strange, knowing how Jasmine felt about her, but everything appearing to be normal. Well, she thought, if I can get through today, it will get easier.

Jasmine sat back down at her desk. Shit, this is harder than I thought it would be. She had been surprised by how strongly Olivia affected her, and wasn't prepared for her reaction of seeing Olivia today. Usually, she was very controlled and reserved, particularly at work. Her mind was whirring. I really should not have said anything to Olivia. Christ, I kissed her. What was I thinking. Well, thinking hadn't really come into it. Jasmine knew that she would just have to deal with it. Olivia seemed to be okay about everything, which was pretty astounding in itself. Things could have gone really badly. Jasmine would just have to go back to putting on a front, as she had become accustomed to do for most of her life. She envied Olivia's freedom, she just seemed comfortable to be herself.

As the week went on, Laura noticed that Olivia and Jasmine were behaving differently around each other. They were polite, friendly still, but there was a tension there that Laura had not seen before. She assumed it must be something to do with the book launch. They had both been working really long hours, they were probably fed up spending so much time together.

Olivia distracted herself with work as much as she could, but she was still having trouble trying to forget what had happened. Certainly, if she was that way inclined, Jasmine was beautiful and sexy, quite a catch. Olivia was surprised that Jasmine was single at all. Of all the people she could be with, Olivia didn't understand why Jasmine wanted her. But it had felt exciting and wonderful to be wanted in that way, to be so desired. Fuck, she was in trouble.

On Friday morning, Emma called out, 'Bye Livvy, I'm off to work now, see you tonight.'

'Mmm, okay, see you later,' Olivia said sleepily as she turned over to look at her clock. It was eight o'clock. She had already decided that she wasn't going into work today, this week was proving really difficult. Jasmine was being professional, to the point of formality, but Olivia still couldn't get her head around what had happened. She knew that Jasmine wasn't going to do anything like that again, she had made that clear. But each time Olivia remembered what had happened, it gave her a flush of excitement. And when she saw Jasmine, she felt like a teenager. At least Laura and Jason didn't know anything about it. Also, Jasmine had said that she could take some time off after the launch, so Olivia not going in wouldn't raise any suspicion. She left a message for Laura. Olivia was well aware that this was only a short term measure, she was going to have to find a way of working with Jasmine. She would just pretend that nothing had happened, and they could go back to the way things were. Still, one more day to herself would be good, and then it was the weekend. Getting back into bed, Olivia turned over and drifted off to sleep again.

Sometime later, Olivia was aware of a noise somewhere. She rubbed her eyes and sat up, and as she came to, realised that someone was knocking on the door. Probably Emma had left her key behind and realised when she got down the road. 'Okay, I'm coming.' She dragged herself out of bed and headed to the door. As she opened it, she stopped short when she saw Jasmine standing there. She felt her whole body flush, and her heart started to pound.

'Hi. Sorry, but I just had to see you. Can I come in?' Jasmine looked tired and concerned.

Olivia hesitated, 'Yes, of course.' She stood back to let Jasmine in, pushing her hair back from her face, and closed the door. For a moment they just stood there looking at each other, then Olivia dropped her gaze.

'Olivia, I'm so sorry. I know this week has been difficult, and I'm not sure what to do or say. You know now how I feel about you, and I know that you don't feel the same way. I want you to know that I will be completely professional from now on. I just thought that we hadn't spoken about this in person since... it happened.' Jasmine had meant to stop, but seeing Olivia again, standing so close to her, she felt a desperate longing, and couldn't help herself. 'You have completely beguiled me, and I haven't been able to stop thinking about you. You are so beautiful, and when I think of that kiss...' Jasmine looked at Olivia with wide, worried eyes.

What surprised Olivia more than seeing Jasmine at the door, was her own reaction. Olivia closed the space between them and kissed Jasmine full on the lips. Jasmine couldn't believe what was happening, and responded passionately. Their hands were in each others' hair, and all over one another. Olivia kissed like she had never kissed before, as if her life depended on it. The passion she felt soared through her body, her skin felt highly sensitised and she felt that twist of excitement in her stomach and an intense heat between her legs. She felt Jasmine's hands slide down to her bottom, and then up her back. In response, she slid her hands down Jasmine's body. Olivia had never touched or kissed another woman in this way, but in this moment, it felt so natural to her, and exciting. Fuck, what is this woman doing to me. She pulled back, breathless, looking up at Jasmine, who looked ecstatic, albeit a bit confused. 'This is not at all what I expected!' laughed Jasmine, her face glowing, the signs of concern and tiredness nowhere to be seen.

'Um, not what I expected either. I've shocked myself, quite frankly!' and they burst into fits of laughter.

Olivia invited Jasmine in, suggesting they talk. She made a cup of tea for Jasmine, and coffee for herself. 'I fell back to sleep, what time is it?' Olivia asked, running a hand through her hair.

'It's ten thirty. Once Laura said that you weren't coming in, I just couldn't stay at work, I had to see you. I was hoping to have a chat with you, if you'd even let me in. I've been worried sick.'

Jasmine watched Olivia making the drinks, and could see that she felt self-conscious. She desperately wanted to kiss Olivia again, but didn't want to make the first move. As it was, she still couldn't believe that Olivia had kissed her like that. Olivia looked down, 'Sorry I didn't call you back when you left me those messages. I was feeling really confused, my head was all over the place, and I needed some time to myself.'

Jasmine touched Olivia's arm, and Olivia lifted her head to meet Jasmine's gaze. Could Jasmine feel that electric connection that Olivia was feeling? 'There's really no need to apologise. I completely understood that I caught you off guard. I felt so bad about what happened, and what you thought of me. I've never done anything like that before.'

Olivia didn't know what to say, and broke her gaze, looking down at herself. 'Forgive the state of me, I need to get showered and dressed.'

'You look very cute in your pj's!' Jasmine smiled, causing Olivia to blush.

'I guess I won't be in trouble for not coming in today, then!' laughed Olivia.

Olivia took the drinks to the coffee table and they sat down on the sofa, Olivia sitting crossed legged opposite Jasmine. They sipped their drinks, smiling at one another. A strand of hair fell over Olivia's face, and Jasmine leaned forward to gently tuck it behind her ear. As Jasmine's hand gently touched her hair and her face, Olivia felt a tingle of excitement. Jasmine looked right into Olivia's eyes, a look that seemed to touch her very soul. 'I can't tell you how happy I am right now,' whispered Jasmine.

Olivia found Jasmine tantalising, and very softly, she said, 'Try.' Her heart was so beating so fast. Jasmine leaned forward and began kissing Olivia softly, lingering and savouring every moment. Now she felt that she had permission, Olivia was asking for this, and it felt so good. Jasmine took her time, she didn't want to do anything that Olivia didn't want to, she didn't want a repeat of last Friday and how it had left her feeling over the weekend. Jasmine still couldn't believe that this was happening. Olivia felt Jasmine's tongue gently exploring her mouth, entwining with her tongue. As they kissed, they became more urgent, more passionate, their hearts beating wildly. Olivia was intoxicated with desire. Now Jasmine moved on top, and began running her hands down Olivia's chest. Olivia was feeling sensations that she wouldn't have dreamed of. Jasmine asked, 'Is this okay?'

Olivia responded with a nod and a shy smile. Jasmine cupped Olivia's breasts through her pyjamas, massaging them, 'You feel so good,' she whispered. It was a long time since she'd been in a relationship. She spent so much of her time working, and of course one of her rules had been to never get involved with anyone at work. But Olivia was irresistible.

Olivia tentatively reached towards Jasmine's chest. She had never done this before, and she experienced a mixture of nervousness and anticipation. Jasmine had an effect on her she had never experienced with anyone else. The kind of thing you see in movies or read about in books, but didn't happen in real life... did it? Jasmine was wearing an open neck blouse, with the first few buttons undone. Olivia could see some cleavage, and reached out to gently touch Jasmine's breasts. Her skin felt so soft. Jasmine arched her back, groaning. Wow. Her response turned on Olivia even more, and she began unbuttoning the rest of Jasmine's blouse, until it was completely open and showing her lacy white bra. Jasmine leaned down again and kissed Olivia hungrily. Then Jasmine rolled over beside her, running her hands up under her pyjama top, feeling her gorgeous breasts, and her nipples hardened in response to her touch. Then she started to trail her hand down Olivia's body, very slowly. Olivia's stomach muscles contracted under Jasmine's touch, and she felt that delicious excitement and anticipation. 'You will say if anything isn't comfortable for you? I can stop any time if you want me to,' said Jasmine softly, thinking please, please don't ask me to stop.

Olivia replied breathily, 'Don't stop.'

As Jasmine's hand slipped down inside the waistband of her pyjamas, there was no part of Olivia's being that wanted this feeling to end, Jasmine made her feel things that she didn't think possible. Jasmine kept watching for Olivia's reaction, making sure it was okay to go on. She could see that Olivia was highly aroused, and leaned down to kiss her again, all the while sliding her hand lower, gently feeling the contours of her body. Olivia ran her hands along Jasmine's back, her skin so soft and supple, Jasmine was so beautiful. As Jasmine slid her hand lower still, Olivia was silently pleading for Jasmine to keep going, and as she felt her fingers sliding up inside her, her body tingled all over with anticipation. Feeling how wet Olivia was, Jasmine groaned, and she began moving her fingers rhythmically and with great skill, as she watched Olivia close her eyes, and throw her head back. Olivia felt light headed with pleasure, this was like nothing on earth. She could feel a delicious building of sensation which was almost unbearable. She panted and groaned with pleasure, crying out as she reached orgasm, and shuddered as it pulsed through her body. Olivia kissed Jasmine urgently, holding her head between her hands, as Jasmine kissed her back and slowly brought her down from climax. 'Oh my god,' Olivia breathed, 'That was amazing.'

Jasmine looked lovingly at her, in the afterglow of orgasm, and said, 'You are so fucking sexy.' She kissed her again, and stroked Olivia's hair. She couldn't quite believe what had just happened. This was so much more than she ever could have hoped for.

As they lay snuggled up on the sofa together, Olivia asked, 'How about you? You could coach me!'

Jasmine smiled, 'I don't want to rush you into it, I know this is all new to you. Let's take things a step at a time.'

'I feel more like I've run a race, actually!' and they both laughed.

They lay there together for a while, taking in what had just happened. 'So what now? What do we do about work?' asked Olivia.

'You know, I really didn't think this through at all. As you can probably tell, I got rather caught up in my attraction to you,' Jasmine paused. 'I think it would be best to keep it quiet for now, until we've had time to let this settle a bit, then we can decide what to do.'

Olivia said, 'It's going to be tricky pretending nothing's going on. At least we don't have to worry about my boss finding out!'

Whilst they were talking, Jasmine was lightly running her hands up and down Olivia's arm. Olivia felt so comfortable, which seemed strange to her when what was happening was so unlike her. 'Look, I'm going to have to get back to work. I told Laura I was popping out to get some notebooks or something, I'm not even sure what I said as I was so stressed. Can I come and see you after work? I could bring a takeaway.'

'That sounds good, but just so you know, my flat mate will be back this evening. We can just say we're going over some work stuff.'

Jasmine popped to the bathroom, then came back re-buttoned and presentable. Despite what had just happened, Jasmine looked suave and unflustered. Olivia walked her over to the door. 'I feel naughty staying at home while you go back to work. I could come in this afternoon.'

Firstly kissing Olivia, Jasmine said, 'No, you have my permission to take the rest of the day off! See you tonight.'

They kissed again, a slow, deep kiss. Eventually they pulled away from each other, and Jasmine left to return to work.

Olivia turned away from the door, and collecting the cups from the coffee table, she took them to the kitchen. She decided that she had better have a shower, as it was almost lunchtime now. She padded through the lounge, to the bathroom and turned on the shower. Holy shit, this morning couldn't have been more different than anything she might have imagined. As she stood under the warmth of the water, she replayed what had happened. Jasmine at the door, so unexpected. Her eyes wide, with a look of longing and desire. Olivia moving in to kiss her. Where did that come from? The way Jasmine looked at her, and how she made her feel, sexy and desired. Jasmine really was intoxicating. And on the sofa, Jasmine touching her so gently and expertly. As Olivia remembered, she had been unconsciously running her fingers over her body, and that now familiar twist of excitement in her stomach kicked in. She was feeling so turned on by what had happened, and needed a release from the ache that she was experiencing between her legs. Her fingers began exploring, and she started to move them faster and faster, knowing that her orgasm was imminent, like a coiled spring, ready to explode. 'Aaahhh...' with one hand against the wall to support herself, she felt her legs weaken as she orgasmed.

SIX

At seven fifteen there was a knock at the door. Olivia went to answer it, and there was Jasmine, standing there smiling, bag in one hand, Chinese takeaway in the other. 'Come in,' Olivia held the door for her, 'Pop it in the kitchen and I'll get some plates.'

'Sorry it's a bit late, but after this morning, I had a bit of catching up to do.'

Olivia followed her to the kitchen, and Jasmine put the bags down on the counter. 'Hi!' She leaned in to kiss Olivia, who suddenly felt shy. They stood side by side, putting the meal on plates. It felt very comfortable and domestic. The kitchen had a dining area, with a small round table, which Olivia had laid earlier, occupying herself whilst waiting for Jasmine. They sat down to eat, chatting about work and catching up on the afternoon. Olivia asked, 'Did Laura say anything about you leaving this morning?'

Jasmine smiled at her. 'No, but I felt really guilty, like a schoolgirl playing hooky! I know it's crazy, but I thought maybe she would guess what was happening.'

'There's no way she could know, I've only just found out myself!' Olivia laughed.

As they sat across the table from one another, Olivia watched Jasmine, how graceful she was. Jasmine looked up with those gorgeous deep brown eyes, and straight into Olivia's eyes. Olivia flushed, and Jasmine smiled at her. Olivia still couldn't believe that this was happening. After eating and clearing up, they went to sit on the sofa, taking their glasses of wine with them. They sat close together, and Jasmine slid her hand over to hold Olivia's hand.

'You know, this is weird,' Olivia said, 'I mean in a good way,' when she saw the worried look on Jasmine's face. 'This is so new to me. It feels really good, and so normal in some ways, but also so out of my comfort zone that I can't explain it. It may take me a bit of getting used to.'

Jasmine smiled, 'Of course. It's new to me too. I mean, I've had relationships with women before, but never anyone I've ever worked with. We'll take it a step at a time,' and she leaned over to kiss Olivia, very gently at first, and as Olivia kissed back, they became more passionate. Suddenly there was a jangle of keys at the door, and Olivia jumped back as if she'd had an electric shock. She quickly moved along the sofa to create some space between herself and Jasmine. The door opened, and Emma walked in. She looked across to the sofa and saw Olivia sitting with someone she had never seen before. 'Hi.'

'Hi, Emma, this is Jasmine, my boss,' said a rather flustered Olivia.

Emma put her bag down and walked over to Jasmine, stretching her hand out. Jasmine stood up, shaking her hand, 'Lovely to meet you, Emma.'

'You too. Don't mind me, I'll just make a drink then I'll be off to my room and you two can carry on... chatting.'

As Emma left, they pulled a face at each other and laughed. They chatted about their families, their interests, and nothing in particular. A couple of hours had passed, and Jasmine got up to leave. She would have loved to have seen Olivia over the weekend, but she already had plans. It was probably best that way, not to rush into things too quickly. Olivia said, 'Thank you for the takeaway, I really enjoyed it, and your company.'

Jasmine smiled, 'Thank you for a lovely evening, see you Monday.'

They kissed, quickly in case Emma came wandering out again.

After Jasmine had left, Emma came into the lounge where Olivia was sitting reading a book. 'So, what's news?'

Olivia looked up, 'Nothing. How about you?'

'Oh, okay. I just wondered. When I came home this evening, you and your boss looked like two rabbits caught in the headlights! Were you discussing some juicy office gossip?' laughed Emma.

Olivia felt her face redden, and hoped that Emma wouldn't notice in the lamplight. 'Yeah, something like that. No-one you know, though. Well, I'm pooped, see you in the morning.'

Getting up hurriedly, Olivia made a bee-line for her bedroom. Emma looked puzzled and amused as she watched Olivia scurry off. 'Goodnight then, sleep well.'

Olivia arrived at the office early on Monday morning, turning on the computer so that she could check her emails. Laura came in about half an hour later. 'Morning. Are you feeling recovered today?' she asked.

Olivia felt her cheeks colour. Damn it, why do I have to blush so easily, 'Yes thank you, I was just a bit tired after the launch. I feel great now.'

'It's amazing the difference a weekend can make.'

You can say that again, thought Olivia. Jason arrived soon after, greeting them both and disappearing into his office, saying that he had some work to do before his meeting at ten. It was just after nine o'clock, and Jasmine breezed through the door. Olivia's stomach turned over with nervousness and excitement. 'Morning ladies, beautiful day,' she said, and went straight to her office.

Laura said, 'She's seems much better today. On Friday morning she was in a very strange mood, although she was better in the afternoon,' and carried on with what she was doing.

There was a lot of work to do, and Olivia busied herself with it. She didn't see much of Jasmine, who had meetings and a lot of reading to do. Having had the weekend to herself without seeing Jasmine, Olivia was getting that feeling that she had been dreaming what had happened, as though it was separate to her. This was strange, that was for sure. Still, Jasmine was behaving normally, maybe it was one of those things that would burn itself out, it felt as though things were back to normal. Maybe now Jasmine had got it out of her system, that would be that. At about three o'clock, Laura knocked on Jasmine's door. 'I'm just popping out to get some drinks, would you like something?'

'No thank you, I'm fine.'

As Laura left the office, Jasmine appeared at her office door. 'Hi. Could you just pop in for a moment?'

Olivia got up, crossing the floor towards the office. Jasmine closed the door behind her, and pressing her up against the door, began kissing Olivia, urgently, passionately. Olivia responded in kind, and suddenly they were all over each other. After what seemed an eternity, Jasmine pulled back, breathlessly saying, 'Sorry, I just couldn't go another second without touching you, without kissing you. I can't stop thinking about what happened on Friday, and how fucking hot you are. Today seems to be lasting forever. Can you come round to my place tonight?'

Olivia, also breathless, giggled. 'I'd love to, but I have plans with Emma. How about tomorrow?'

Jasmine said, 'Damn, I can't, I've got arrangements most of this week. Is Friday good for you?' Olivia nodded eagerly. 'Great. Would you like to go out for dinner, or I can cook for us.'

'Either sounds great, thank you. Look, I'd better get back to my desk, Laura will be back soon.'

'Okay,' Jasmine replied, giving Olivia a quick kiss on the lips.

Sitting back at her desk, Olivia couldn't stop smiling to herself. This thing, whatever it was, certainly hadn't burnt out. Quite the opposite, Jasmine excited her so much, and she could feel her heart pumping so fast. She had better have some control, or this could be really difficult, however exciting it may be. Still, it was going to be a few days before they would be spending time together properly. Maybe that was a good thing, things were happening pretty quickly. Laura returned from the coffee shop with Jason's drink, and one for each of them. 'I forgot to ask you, so took a chance and got you a latte,' as she handed Olivia a recycled cardboard cup, the delicious smell of coffee wafting from it.

'Thank you, that's so kind.'

Laura had been brilliant at helping Olivia get settled in, and teaching her the job. It was a lovely atmosphere in the office, and having left her family and friends in Cornwall, it was beginning to feel like having a little family here.

The next few days were busy and Olivia found that the time flew by. On Friday afternoon, as Laura was packing up, she asked Olivia, 'Have you got any plans for the weekend?'

'Not much really, I might do something with Emma tomorrow, nothing definite.' She felt her face flushing, knowing that tonight she was going out with Jasmine. 'How about you?'

'I'm going out with some friends tomorrow, which I'm looking forward to. We don't get together as much as we used to. Everyone's so busy now, and a few of us have to arrange babysitters. Well, have a good one, see you Monday.'

'Yes, you too.'

Jason appeared at his office door, 'Hey, I'm off in a minute. Have a good weekend.'

Jasmine had told Olivia earlier that she had booked a table for them at a restaurant in Covent Garden. She said goodbye to Jason, and left with Olivia. Olivia was feeling nervous now, this was like going out on a date. Then the realisation hit her, that this was a date. When she thought about it like that, it seemed really strange to her. When she wasn't thinking, when she was just being in the moment, it felt like the most natural thing in the world.

Jasmine and Olivia left the office and headed towards Covent Garden. It was a beautiful September evening, and they decided to walk. It was often easier and quicker to walk around London rather than use public transport at busy times of day. As they walked side by side, Olivia felt Jasmine's hand gently touch hers, and a jolt of excitement ran through her. She had never had a reaction like this before, and it took her breath away. Olivia wondered how she was going to get through this meal without going to pieces, and thought maybe they should have eaten at Jasmine's. She looked at Jasmine shyly and smiled.

On Friday, Jasmine had been getting more nervous as the day went on. She kept herself busy, and was relieved when five o'clock eventually arrived. It was all she could do to not go to Olivia's desk, take her in her arms, and kiss her right then and there. She knew that Jason was still in though, and didn't want any chance of him knowing anything, certainly not at the moment. Jasmine had always prided herself on keeping her private life private. As they left the office and walked down the road, she tentatively brushed her hand against Olivia's. She felt Olivia's reaction, and as Olivia turned to look at her, it was all she could do not to kiss her right there in the street. That wasn't her style though, and she wanted to take things slowly with Olivia, as she was still adjusting to their relationship. Jasmine smiled back at her, and they continued to the restaurant.

Covent Garden was a bubbling mass of people and noise as usual. They arrived at the restaurant, which had steps leading up to it on the first floor. Jasmine had reserved a table on the veranda, giving an excellent view of everything going on below. Olivia thought this was perfect for people watching, although this evening she thought that she probably wouldn't be looking at many other people tonight. As the evenings were beginning to get cooler, the outside heaters were on, so although they were on an open veranda, it felt very cosy. As Jasmine was looking through the menu, she said, 'Ah, this is nice. We can relax now, and we have the whole weekend ahead of us.'

Having placed their order, the waiter went off to get their drinks. Olivia looked across at Jasmine, 'So, have you always lived in London?' she asked.

Jasmine explained that she was born in London, and lived in Chelsea, quite near where she grew up. 'I feel it's so vibrant here, and also I always knew I wanted to be involved with publishing, and London seemed the perfect place. Are you enjoying being in London, now you've been here a few months?'

'Yes I am. It has been a bit of a culture shock, although I knew it would be, that's one of the reasons I wanted to come here. Emma has been great, showing me around, and letting me stay at her place. What's happening now, with us, that has really thrown me,' Olivia smiled shyly.

Jasmine looked right into her eyes, 'Sometimes you just have to go with what feels right. You don't have to do anything you don't want to.'

They sat across the table from one another, Olivia lost in thought for a moment. Over the sound system they could hear Bruno Mars' Just The Way You Are. Jasmine broke the silence, 'I love this song, it's beautiful, and the lyrics are very appropriate, I think,' she said, as she looked directly into Olivia's eyes.

Olivia blushed, smiling at Jasmine. Over dinner, they chatted about books that they loved, and comparing film adaptations of books. When Olivia spoke, Jasmine listened so intently, absorbing everything that she said. Olivia felt as though she was the only person in the world. To Jasmine, she was. The conversation flowed freely, through the meal and desserts. The waiter came over to clear the plates, and asked whether they would like a coffee or anything else to drink. Jasmine looked at Olivia, who shook her head. 'No thank you, just the bill please,' she smiled at the waiter.

Turning back to Olivia, she said, 'Would you like to come back to mine for a drink?'

Olivia hesitated. Jasmine didn't want to rush Olivia, but she was desperate to have her to herself, this week had felt so long. Olivia said yes, and Jasmine paid the bill. After putting their jackets on, they made their way down the steps. 'Thank you so much for dinner, that was lovely.'

Jasmine responded, 'You are very welcome, thank you for your company. I still can't quite believe we're doing this, I really thought that I had messed up when I told you how I felt about you.'

Olivia looked down, 'Well, you did freak me out, to be honest. But there was another part of me that felt it was so right. It was like my head was screaming no, and my very being was saying yes, go with it... It's really hard to describe.'

They walked through Covent Garden, still chatting, then headed to Jasmine's place. She did have a car, but generally used public transport to get around the centre of London. Once they arrived, Jasmine said, 'This is it.' Olivia looked up to see a beautiful town house, with regency windows and a white front door. Jasmine opened the door and invited Olivia in. 'Welcome to my home. Let me take your jacket.'

Handing Jasmine her coat, Olivia said, 'Thank you.' Olivia followed Jasmine to the kitchen.

'What would you like to drink? A glass of wine, coffee?'

'A coffee would be good, thank you.'

Once the drinks were made, they went through to the lounge. 'You have a beautiful home.' Olivia said, looking around.

The walls were pale blue, and the furnishings were white and pale wood. There was a large cream sofa, and two armchairs either side of it. 'Thank you, I'm very happy here,' replied Jasmine.

'Have you always lived on your own?'

Jasmine nodded, 'Apart from when I was at University, I've always lived here. I was very fortunate that my parents bought this place and gave it to me when I started working. I do love to have my own space. Let's sit down, I couldn't wait to get you alone so that we could talk. I've been going mad this week, waiting for this evening. I know this week has been unusual, shall we say,' Jasmine laughed, 'and I so want to spend time with you. I also don't want to rush you into anything, and you must tell me if anything is uncomfortable for you at all.'

Olivia looked back at her, 'Thank you. I might just need a bit of time to... adjust I suppose. But the way I've been feeling...' and she smiled at Jasmine.

When Olivia smiled at Jasmine like that, it made her heart soar. She had been using all of her self restraint this evening to not grab Olivia, kiss her, hold her. She had never felt this way about anyone before. As they sat together on the sofa, Jasmine reached across for Olivia's hand. Olivia felt the electricity race through her body. She turned towards Jasmine, who responded by kissing her full on the mouth. Olivia reciprocated eagerly, and Jasmine pulled her closer. Then Olivia whispered in Jasmine's ear, 'I want to make you feel as good as you made me feel the other day.'

Jasmine felt her insides melt, and she kissed Olivia deeply, holding her close. She could feel her heart beating, pounding with excitement. Jasmine moved herself over, and sat astride Olivia's lap. Olivia gently ran her hands down Jasmine's back. Tentatively holding the waistband of Jasmine's trousers, she slowly undid the button and lowered the zip. Jasmine watched Olivia as she did this, she couldn't believe how lucky she was, that this gorgeous woman wanted her too. Olivia looked up at Jasmine, and caught her eye. The look on Jasmine's face made her blush. Olivia touched Jasmine's body gently, feeling nervous. Although she knew what she wanted to do, she had never done this before. She started to move her hand down the front of Jasmine's trousers, and Jasmine groaned in response. This gave her the encouragement to carry on and go further. She slid her hand down, and then slowly entered her with her fingers. Jasmine was so wet and ready, and Olivia began massaging Jasmine, eliciting sounds of pleasure. Olivia moved faster, and Jasmine threw her head back in ecstasy, her body writhing. Olivia was really turned on by how she could make Jasmine feel, and moved her fingers in a circular motion, building the speed. Jasmine was so responsive to Olivia's touch, and the feelings that she could elicit, feelings of ecstasy. Jasmine's breathing was becoming more erratic, then she cried out with pleasure, and Olivia could feel the pulses of Jasmine's orgasm rippling through her. Jasmine said, 'Holy fuck,' and leaned forward to kiss Olivia.

Olivia was so turned on and throbbing down below. Jasmine undid Olivia's top, and discarded it. She leaned down to kiss Olivia's neck, savouring the softness, and running her tongue along the contours of her neck. Each time Olivia felt Jasmine's soft lips on her skin, it sent an amazing sensation through her. Jasmine kissed her breasts, her stomach, and Olivia felt that now familiar twist of anticipation. Jasmine slid her hands down, and unbuttoned Olivia's trousers, revealing her lacy pink pants. As Jasmine kissed Olivia, she slid her hands further still, and entered Olivia. She felt so good. Olivia was so aroused and close to coming, that it didn't take much before she was bucking and sighing with pleasure. As Jasmine looked at her in awe, she said, 'You're amazing. Stay with me tonight.'

Olivia was unsure, then Jasmine said, 'It's late now, and it's the weekend. It will be like a slumber party! We can have a lay-in, I'll make us breakfast.'

'Mmm, that does sound nice. But I haven't got any of my stuff.'

'I think I can find you a spare toothbrush, and you can borrow a pair of pj's, not that you'll need them,' said Jasmine, smiling cheekily.

Olivia agreed, why not. They snuggled up together on the sofa, chatting about nothing in particular, just enjoying one another's company. Rocky came along to join them, curling up on the end of the sofa, purring contentedly. At midnight, they decided it was time to get some sleep. Jasmine handed Olivia a toothbrush, and they got ready for bed. Olivia slipped under the covers naked, and Jasmine snuggled in beside her, and they drifted off to sleep. Jasmine was so happy, she couldn't have wished this to be any better.

SEVEN

Olivia awoke to bright sunshine streaming in through the bedroom window. For a moment, she was disorientated, then saw Jasmine standing by the bed looking at her. 'Morning, beautiful!' Jasmine said, and climbed back into bed, under the soft cotton covers. Olivia smiled back. 'Did you sleep well?' asked Jasmine.

'Yes thank you. Did you?'

'I had the best sleep that I've had in a long time. I still can't believe that you're in my bed.'

'Um, nor can I. I think I may be dreaming, or perhaps I've just been dropped into someone else's life.' Olivia looked a bit bemused.

Jasmine sat up and removed her top, revealing her beautiful breasts. She moved closer, whispering into Olivia's ear, 'Perhaps I can give you something to dream about...' and Olivia felt Jasmine's fingertips trail from her breasts, very slowly down her stomach, moving slower still, further down. Olivia felt that now familiar tightening of her stomach, and that tingle down to her core. Jasmine leaned forward and kissed Olivia, slowly and sensuously at first, then harder and faster. Olivia responded, holding Jasmine close. Olivia felt as though she was floating on air. But she still kept getting the feeling that she was having an out of body experience, like part of this wasn't her, or was perhaps a different version of her. As she was having these thoughts, sensation took over again, and now she was feeling Jasmine's warm breath on her neck, soft kisses being rained down on her. Olivia felt Jasmine's lips move down her neck, to each of her breasts in turn. Jasmine breathed, 'You have amazing tits,' and Olivia couldn't help giggling.

Jasmine continued down Olivia's body, gently kissing her stomach, her hips, going lower and lower still. She slid her hands to her thighs, and gently started pushing them apart. Olivia started to feel shy, thinking, surely not... And then she felt Jasmine's warm breath between her legs, her mouth on her, her tongue exploring Olivia. 'Oh, fuck!' Olivia cried out, the feeling was amazing, her body writhing in response to Jasmine's touch.

'I couldn't wait to taste you. Fuck, you taste so sweet.' Jasmine was relentless, and Olivia threw her head back, breathing heavily. Olivia could feel her orgasm building, her body a mass of sensation, feeling Jasmine's hands on her skin, her tongue in her sex.

'Aaahhh, aaahhh, aaahhhhh', Olivia cried out as her hips bucked, and she orgasmed again and again. 'Oh my god. Oh my fucking god,' breathed Olivia.

Jasmine moved back up the bed, searching for Olivia's mouth. She kissed her passionately, she was falling for Olivia so hard, she couldn't get enough of her. Olivia kissed her back with an intensity she felt she was not in control of. She'd heard of people talking about two becoming one, now she was getting a sense of what that really meant. Jasmine looked lovingly into Olivia's eyes. When Jasmine looked at her like that, Olivia felt that she could see into her very soul, her being. Olivia looked straight back at her, smiling, 'Are you the orgasm fairy or something? That was mind-blowing.'

Jasmine laughed, then looked serious, 'I think I'm falling in love with you.'

Olivia sat up, drawing her knees up to her chest. She pulled the covers over herself, and pushed her hair away from her face. Looking down, she said, 'Jasmine, this is amazing, the way you make me feel. You are a gorgeous woman, and to be honest, I'm not sure what you see in me. But as amazing as this is, I'm still trying to get my head around this. I'm straight, well, I always thought I was, now I just don't know. I've never been attracted to a woman before, but believe me, if I was going to be with a woman, it would be you.'

Jasmine felt her heart drop heavily. Suddenly her colourful world felt black and white. Oh shit, she thought, I moved too fast. I can't believe I've blown it, what on earth is wrong with me. Jasmine reached out, gently lifting Olivia's chin so that she could look into her eyes, 'I'm moving too fast, I'm so sorry. I said I was going to take things slowly with you. It's just that you have this effect on me, and any logic goes out of the window. You drive me wild with desire.'

Jasmine dropped her hand, and sat back on the bed. Olivia couldn't bear the sadness in Jasmine's eyes. 'Look, I'm not saying we can't do this, I'm just saying I'm having some difficulty with it.' At Olivia's words, Jasmine felt some hope spring back. 'Have you always liked women?' asked Olivia.

'Yes, it was something I realised at an early age, when I fell in love with a girl in my class at school.' She paused for a moment, 'Look, what do you want me to do? We can slow things right down, I promise.'

Olivia leaned over to gently kiss Jasmine. Jasmine felt such a longing that it hurt. She composed herself, 'Why don't you have a shower, and I'll make us some breakfast.'

Over breakfast, Jasmine asked Olivia what she wanted to do that day, suggesting perhaps a visit to a museum or art gallery. Olivia said, 'That would be great, but I need to pop home and get a change of clothing. I was wearing these clothes for work yesterday.'

They decided to visit the National Gallery, with a stop off at Olivia's place so she could get changed.

On their way to Emma's, Jasmine said that she would wait outside whilst Olivia popped inside. Olivia put the key in the door, and walked in. Emma and Matt were on the sofa, looking at the newspapers.

'Morning!' Olivia said brightly, 'I just came back as I forgot something.'

Emma looked at Olivia, noticing that she was in the same clothes as the previous day. 'Okay,' she replied, smirking, and she and Matt gave each other a look. Emma thought, I'll ask her about it later. I wonder whether it's her boss, she certainly seems to fancy him.

Olivia re-emerged from her room, wearing jeans and a white shirt, with her favourite brown biker jacket. 'See you tonight, then. Have a good day guys.'

Emma replied, 'I'm staying at Matt's tonight, so I'll see you Sunday.'

Closing the door behind her, Olivia walked down the steps to where Jasmine was waiting for her. Jasmine watched Olivia, and the way the sunlight caught her hair, giving her an ethereal glow. Jasmine looked right at Olivia, in that way that she had, and said, 'You are so beautiful.'

Olivia smiled back shyly. Jasmine had a way of saying things which made Olivia feel as though the floor had been taken away from under her feet, and she was free-falling.

Jasmine and Olivia walked along side by side, idly chatting. Olivia said, 'When I was a kid, we had a school trip to the National Gallery. I remember loving Monet and Renoir, and I did a school project on the French Impressionists. The school trip was also the first time that I had seen a Turner painting. I remember, the one that struck me the most was The

Fighting Temeraire, and I bought a postcard of it. I thought that the ghost-like ship was one of the most beautiful paintings I had ever seen. I've loved Turner ever since.'

It was at these moments, when Olivia was lost in the beauty of something, and the way she expressed herself, that Jasmine could feel herself fall that little bit more for Olivia. She wanted to hold her in her arms and kiss her, right there in the street. Instead, she looked at Olivia and smiled.

It was a typically busy Saturday in Trafalgar Square. As it was approaching lunchtime, Jasmine suggested that they go to a nearby cafe first to eat. They ordered paninis and hot drinks. After lunch, they made their way across Trafalgar Square, to the National Gallery. Walking up the steps, Olivia paused to look around her, taking in the marble pillars and golden arches. At the top of the steps she stopped to look in wonderment at the mosaic floor. Within the mosaic were various pictures. She noticed that one of them was called 'wonder', which she thought was very appropriate. Jasmine stood alongside her, watching Olivia taking everything in. 'It's so beautiful.'

'Beautiful, certainly,' Jasmine said softly, looking at Olivia.

Jasmine realised that it was so easy to take things for granted when you are surrounded by things that are familiar to you, whereas Olivia was seeing with fresh eyes. In that moment, Jasmine felt a wave of love for Olivia, and gently touched her hand. She felt a connection, and as Olivia turned her head to look into Jasmine's eyes, knew that Olivia felt it too.

They wandered around, taking in the paintings, standing back to get a good perspective. There were so many paintings to see, but Olivia particularly wanted to see the Turners. They walked through a set of doors, and on the left was The Fighting Temeraire. All over again, it took Olivia's breath away. Jasmine stood back, watching Olivia's reaction. She noticed a tear run down Olivia's cheek, which she quickly brushed away. Jasmine didn't say anything, she just walked over to Olivia and stood beside her in silence. As they walked slowly around the room, its deep blue walls giving the room a subdued feeling, they came to Turner's The Parting of Hero and Leander. Olivia exclaimed, 'Oh, I remember this painting now, I used to have a postcard of this one too. I had completely forgotten about it. It is so exquisite, I don't think that there are words to describe it.' Olivia stood for a long time, absorbing the beautiful painting.

At about half past three, Jasmine suggested that they go to the coffee shop. While Olivia went to find a table, Jasmine ordered the drinks. Jasmine couldn't help noticing how quiet Olivia was, but decided not to ask her why at the moment. Returning with their drinks on a tray, Olivia looked up, thanking Jasmine as she took her coffee. Jasmine waited for her tea to brew for a bit longer, before pouring herself a cup.

They spent another hour or so wandering around, before making their way to the shop to have a look around before they left. Jasmine noticed that Olivia spent a long time looking at a book on Turner's paintings. Around the shop were some glass cabinets, and there was one with an unusual vase of The Fighting Temeraire. 'Oh, isn't it beautiful!' exclaimed Olivia.

Looking at Olivia, the contours of her face, her wonderment, Jasmine softly said, 'Yes, it is.'

For a moment, Jasmine felt light headed, and knew that she was deeply in love with Olivia. Olivia turned to look at Jasmine, and held her breath. She could feel it too. After a while, Jasmine asked, 'Are you ready?'

Olivia nodded.

On their way back, Jasmine tried to make conversation, but Olivia seemed lost in her thoughts. They arrived at Olivia's, walked up the steps, and Olivia searched for her keys in her bag. 'Would you like a cup of tea?' she asked, as Jasmine followed her up the steps.

'That would be lovely, thank you.'

As they went inside, Olivia dropped her bag on a chair, and headed for the kitchen, filling the kettle with water. Jasmine followed her, asking, 'Is everything alright, you've been really quiet this afternoon.'

'I'm fine, I just feel really tired, that's all. Things have been so busy recently.'

Having made the drinks, she carried them through to the lounge, where they both sat on the sofa. 'Is Emma here today?' asked Jasmine.

'No, she's at Matt's. She'll be home tomorrow.'

Jasmine looked concerned, 'Olivia, do you want to talk? I know something's up.'

Olivia sighed, 'I don't know, really. Since that day when you kissed me, it's been a bit of a rollercoaster.'

Jasmine reached out for Olivia's hand. 'I guess things have moved pretty quickly for you. I should have been more thoughtful.' Shit, Jasmine was getting really worried she'd screwed things up.

'Don't get me wrong, I've been feeling things that I never thought possible. It's been really exhilarating, and also so overwhelming,' she looked at Jasmine, smiling weakly.

Jasmine said, 'I couldn't help watching you when you were looking at The Fighting Temeraire. Standing there, lost in thought. You looked so beautiful, I wanted to hold you, then and there. What were you thinking about?'

Olivia hesitated, and looking down as she spoke, said, 'I saw again how beautiful and sad it was. It took my breath away.'

'You take my breath away,' whispered Jasmine, and she leaned over to kiss Olivia gently on the lips. Jasmine continued, 'It was more than that, wasn't it?'

Now Olivia made eye contact, how could Jasmine know? 'As I looked at the painting, I thought about how it hadn't changed in nearly two hundred years, how it captured a moment in time. It took me back to being a kid, standing opposite the painting, when things seemed more certain. I suppose what with breaking up with Liam, leaving home and moving here, new job, new life, not to mention what's been happening with us... I felt like I didn't know anything anymore, and it scared me. Sorry, I haven't been very good company this afternoon. Did you enjoy the gallery?'

As Olivia looked up at Jasmine, she simply said, 'Yes, it was lovely.'

Jasmine put her arm around Olivia, who snuggled up beside her. What Jasmine really wanted to say, was that Olivia was the most beautiful person that she had ever met. That sharing moments with her made her heart sing in a way she never dreamed it could. That today, she had fallen in love.

They must have drifted off to sleep on the sofa, for Olivia came to with a start. She looked at the clock, seeing that it was nearly ten. She started to get up, and Jasmine opened her eyes. 'Oh, did I fall asleep? Sorry.'

'We both did,' said Olivia, stretching, then getting up.

Jasmine looked at her watch, 'It's getting late, I'd better be going.'

'Would you like to stay here tonight?' asked Olivia.

Jasmine hesitated, wondering whether it would be better if she gave Olivia some space, and searching her face for a clue. 'If you're sure that's okay, I'd love to. I'll go home after breakfast.'

Having got ready for bed, Olivia climbed under the covers, and rolled onto her side. Jasmine slid in beside her, and turned over to cuddle her, her front snuggled up to Olivia's back, with her arm around her. Jasmine listened to Olivia's breathing slowing down as she drifted off to sleep. Jasmine lay awake, praying that she hadn't rushed things with Olivia.

In the morning, Jasmine woke up to see Olivia lying next to her, smiling. 'Hello,' she said sleepily.

Jasmine smiled back at her. Waking up next to Olivia was amazing, something she had dreamed of, and thought would never happen. Jasmine spoke softly, 'Hello. You look beautiful this morning.'

Olivia smiled, 'So do you.' She leaned over and kissed Jasmine, her tongue searching Jasmine's mouth. Jasmine groaned, and kissed her back. Olivia broke the kiss, saying, 'I'm sorry about yesterday. I just got overwhelmed. I feel better for having a good sleep.'

Jasmine looked into Olivia's eyes, 'That's okay, there's no need to apologise,' and kissed her.

After breakfast, they showered and dressed. Jasmine said that she was going to head home. As much as she would love to spend another day with Olivia, she thought that Olivia could do with a day to herself. 'I'll see you at work tomorrow, have a good day,' and kissed Olivia.

'Yes, see you tomorrow. Thank you for yesterday.'

Olivia watched Jasmine walk down the steps. As she walked along the road, she turned to wave at Olivia. Olivia waved back, then closed the door. She decided to spend the day relaxing at home. Thinking back over the last couple of days, it had been quite a whirlwind. Although she had felt overwhelmed yesterday, Olivia had also never felt more alive in her life.

EIGHT

Walking into the lounge, Olivia noticed a book on the coffee table that she hadn't seen before. Maybe Jasmine had left something behind. She walked over, and saw that it was the Turner book she had been looking at yesterday in the gallery shop. There was a little note on it that simply said, 'For you.' Olivia picked it up, thinking how thoughtful of Jasmine it was. She opened the cover, and saw Jasmine's beautiful, flowing handwriting. 'Olivia, I have had the best weekend of my life. Thank you for sharing it with me. All my love, J x.'

Olivia clutched the book to her chest, smiling to herself.

Emma returned home about eight o'clock that evening, whilst Olivia was sitting on the sofa, flicking through a magazine. 'Hi, did you have a good weekend?' Emma asked.

Olivia looked up from her magazine, pushing her fringe off of her face, 'Yes, good thanks.'

'Only good? Come on, you appeared Saturday morning wearing the same clothes that you wore for work on Friday. Spill the beans!'

Olivia felt her cheeks colouring, as she remembered Friday night. 'I just stayed with a colleague from work. We had eaten out after work, and it was getting late, so it was easier to stay over.'

Olivia knew that she didn't sound very convincing. Emma reached towards the coffee table, and picked up the Turner book. 'Ooh, this a lovely book,' and before Olivia could stop her, she saw the inscription.

'Well, I think there might be a bit more to the story here,' she smiled at Olivia, and Olivia knew that she wouldn't be able to fob Emma off.

Olivia's head started buzzing, how was she going to explain this. She could not tell Emma that she had gone on a date with her boss, not to mention, her *female* boss, and they had gone back to her place for a night and morning of passion, and the best sex that she had ever had. Fuck. She still couldn't get her head around what was happening, and she certainly wasn't ready to start talking about it.

'Oh my god,' exclaimed Emma, 'I knew it. J, that's that Jason you fancy from work!'

Olivia started to laugh, then thought actually this is quite good. 'Umm, well, things just sort of happened. My boss is single, I'm single, so, you know...'

'Oh my god, was that what you and Jasmine were talking about the other evening on the sofa? You both looked as guilty as hell,' Emma laughed, 'I knew you were smitten. So, how was it?'

Olivia playfully threw a cushion at Emma, 'I don't kiss and tell!' and they both fell about laughing.

On Monday morning, Jasmine was already at work when Olivia arrived. Olivia went to the door and tapped on it. 'Come in,' Jasmine looked up, and smiled broadly when she saw Olivia.

'Hi. I just wanted to say thank you so much for the book, it was really sweet of you.'

'It's my pleasure. You seemed engrossed in it at the shop, and I really wanted to get you a memento of our weekend,' Jasmine smiled, giving Olivia a look which made her blush.

Olivia walked over to Jasmine, and bent down to kiss her. Suddenly they heard a noise in the outer office, Laura had just arrived. They pulled away quickly, and Olivia's heart was beating fast. Jasmine looked at Olivia, 'I think it would probably be a good idea to talk about how we're going to handle work. Would you like to come back to mine after work today?'

Olivia agreed, and went out to her desk. 'Morning, Laura. Good weekend?' she asked.

'Yes, it was lovely. Pete and I took the kids to Regents Park and we had a picnic and played football and rounders.'

'Oh, I used to love playing rounders. It's years since I played.'

'Well, how about we get together one weekend for a game? It's better when there are more people. We can ask Jason and Jasmine too,' Laura said excitedly.

After work, Laura had left, and Jason was still ensconced in his office. Jasmine and Olivia headed off home. Jasmine prepared a meal for the two of them, and they chatted about how they were going to handle work. Jasmine was very mindful not to rush Olivia in any way, and thought a slow approach would be best. She longed to make love to Olivia again, but after how Olivia was at the weekend, when Jasmine thought that she had screwed up by telling Olivia that she was falling in love with her, she knew that she would have to take things carefully.

They decided that at work they would be completely professional, or things might get difficult with Laura and Jason. They also agreed that they would only see each other socially at weekends, to make things easier. Olivia wasn't ready for people to know about her and Jasmine yet. She said, 'I haven't told you yet about last night, when Emma came home. She asked me about Friday night, and coming home Saturday in the same clothes. I said I stayed with a colleague, which actually was true! Then she picked up the book, and read the inscription.'

Jasmine looked worried, 'Oh, no, how did you explain that away?'

'As it happens, Emma jumped to the wrong conclusion, thinking J is Jason. So I was just vague, and said I wouldn't kiss and tell!' laughed Olivia.

'That could have been very awkward,' Jasmine paused, 'Come to think of it, why would she think it would be Jason?'

Olivia flushed, feeling really embarrassed. 'Er, um... after my interview, Emma was asking me about everyone. Because I said I thought Jason was sweet, she's been teasing me a bit. I said that I wasn't into him that way, and I'd never get involved with my boss. Ironic really,' and she laughed.

After dinner, Olivia was getting ready to go home. 'Thank you for dinner, it was lovely.'

Standing by the door, they kissed. A slow, deep kiss. As they pulled apart, Olivia was feeling breathless, her chest rising and falling rapidly. Jasmine looked at her with those deep, dark eyes, 'Stay with me this weekend. Bring your overnight bag and you can come back with me after work. I'd like to take you to the theatre.'

Olivia thought for a moment, 'That would be lovely, thank you.'

Back in the office, Olivia was pleased that they had decided to keep work separate to their social time. It would make work easier, and it also helped her because she was still getting her head around what was happening. It was almost like she was living two lives, one which was familiar to her, the one where she had moved to London and was starting a new career. The other life, she just didn't know at the moment. It was exciting, and unlike anything that she had ever done, or been before. Was this the real me, she wondered. Had Jasmine unleashed a side of her that she never knew existed. If she hadn't come to London, and got the job with Jasmine, none of this would be happening. Still, Jasmine had awakened something in her. When Jasmine had told her that she wanted to kiss her that first time, she could have said no. Olivia had let it happen, and not only that, but she had kissed her back. Afterwards, Jasmine had made it clear that she would never do something like that again. But Olivia had wanted it, and she hadn't realised how badly, until Jasmine had shown up at her door. Olivia came to, to see Jasmine walking towards her, with a smile on her face. She realised that she had drifted off with her thoughts, and sat up straight, smiling back at Jasmine. Jasmine handed her some letters to deal with, and Olivia brushed her hand as she took them. She looked up at Jasmine, into her dark eyes, and saw the look of longing in them. Then she suddenly remembered where she was. 'Okay, leave them with me,' she said, clearing her throat.

Jasmine went back to her office, and sat down. She couldn't wait for Friday to come around. She found it almost unbearable to be around Olivia all week and not be able to touch her or kiss her. Especially just now, watching Olivia as she walked towards her, seeing that look on her face, and feeling the gentle touch of her hand. Still, work had to be work, they would have plenty of time together at weekends. Jasmine also knew, after the day that they had been to the gallery, that she did not want to overwhelm Olivia.

Friday eventually arrived, and as they were leaving work, Olivia said that before the play, she would like to take Jasmine to dinner at her favourite Mexican restaurant in Covent Garden. As they arrived, it was already starting to get busy, with people chatting noisily at the bar. They sat down, and ordered some drinks. Olivia said she would have the fajitas, and Jasmine ordered the same. Jasmine told Olivia about the play that they were going to see. 'It's a new play, called Farinelli and the King. It's about King Philip V of Spain, and Farinelli, the eighteenth century's most celebrated castrato, who restored the King's sanity with his beautiful voice.'

They chatted about the theatre, which Jasmine loved. Olivia had only seen a couple of West End shows when she was a child, and she was excited about going to the theatre.

Jasmine said, 'These fajitas are delicious, I can see why you like it here.'

'Emma introduced me to this place. Actually, that day when you rang me to offer me the job, we came here to celebrate,' Olivia smiled at the memory.

Jasmine looked at Olivia. 'I remember the conversation clearly. You were so excited, so vibrant. I was thrilled when you accepted.'

After dinner, it was only a short walk to The Duke of York's theatre. London on a Friday evening was buzzing as usual. Olivia loved it, it was so different to back home. The thought gave her a strange feeling. This is my home now, she thought, although it still felt a bit temporary to her. Jasmine led the way in to the theatre, and they took the stairs down to the stalls, where their seats were at back of the theatre. It had been tricky getting tickets at all, as it was a limited run and very popular. Jasmine was so pleased that Olivia wanted to come to the theatre with her, it was one of her passions, and she loved that she could share it. She watched enthralled as the musicians arrived on stage and began to play, the music drifting into the auditorium. The stage was lit by candlelight, with candles around the lavish set and descending from the ceiling in chandeliers, giving the theatre an intimate feel. Jasmine was enchanted by the play. As it ended, she turned to look at Olivia, who had been completely engrossed in it. They smiled at each other, and got up to leave. They discussed the play as they headed back to Jasmine's place. 'Thank you so much, I really enjoyed it.'

Jasmine looked at Olivia, 'I'm so glad you did. Thank you for dinner, it was lovely.'

When they were back home, Jasmine took Olivia's jacket and hung it up. For a moment, they stood there looking at one another, then they drew closer and kissed, becoming more and more passionate. Jasmine breathed in the scent of Olivia, relishing the feel of her. Olivia still couldn't believe that Jasmine wanted her, but as they sank into the kiss, all thoughts disappeared. They drew apart, and went into the kitchen to make drinks. Rocky appeared, purring, and Jasmine prepared him some food. Olivia watched Jasmine as she busied herself, taking things from the cupboards, and thought how graceful she always looked. She remembered when she had first laid eyes on Jasmine, walking into the office for her interview. She had thought then how beautiful she was. Olivia would never have dreamed in a million years that she would wake up in Jasmine's bed. 'A penny for your thoughts.'

Olivia suddenly came to, realising she had drifted off into her own world. She looked up to see Jasmine watching her with an amused expression on her face. 'Oh, sorry. I was remembering when I first laid eyes on you. I thought you were so beautiful. I was just thinking that I never would have imagined what was going to happen with us.'

'You thought I was beautiful?' Jasmine was beaming at Olivia.

Olivia nodded shyly, then looked down. Jasmine asked, 'What did you enjoy most about the play this evening?'

Olivia thought for a moment, 'I think how Farinelli's voice touched the King's soul, and how the King described it as transporting him to the stars.'

Olivia looked up to see Jasmine looking right into her eyes, in that way that she did, 'You transport me to the stars.'

Jasmine spoke to Olivia in a way that no one had ever done before, as if she was the only person in the world that mattered. Olivia closed the space between them, and kissed Jasmine on the mouth. Jasmine responded eagerly, and they were all over each other, hands everywhere. 'Oh, I've been longing for this week at work to finish, I don't know how I managed to wait all week,' Jasmine said through their kisses.

They moved to the bedroom, beginning to undress one another urgently, then fell onto the bed. Jasmine began kissing slowly down Olivia's neck, her breasts, her stomach, savouring each piece of bare flesh. Olivia rolled over, and she was now astride Jasmine. She moved back, and slid Jasmine's trousers down thighs and discarded them. Jasmine was a mass of sensation as she felt Olivia's fingers softly sliding her lacy white panties down, trailing down her hips, her thighs, down to her ankles. Olivia climbed back on the bed, kissing Jasmine on the mouth and moving slowly down her body, her fingertips tracing along her skin, kissing her body as she continued moving downwards. Jasmine was writhing with sensation and pleasure, and her responses turned Olivia on even more. Olivia was highly aroused, and knew what she wanted to do, but she was feeling nervous. She had never done this before, and she wanted to do it right. As her lips reached the apex of Jasmine's thighs, she paused. Jasmine whispered, 'You don't have to do this...'

Oh my god. Jasmine couldn't believe it. She was so highly sensitised, and she didn't want the feeling to stop. Olivia was determined, 'I want to...' and Jasmine felt Olivia's soft sweet lips on her, tentatively searching and stimulating her. Holy fuck, that feels amazing. Jasmine felt lightheaded with sensation, with desire, with love. She had never felt this way before, and it overwhelmed her. A tear escaped, and ran down her face.

Olivia was rhythmically exploring Jasmine. She loved how she could have this effect on Jasmine, and elicit such pleasure. Olivia could hear and feel Jasmine nearing orgasm, and held her as she cried out, convulsing and groaning with pleasure. Olivia pulled back, laughing, 'Not bad for my first time!'

Jasmine was breathless, practically speechless. As she began to reclaim herself, she breathed, 'Holy fuck, talk about a trip to the stars.'

Olivia moved up the bed, and Jasmine kissed her with fervour. 'I can't wait to taste you again,' she whispered in Olivia's ear.

She moved down Olivia's body, and Olivia's stomach twisted with that familiar feeling of expectation and excitement, knowing what was about to happen.

As they lay in bed together afterwards, Olivia's body subsiding from her orgasms, Olivia was thinking that she didn't know she could feel so connected with someone, both physically and spiritually. It was an amazing feeling. She turned and smiled at Jasmine, who licked her lips seductively and whispered, 'You taste so sweet, I can't get enough of you.'

Olivia thought, holy mother of fuck, that was hot. They kissed again, and then fell back on the bed. 'I never knew a night at the theatre could be so exhausting!' laughed Olivia.

They both lay there, holding hands, laughing.

NINE

A few weeks later, the weekend was approaching. Laura had arranged for everyone to get together for a rounders game. Although it was now November, Sunday's forecast was dry and bright. Never mind if it was a bit colder now, they would soon warm up once they were running around.

Sunday morning was as good as the forecast. Olivia and Jasmine had decided to travel to Regent's Park separately. Emma had been quite surprised that Olivia was home on Saturday evening. Lately, she had hardly been there at weekends. She assumed that Olivia must be spending more time with Jason, although whenever she tried to ask questions, Olivia was very vague. Ah well, at least she seems really happy. Come to think of it, she always seemed happy, with a rosy glow on her cheeks. Well, something was obviously agreeing with her.

'Okay Emma, I'm just off out. Laura has arranged for us to play rounders with her hubby and kids, so I'll see you later.'

Emma replied, 'Have a great time, then.'

When Olivia arrived at Regent's Park, Jason and Jasmine were already there. 'Hi,' she said, walking towards them. Jasmine beamed at her. Just then, Laura and her family arrived, and as Jason went to greet them, Jasmine took the chance to speak to Olivia alone. Very quietly, she said, 'I missed you last night. The bed felt so empty without you.'

Olivia felt a longing to kiss Jasmine, but there was no way with the others around. Instead, she said, 'I missed you, too.'

They walked over to the others, and Laura introduced Olivia to Peter, and their children, Felicity and Harry. Olivia shook hands with Peter. They got the game set up, and took it in turns to bowl, with the other six making two teams. Jason, it turned out, was excellent at whacking the ball really long distances, and consequently he scored a lot of rounders for his team. Thankfully, the children loved to run and run, so they did a lot of the chasing. At lunchtime, they all sat down in a heap, ready for the picnic that Laura and Peter had prepared. Jason said, 'Thank you, guys, for arranging this, it's great fun. Also, it's good to get together out of work. We should do it more often.'

At this comment, Jasmine and Olivia stole at look at each other, and smiled. Laura noticed the exchange of looks, but thought nothing more of it. After lunch and a rest, Felicity and Harry were desperate to start playing again. 'Come on Olivia, come and play,' said Felicity, pulling on Olivia's hand.

Olivia got up, and the three of them ran around playing tag. Jason said, 'She certainly has a lot of energy. And she's great with the kids.'

Jasmine looked on, watching Olivia running around, laughing, she seemed so free and happy. Again, Laura noticed Jasmine watching Olivia. Jasmine turned and caught Laura's eye, and they smiled at one another. After a couple more hours playing, the children were finally worn out. They packed up their things, kissed and hugged each other goodbye, and everyone started to head off home. Jasmine and Olivia walked to the exit of the park with Jason, and they said goodbye. Once he was down the road, Olivia asked whether Jasmine would like to go back to her place for the evening.

Sitting on the sofa after tea, Jasmine said, 'I had a lot of fun today. You seemed to really enjoy running around with the kids.'

Olivia looked at her, 'Yes, I did. They are really cute kids. Laura has such a lovely family.'

Jasmine asked, 'Would you like to have children one day?'

Olivia thought for a moment, 'I don't know. I guess when I was younger I just assumed that I would meet a guy, get married and start a family. It's not something I've thought about recently, though. How about you?'

Jasmine replied, 'Not particularly. Obviously, I knew I wasn't going to settle down with a guy, so just thought I'd wait and see what happens.'

There was a noise at the door, as Emma let herself in. 'Hi Emma, you know Jasmine. We're recovering from a fun and exhausting day running around Regent's Park.'

'Hi Jasmine. Did you all have a good time?'

'Yes, it was great fun. I was a bit rusty, but managed to score a few rounders,' replied Olivia.

Jasmine said, 'Well, I'd better head off home now, we've got work tomorrow. Nice to see you again, Emma. I'll see you in the morning, Olivia.' Olivia walked her to the door, but didn't kiss her as Emma was there.

Laura arrived at work on Monday morning, putting her bag down on her desk, and taking off her coat. 'Hi, Olivia. Yesterday was fun. I have to tell you, my kids love you. All they've been talking about since yesterday, is when can they see you again.'

'Oh, that's so sweet, your kids are gorgeous. I remember you once said you and Peter don't get out much on your own. How about I babysit sometime, I can do something with the kids, and you two get some time on your own.'

Laura looked thrilled, 'Really? That would be wonderful. Felicity and Harry will be ecstatic when I tell them. Thank you, thank you so much.'

Jasmine appeared in the outer office, and had caught the conversation. She saw how happy Laura looked, and how pleased Olivia was. Jasmine thought again how grateful she was that Olivia was here.

Over the next few weeks, things seemed to be settling into a pattern. Jasmine and Olivia saw each other at the weekends, and Emma assumed Olivia was dating Jason. A few times, Emma did ask about meeting him, and Olivia managed to think of some excuses, then Emma would stop asking for a while. Jasmine wanted to see Olivia in the week as well, but decided not to say anything at the moment, as things were going really well with them. They tended to keep to themselves, visiting art galleries, museums and the theatre or cinema, and often staying in. Olivia always stayed at Jasmine's, as she had her own place, whereas Olivia had a roommate who liked to ask questions. Jasmine loved the weekends, where she and Olivia could be free to be themselves. She hoped that soon, Olivia would be ready to be open about their relationship.

At lunch one day, Laura asked if she could take Olivia up on her offer of babysitting. Pete had a works do, and Laura was invited. Olivia said of course, and it was arranged. When the evening arrived, Olivia turned up at Laura's at six thirty. Laura answered the door wearing a beautiful black dress and a stunning red necklace. 'You look gorgeous,' Olivia smiled.

Laura blushed, 'Thank you, I don't get dressed up very often. Pete is just putting his suit on.'

Felicity and Harry came running up to see her. 'Hi, how are you?'

The children were so excited to see Olivia. All at once, they wanted to show her their toys, draw, make things, and watch a film together. Laura laughed, 'Give Olivia a chance to get in the door! You have all evening to play.'

Laura showed Olivia where everything was, inviting her to make herself at home. She said that as it was the weekend, the children could stay up, but not too late. Pete appeared downstairs, doing up his tie. Olivia said that he looked very handsome in his suit, and that they made a lovely couple. Pete looked lovingly at Laura, and kissed her, which made the children giggle. They all said goodbye, and Laura and Pete left for their party. Felicity grabbed Olivia's hand, taking her to her bedroom to show Olivia her teddy bears. Harry couldn't wait to show Olivia his toys too, and they both wanted help building the wooden train set. All three of them set to work building a track across the floor, and when it was finished, they played happily, making chuffing noises and train whistles. A while later, they all snuggled up on the sofa to watch one of their favourite films. Once the film had finished, Olivia said that it was time for bed. She read them both a story, and tucked them in. Felicity looked up at Olivia, with big eyes, and asked, 'Will you come and look after us again please.'

Olivia said of course she would, and said goodnight. Harry gave her a big hug, and snuggled under his covers. Laura and Pete returned home about midnight, and Olivia was half asleep on the sofa. She heard the key in the door, and looked up, 'Hi guys, did you have a good time?'

Pete said, 'Yes thank you, it was great. Sorry we're a bit late. How were the kids?'

'Brilliant. You have the cutest children. Any time you need a babysitter, just ask.'

Laura was thrilled to bits, 'Thank you so much.' Pete booked a cab to take Olivia home.

It was coming up to Christmas, and the office was closing for the week. Olivia was going back to St Ives for the holiday, and it would be the first time that she had been back since moving out in June. She had thought that she would visit before now, and wondered where on earth the time had gone. Olivia did talk to her parents and Becky regularly, so they each kept the other updated with what was going on. Olivia was going to leave for Cornwall from Jasmine's. Lying in bed that morning, Jasmine said, 'I do wish you weren't going away. I know it's your first time back, but I'm really going to miss you.'

Olivia leaned over and kissed her, 'The week will fly by, and before you know it, I'll be back. Anyway, you'll be able to catch up with your friends and family too.'

Olivia arrived at St Erth station, to see Ella waiting expectantly. 'Darling! It's so good to see you.' Her mum wrapped her in a big hug.

'Hi Mum, it's good to see you too.' Olivia suddenly felt very emotional, she had missed her mum, and this was the longest time that she had been away from her.

They chatted animatedly on the drive home, and Ella asked her daughter lots of questions about her new life in London. 'I thought you might be too tired after the long journey to go out tonight, so I'm going to cook at home. I've booked a restaurant for tomorrow so we can all go out together then.'

'Lovely, thanks Mum. So, what's news with you?'

After dinner, Olivia went to help clear up. Her dad told her to sit down, he would do it. Olivia sat herself down in the armchair, and her mum sat on the sofa. Ella was asking her more questions about the people that she had met in London. Olivia knew that really she was angling to find out whether she was dating anyone. Eventually, she came out and asked outright. 'Mum, there's so much going on with work, and I socialize with them too sometimes, I'm still getting settled in.'

Then Olivia told her mum about the rounders day in the park, and how she had babysat for Laura's kids. This kept Ella distracted, and the inquisition stopped for the time being. Between Emma and her mum, Olivia was running out of excuses.

The next day, Olivia was feeling refreshed after a good night's sleep. Today she was meeting up with Becky, Dan and Liam. Waiting in their usual cafe, Olivia saw the others arriving. Becky squealed and rushed towards Olivia, giving her a crushing hug. 'I've missed you so much, the gallery isn't the same without you.'

Olivia replied, 'I've missed you too,' and suddenly felt emotional as she hugged her dear friend. Becky was really missing Olivia, they had never spent this much time apart before. Becky dearly hoped that she would get this London business out of her system, and move back home. They hugged each other for a long time, then Liam said, 'I think it's my turn, can I have a look in!' then grabbed Olivia and hugged her, lifting her feet off of the ground. He put her down, and Olivia hugged Dan.

'It's so good to see you all,' she said. They sat around the table talking endlessly. Dan looked at Olivia, 'Something in London obviously agrees with you, you look fantastic.' Olivia blushed.

Olivia's parents held a party on Christmas Eve. They had a beautiful Christmas tree, with lots of multi coloured fairy lights. There were still decorations on the tree that Olivia and Ben had made when they were children. Ella wouldn't hear of getting rid of them, they meant a lot to her. Friends and neighbours were invited, and the evening was in full swing. Everyone wanted to hear about Olivia's new life, and by the end of the evening she was getting quite tired, having answered the same questions multiple times. Becky and Dan were still dancing, and some of the neighbours were getting a bit tipsy. Liam had been watching Olivia, he found it hard keeping his eyes off of her. She seemed different somehow, but he couldn't say how. Was it confidence from working in London, maybe. She seemed to have a freedom about her that he hadn't seen before. After the party, when Olivia was helping her mum and dad clear up, Steve asked, 'So, has it been good catching up with your friends again?'

Olivia stopped wiping up the plates for a moment, and leaned on the worktop. 'Yes, I have missed them. At the same time, I know that I made the right decision moving to London. That's not to say that I'll stay in London indefinitely, but at the moment I am having an amazing time,' she smiled at her dad.

'I noticed that Liam couldn't keep his eyes off you, I think he's still rather smitten. I don't think he's been seeing anyone.'

'Dad, I'm really happy as I am, thank you! Liam is great, but it was time for us.'

Ella said, 'Steve, stop trying to match make, Olivia is fine,' and smiled at her daughter.

On Christmas morning, Olivia woke up to see a stocking at the end of her bed. It didn't matter how old she was, she loved this, and felt like a child again. She went downstairs to turn on the Christmas tree lights, and sat down by the tree. She remembered the many times that she had done this over the years, and now was the first time that she wasn't living at home. Home was a changing feeling for her now. She thought about Jasmine, and decided to call her, although it was still early. Olivia heard Jasmine's sleepy voice on the end of the phone, and she was delighted to hear from Olivia. 'Happy Christmas. I really miss you.'

Olivia replied, 'I miss you too. Are you going to your parents today?'

'I'm going to Phoebe and Fran's today, and my parents tomorrow. I can't wait for you to come home.'

Home, there it is again. They chatted for a while, then Olivia heard her parents getting up. She said that she would have to go, and would speak to Jasmine soon.

Olivia had a wonderful Christmas, although she really missed Jasmine. It was great to be with her parents, Ben and Tina. Ben and Tina had been together for a couple of years now, and seemed pretty serious. Tina had really become part of the family.

Olivia knew that she would soon be heading back to London, as she had said to Jasmine, the week was flying by. She was loving seeing her family and friends again, but at the same time she really missed Jasmine. One morning she was sitting in her room, with its white furniture and blue and white check duvet cover, looking out of the window. It was lovely being back, but she also knew that a part of her didn't belong here now. She thought about Jasmine, and wondered what she was doing now. It was a shame that Olivia couldn't talk about her in the way she wanted to. She would when she was ready, but at the moment she was still trying to work out how she felt about it herself. As she looked out of the window, her mind wandered. She didn't know when it started, when things changed. Had there been signs, and she had been too caught up in other things to see them... Maybe it was just a phase, or was she starting to lose it? Or maybe she was beginning to find herself. Perhaps she could just give in to it, let herself go...

Olivia had one more get together with her friends before catching the train back to London. When it was time to leave, Becky said, 'Ring me when you're back, have a safe journey.'

Liam gave her a hug, 'It's been so good to see you, really good.'

'You too,' she replied.

The train was running a bit late, and Olivia had received a text from Jasmine, asking when she would be arriving. Eventually, the train pulled into Paddington station. Olivia was walking across the concourse, then noticed Jasmine walking towards her, beaming from ear to ear. 'Welcome home!' Jasmine flung her arms around Olivia.

'Thank you, this is a surprise. I didn't think I was seeing you until tomorrow.'

Jasmine said, 'I know, I just couldn't wait another minute to see you. I've got my car, come back with me and I'll drop you home in the morning.'

Arriving home, Jasmine opened the door and turned on the hall light. Olivia followed her in, and closed the door behind her. Immediately Jasmine's lips were on hers, and Jasmine started undoing Olivia's coat. Olivia started unbuttoning Jasmine's coat, and pushed it off of her shoulders, then she slipped her own coat off. Their hands were all over each other. 'I've missed you so much,' said Jasmine between kisses.

'I missed you too.'

They moved into the lounge, undressing as they went, and onto the sofa. Jasmine ran her hands over Olivia's body, feeling her contours, her softness. Oh, how she had missed Olivia, she didn't know how she had managed a whole week without her. Olivia was revelling in the feeling of Jasmine's soft skin against her own. Kneeling opposite each other, Olivia felt Jasmine's hand slide down her pants, her fingers exploring and entering her. Jasmine breathed, 'You are so wet, you make me so fucking horny.'

Olivia deepened their kiss, and Jasmine could feel Olivia's fingers moving down her body, then inside her. Jasmine felt a renewed explosion of desire, so much sensation, it was almost unbearable. They had missed each other so much, and Olivia's senses felt ever more heightened. She felt as though she had been starved, and now she was at a banquet. As their desperate longing for closeness increased, so did their momentum, and the inevitable build towards climax. They groaned with pleasure, and came together, crying out, and holding one another as their bodies shuddered, and their orgasms dissipated. Jasmine pulled a blanket over them, and they curled up together on the sofa.

TEN

Olivia arrived back at home the following morning, to find Emma in the lounge. 'Hello, did you have a good Christmas?' she asked.

Olivia replied, 'Yes, it was lovely being back and seeing everyone. I did get a million questions, though!'

'Well, you look great. If I didn't know any better, I'd say that you got laid last night, big time.'

Olivia flushed bright red, and lent down, pretending she was getting something from her bag. Fortunately Emma hadn't noticed, and continued, 'Did they ask you about Jason, did you tell them anything?' Emma was eager to know.

'No I didn't, it's a bit soon. How about you, did you have fun?'

Emma nodded, 'Yes, it was great. I've been to a few parties, and danced my socks off!'

That evening, Jasmine came over to see Olivia. Emma was out with Matt, so they could talk freely. Jasmine said, 'I'd like you to come to a party with me tomorrow night that my friends are holding. It will be just women, not too many people, probably ten of us in all. It would mean that we could be a proper couple there.'

'Okay, that sounds nice. I've not yet met any of your friends.'

Jasmine looked at Olivia, in that way she did, and leaned forward to kiss her. 'Wonderful, I'm so pleased. You can stay at mine.'

Olivia had decided to wear a dress for the party, with some high heeled knee high boots. It was a deep red shift dress, with a slight shimmer when it caught the light. Emma was getting ready to go out when Olivia was getting ready. 'You look fabulous. I love your boots.'

'Thank you. I don't know if it's a dressy party or not, but I thought, why not!'

Emma said that she was off out with Matt, and left saying, 'Have fun!'

About twenty minutes later there was a knock at the door. Olivia opened it, and Jasmine looked at her wide eyed. Walking inside, Jasmine said, 'Holy fuck, you look gorgeous,' and kissed Olivia passionately.

As they pulled apart, breathing heavily, Olivia laughed, and Jasmine asked her what was so funny. Olivia smiled at her, 'Well, when I first met you, I thought how sophisticated you were, and I would have never dreamed what a potty mouth you have!'

Jasmine gave her a look, 'Well, you just do something to me that drives me wild!', and pulled her into another passionate embrace.

When they pulled apart, Olivia said, 'You look amazing.'

Jasmine was wearing that long midnight blue dress, with satin shoes to match. She had tied her long hair up, exposing her delicate neck. She wore beautiful dangling platinum earrings with a single diamond on them. She looked stunning. Olivia still didn't know why Jasmine wanted to be with her.

The party was a relaxed affair, but everyone had dressed up, so Olivia was glad that she had chosen her dress and boots. Back in Cornwall, the few parties she went to were usually college friends having a party at home, wearing jeans and t shirts. Arriving at the front door, Jasmine said, 'Hi, I'd like you to meet Olivia. Olivia, this is Phoebe, and this is Fran.'

They all shook hands and kissed cheeks. Phoebe said, 'We've heard so much about you, it's so lovely to finally meet you.'

Jasmine's friends were mostly a bit older than Olivia. Jasmine introduced Olivia to everyone, she didn't want her feeling left out in any way. Jasmine's friends were very interested in hearing about the gallery where she used to work, and the artists she met. Most of the guests at the party were couples, and Olivia thought that they were all very friendly. Jasmine frequently touched Olivia's hand, and put her arm around Olivia's waist. Away from home, this felt unusual, as they had been careful not to have too much physical contact at the office, or out in public. Here, it felt really good to be able to relax with other people.

Jasmine was having a wonderful evening. She watched Olivia chatting with her friends, and felt so pleased that at last they had met her. Jasmine's friends had been keen to meet Olivia, the woman who had stolen Jasmine's heart. They had never seen her so happy before. There was music playing in the background, and people were beginning to dance. Jasmine walked over to Olivia, 'Dance with me,' and took her hand. 'You look so beautiful, thank you for coming with me tonight.'

Olivia looked into Jasmine's eyes. With her heels on, Olivia was almost the same height. Jasmine leaned in to kiss Olivia, who instinctively moved her head back. 'It's okay, we're amongst friends,' she whispered, and tentatively kissed Olivia, who now responded.

It seemed strange to Olivia, being kissed in front of other people. She guessed she would get used to it at some point, and she knew she wouldn't be able to keep their relationship secret forever, nor would she want to. At the moment though, it still felt too soon, so much had changed for her in such a short period of time. Jasmine had been very understanding and patient. They had been seeing each other for nearly three months, and this was the first time that Jasmine had suggested meeting her friends. With their arms around one another, they danced for the rest of the evening. When it was time to leave, Jasmine and Olivia said their goodbyes. At the door, Phoebe and Fran

133

hugged Olivia. 'Thank you for this evening, I've had a wonderful time,' said Olivia.

Phoebe smiled, 'Thank you for coming, I can see how happy you and Jasmine are, it's wonderful.'

Back home that evening, Jasmine said, 'Thank you so much for coming to the party with me, it made me so happy. My friends love you!'

Olivia replied, 'I had a really good time tonight. It did feel a bit weird to start with, being a couple in front of other people, but I guess I'll get used to it. Your friends made me feel very welcome.'

It was a couple of weeks into January, and Olivia was just walking from Jasmine's office, back to her desk. She noticed that someone was sitting on the sofa, and couldn't believe it when she realised that it was Liam sitting there. He stood up as he saw her. 'Hi Olivia, how are you?'

She walked over to him and they hugged. 'What on earth are you doing here?'

Liam explained that he was in town, and thought he would pop by. He wanted to take her out for lunch. Olivia said that she would just let Jasmine know that she would be popping out. Jasmine looked up at the tap on the door, smiling when she saw Olivia. 'Hi. Um, Liam has turned up out of the blue. He wants to go for lunch, is it okay if I pop out now? If you like, I'll introduce you.'

Olivia walked back out to Liam. She introduced him to Laura, and then Jasmine appeared from behind her. 'Liam, I'd like you to meet Jasmine. Jasmine, this is Liam.'

As they shook hands, Jasmine said, 'It's very nice to meet you.'

Liam smiled, 'Very nice to meet you, too.'

They chatted for a few minutes, and Jasmine noticed how easy and relaxed Olivia was with Liam. She also noticed that he hardly took his eyes off her.

Olivia suggested a nearby sandwich bar for lunch. After ordering their food, they sat down with their drinks. 'So, what are you doing in London?'

'Actually, I'm looking for a job here. Seeing you back home at Christmas, it got me thinking. I thought maybe it was time to explore somewhere outside Cornwall too. I was thinking of taking on a short term contract initially, to see how I get on.'

Liam was a software engineer, and tended to work contracts. The pay was excellent, and if he wanted time off for holidays, it was very flexible. 'Look, will you have dinner with me tonight? I'd like to chat with you a bit more.'

Olivia was really surprised that Liam would want to come to London. He had never before shown any interest. In fact, when she had first talked about moving to London, he had tried to put her off, saying it was one of the last places that he would ever want to work. Still, she thought, people do change. Take her situation, for example. She would never have imagined what was going to happen with her and Jasmine.

After lunch, Liam walked Olivia back to the office. Later that afternoon, Jasmine asked whether Olivia had had a nice lunch. When Olivia explained that Liam was looking for work in London, and he was going to tell her more at dinner that evening, Jasmine couldn't help feeling a pang of jealousy. Liam and Olivia had a long history together, and she saw the way that he looked at her. She knew that look so well, and at the party her friends had seen it in her. In fact, after the party, Fran had commented to Phoebe, 'Boy, Jasmine has got it bad. Did you see, she didn't have eyes for anyone in the room but Olivia.'

Over dinner that evening, Olivia asked Liam what he wanted to talk to her about. Liam looked at her, 'I'm just going to come out and say it. I can't stop thinking about you. I think I made a huge mistake letting you go. I want you back.'

Oh. Olivia was speechless.

'When I saw you at Christmas, I was watching you at the party, thinking what an idiot I was. I still love you.'

Olivia looked at Liam, his expression so earnest. 'I don't know what to say. We discussed it all back in the spring. I do love you, but as a friend. We had our time together, it's over now, I'm sorry.'

Liam apologised, then laughed to himself. 'I guess I was crazy, thinking I could just turn up, declare my love, and you would fall into my arms.'

Olivia smiled, 'You are such a sweet guy, and you will meet the girl for you.'

Liam looked up sadly, 'I think I already did.'

Liam walked Olivia home, and she invited him in to meet Emma. He told Emma about his plans to work in London for a while, and omitted the part about trying to get Olivia back. After he had left, Emma plonked herself on the sofa next to Olivia. 'Liam is lovely, and he's obviously crazy for you. Now he's coming to London, you could get back together.'

Olivia said, 'He's lovely, but I just don't feel that way about him now. Actually, at dinner he told me he thinks he made a mistake in letting me go, and that he still loves me.'

Emma looked surprised and excited, 'Oh, that's so romantic.'

Olivia smiled, 'Yes, but it's not just a case of him letting me go. I wanted to go.'

Liam got a six month contract in the city. Emma put him in touch with someone who had a place to rent, and he moved into a flat near his work. Over the next few weeks, Olivia and Emma helped him get settled. He found London quite overwhelming, and much more pressured than he was used to in Cornwall. Still, he loved spending time with Olivia again, even if it was just as friends. They saw a lot of each other after work, although at weekends he found that Olivia often had plans with a friend. Olivia was rather vague about who it was, though. Liam got on well with Matt, and sometimes they would go out for a drink or to watch a film if it was one that the girls didn't want to see. Olivia was enjoying hanging out with Liam because it was so easy. She felt that she could be herself around him all of the time. He fitted in with the part of her life that was safe and familiar to her. Also, they made up a good foursome with Emma and Matt. Olivia really cared for Jasmine, and they certainly had an amazing connection, that was without doubt. But there was still a part of her which was unsure. When she was with Jasmine at weekends, everything felt perfect, but when they were apart during the week, being just colleagues, she was feeling as though she was living two different lives. One was exciting, and she felt so alive, but it was also partly secret. Was that what made it exciting, she wondered. The other part of her life was comfortable and easy, because it was familiar to her.

As the weeks went by, Jasmine had the feeling that she was starting to lose Olivia. She understood that Liam was a close friend, and she knew that Olivia didn't want to get back together with him. But when she saw them together, it made her heart ache. One Saturday morning, they were having breakfast at Jasmine's. Olivia seemed really distracted. Jasmine looked across the table at her. 'Is something up? You haven't been yourself recently.'

Olivia sighed, and as she raised her head, Jasmine saw tears running down her face. Olivia sobbed, 'I'm sorry, I'm so sorry. I don't think I can do this anymore.'

Jasmine felt the colour drain from her face, and was glad she was sitting down, as she felt the bottom fall out of her world. No, no, this can't be happening. 'What do you mean?' Jasmine was trying to stop her voice from quivering.

Olivia was now sobbing really hard. Once she had calmed down a bit, she said, 'You know I've been having some trouble getting my head around what's been happening. You are so beautiful and sexy, but it all happened so quickly, and I thought it would be easier by now. I really don't want to hurt you. I think I just need some time, some time alone. I'm so sorry, please forgive me.'

Jasmine didn't know what to say, her mind went numb. She couldn't move, she just sat stock still at the table, as though her legs were encased in concrete. Olivia went to get her things, then walked over to Jasmine, and kissed the top of her head. 'I'm going to go, I'll call you later. I'm so sorry,' and the tears started to flow again.

As Jasmine heard the door close, she came to, and let out a howl of pain and sadness that emanated from the core of her being. She sobbed uncontrollably, hugging herself and shaking.

Olivia arrived home, although she didn't remember how she got there, and went straight into her room. She lay on the bed, sobbing. What had she done. She thought she was doing this for Jasmine, and she was the last person that she wanted to hurt. Olivia felt so sad. Deeply, painfully sad. At the same time, she knew that she needed some head space. Being with Jasmine was amazing, but along with their relationship, she felt that she had to keep a part of herself hidden. She knew that was her choice, to an extent. Surely, it was best this way in the long run.

Olivia came to, and sat up. She must have fallen asleep. Looking at the clock, she could see that it was nearly eight in the evening. Suddenly feeling hungry, she got up to get something to eat. As she walked past the mirror, she caught her reflection. Shit, she looked terrible. She quickly went to the kitchen to make some coffee and a piece of toast, taking it back to her room. She didn't want to talk to Emma tonight.

At some point, Jasmine must have moved to the sofa, for that is where she was when she woke up. Coming to, she opened her eyes, then the reality of that morning smacked her right in the face like a bucket of cold water. A feeling of desolation coursed through her, and she didn't think that she could stand the pain. Her tears began again, uncontrollable, seemingly unending. Rocky had been curled up on the end of the sofa, and now padded over to Jasmine, purring and rubbing his face on her. She cuddled him, her tears dripping onto his fur.

On Sunday morning, Olivia realised that she hadn't called Jasmine, as she had said she would. She nervously dialled her number. Eventually, she heard Jasmine pick up. 'Hi,' Jasmine's voice sounded hollow.

Olivia said, 'I'm so sorry. I hope you can forgive me. I couldn't carry on with things while I'm feeling so confused. Please forgive me,' and Olivia's voice broke.

Jasmine hated hearing Olivia like this, although she was still feeling a combination of intense pain, followed by numbness. She simply said, 'Is it Liam?'

Olivia replied, 'No, there's no-one else. I just need some time for me.'

Jasmine sighed, 'Okay, look, I have to go,' and hung up.

She dropped the phone, and bent forward, hugging herself, the tears flowing down her cheeks like waterfalls.

Olivia put her phone down. Shit, this was so hard. She started sobbing again, and curled up on the bed. After some time, Olivia heard a tap on the door. Emma asked if she could come in, and opened the door. She looked at Olivia, her face red and puffy, and went over to give her a hug. 'Oh my god, what on earth happened? I heard you crying, I had to check you were alright.'

Olivia sobbed in Emma's arms. Emma held her until the tears started to subside. Eventually, she began to talk. Olivia told Emma that she had been in a relationship, but she had ended it because she needed to figure out some things, and it was best that she did it alone. Emma said, 'But you've been so happy these last few months. Well, whatever you need to sort out, I'm sure you've made the right decision.'

Olivia was grateful for Emma's support. 'But it feels so bad, and I can't stop crying,' Olivia wailed.

'I know, I know. It will get easier,' Emma stroked her friend's hair away from her tear stained face. 'Look, let's put on a movie, I'll get some drinks, some chocolate and popcorn, take your mind off things for a bit.'

On Monday morning, Laura was just getting set up for work. Jason wasn't going to be in until later as he had a meeting elsewhere at nine this morning. Laura thought that she would see if Jasmine wanted a drink. She tapped on the door, and opened it. Jasmine was sitting at her desk, and she looked terrible. Her face was drawn, with dark shadows under her eyes. Laura wondered if she had slept at all over the weekend. Laura had never seen Jasmine like this, and went and called for a taxi to take her home. Laura was concerned, 'You need to go home and sleep. Call me later and let me know how you are. If you need me to, I can come and see you after work.'

The taxi soon arrived, and Laura helped Jasmine with her coat and bag. She got Jasmine into the taxi, and gave the driver the address. Olivia arrived as the taxi was pulling away. 'Hi, Laura. Was that Jasmine in the taxi?' she asked, wondering what was going on.

They walked into the office, Laura saying, 'Yes. I think she must be poorly, or something. I went to ask whether she wanted a drink, and she was just sitting at her desk, staring at nothing. She looked like death, so I sent her home.'

Olivia felt terrible, 'Oh, the poor thing.'

When Jasmine got indoors, she took off her shoes and coat, and went straight to her bedroom. She fell onto the bed, exhausted. As she turned over, she could smell Olivia's perfume on the pillow next to her. She hugged the pillow, sobbing silent tears into it.

That evening, Olivia rang Jasmine. 'Hey, I just wanted to check that you're okay.'

Jasmine sighed, 'I will be. How are you?'

Olivia hesitated, 'Okay, I guess. Actually, I'm not okay, I feel terrible. The last thing I wanted to do was hurt you.'

Jasmine replied, 'I know you need some time, it will work itself out.'

Olivia said, 'If you want me to leave work, I will.'

'No, that would be ridiculous. We're both professional, Laura and Jason know nothing of our relationship. It'll be fine.'

Whilst Jasmine had been at home, the reality of what was happening had started to kick in. Olivia needed time, she got that. This was why she didn't get involved with colleagues, it could get very messy. After three days of hurting and crying, she really did think she was empty now, and the numbness was easier to deal with than the pain.

Olivia got into work early on Tuesday morning. She was feeling nervous, but knew if she could get through today, she would be okay. She tapped on Jasmine's door, and went in. Jasmine looked up, and smiled weakly. Olivia was shocked at how drawn she looked, and her stomach turned over. 'I just wanted to say hi. Can I get you a drink?'

Jasmine's voice was quiet and flat, 'No, I'm fine thank you, I've just got a lot to catch up with today.'

'I'll leave you to it, then,' and Olivia left, closing the door behind her.

For a moment, she just stood there, leaning on the door. Shit, Jasmine just looked so sad. She hated seeing her like that, and hated more that it was because of her. Olivia started as the outer door opened, and Laura arrived. 'Morning, how are you? Oh, is Jasmine here today, I hope she's feeling better.'

Olivia managed to smile, 'Yes, she's got lots to do today, I better get on as well,' and she went to her desk.

Laura didn't think that Olivia seemed herself today, but didn't say anything. Maybe she had caught the same thing that Jasmine had.

Over the next few weeks, things continued as they had at the beginning, although Jasmine kept much more of a distance. Laura and Jason commented on it one day, and they put it down to assuming that she had a lot of work on. Jasmine had seemed to take on a lot of extra work at the moment.

Olivia was spending more time with Liam now. He was getting on well with his job, but he still found London very busy. Still, this way he got to be with Olivia, and he was dearly wishing that they could start dating again. Olivia found that spending time with Liam helped her to keep her mind off of Jasmine a bit. It was still difficult though, and at times she wondered why she was doing this. Olivia had thought that this would be the easier way, but it felt anything but.

Jasmine was functioning at a minimum. She kept herself busy at work, and was mostly in her office with the door closed. She worked late nearly every night. One evening, Jason tapped on her door. He asked if he could sit down, and Jasmine nodded. He sat down on the sofa, looking at Jasmine. 'Jasmine, I'm really worried about you. You've become withdrawn, and you're working way too much. I think you should take some time off.'

Jasmine sighed, and looked up, 'I'm fine, just busy.'

Jason hated seeing her like this. He also knew that she was fiercely independent, and liked to sort things out for herself. 'Look, if you need anything, or you want to talk, you know where I am.'

Jasmine looked up at Jason, and just about managed a smile, 'Thank you.'

Later that evening, Jasmine was back at home and had the radio on whilst she was preparing some food. 'Just The Way You Are' came on, and it reminded Jasmine of her first date with Olivia. The tears started to flow, and Jasmine didn't think that she could bear it.

ELEVEN

Olivia found that she and Liam slipped into an easy friendship again. They knew each other well, and would finish each other's sentences. They often went out with Emma and Matt, who couldn't work out why they didn't get together. One Friday evening, they had returned from the cinema late, and Liam asked if he could sleep on the sofa. Emma said that was fine, of course. Matt and Emma went off to their room, leaving Liam and Olivia in the lounge. Liam took Olivia's hand, saying 'I've really enjoyed these few weeks with you. You know I want to be with you again,' and he pulled Olivia close and kissed her.

Olivia kissed him back, and it suddenly felt so familiar, so comfortable. Olivia looked up at him, he really hadn't changed much in six years, he still had that boyish look. She took his hand, and led him to the bedroom. They began kissing again, and started to undress. Liam couldn't quite believe this was happening, and he held Olivia's head, kissing her deeply. They fell onto the bed, a tangle of arms and legs. Liam ran his hands down Olivia's body, down her thighs, touching her between her legs. Olivia took in the familiar scent that was Liam, clean and slightly musky. She ran her hands over his shoulders, down his chest. It had been such a long time, and Liam was very ready. He reached over for his jeans, and pulled a condom out of the pocket. Tearing open the wrapper, he pulled it out and rolled it on. He was back on top of Olivia, kissing her. He said, 'You're sure?'

Olivia nodded, and Liam entered her, groaning with pleasure, 'I've wanted you for so long.'

He kissed her, and moved rhythmically, building up momentum. He could feel his imminent climax, and groaned as he came. Olivia could feel him inside her, throbbing. Liam kissed her, her mouth, her face, her shoulders. Liam pulled out of Olivia, and discarded the condom, and lay beside her. 'You didn't come,' he said, 'We'll have to do something about that,' and slid his hand down her body.

'No,' she looked at him, 'Not with your hand, with your mouth.'

Liam looked at Olivia, she had never asked for that before. He slid down the bed, and Olivia parted her legs. Liam was hesitant at first, then started finding his way. It seemed to take a long time, but eventually Olivia came, and they cuddled up together on the bed.

In the morning, Olivia woke up with Liam looking at her. He smiled at her, and went to kiss her. Olivia pulled back. She knew that last night had been a big mistake. Oh shit, not another one of these conversations. What on earth am I doing. Liam looked at her, 'I know what you're going to say. I can see it in your eyes. Look, it's fine. You've changed, our lives are different now. We can still be friends, though, right?'

Olivia looked into Liam's blue eyes, 'Liam, you are the sweetest guy. There was a part of me that thought it might work, and I wanted it to. But it just isn't the same now. I'm really sorry.'

They hugged, and Liam breathed in the smell of Olivia, knowing that he had to finally move on now.

Over drinks, a couple of weeks later, Liam and Olivia were out with Emma and Matt. Liam said, 'I've decided to go back to Cornwall after this contract finishes. It's been fun, but I find the pace a bit too fast for my liking, so I'm searching out opportunities nearer to home.'

Emma said, 'We'll miss you, it's been great having you around.'

Emma wasn't surprised, though. Olivia had told her what had happened, and how she felt that she had had closure with Liam. No doubt, he felt it too, he needed to get on with his life now. Also, it was clear that he wasn't suited to London life, whereas Olivia thrived on it.

Jasmine was still operating in numbness mode. She was pretty sure that Olivia was back together with Liam now. Her friends were getting worried about her, as she couldn't seem to snap out of it. Usually nothing would phase her, and they had never seen her like this before. One evening, at Phoebe and Fran's place, Phoebe said, 'This is crazy. You're a beautiful, professional woman. You can't carry on like this. It doesn't help that Olivia is still working with you, that you have to see her every day.'

Jasmine replied, 'I want her there. She's really good at her job, by far the best person that we had. But I knew I wanted her the moment I saw her, which was not professional of me in the slightest. I've never felt like this about anyone, or come undone like this. I feel so stupid.'

Fran said, 'It's okay, you fell in love, and you fell hard. Don't beat yourself up about it, but you have got to pull yourself together. I think you should take some time off, like Jason suggested. You could go on holiday,' Fran looked concerned.

Jasmine looked at them both, sighing, 'Yes, I know you're right. Starting from now, I will make a real effort.'

Phoebe said, 'We were thinking about having a dinner party soon, and there's someone that we think you'll get on well with.'

Shaking her head, Jasmine said, 'No, no way. I don't want to be set up. Anyway, I'm nowhere near ready to meet someone else at the moment.'

Phoebe said, 'Okay, but will you come to the party?'

Jasmine looked at her, sighed and nodded. She was coming to terms with the fact that Olivia was with Liam, and she would have to think about moving forward.

Phoebe and Fran were Jasmine's closest friends, and they were being great whilst Jasmine was trying to get over Olivia. They had met at an art exhibition in Hampstead when Jasmine was nineteen. At that time, the two of them were friends, and not yet a couple. They had all got on so well together, and started to socialise, going to events and the theatre. When, a year later, she came out to her parents, Jasmine really appreciated their support. Jasmine had had a middle class upbringing, and her father was strict and quite distant with her. He believed that young ladies should behave in a certain way, and Jasmine knew that that wasn't quite her. Her mother, on the other hand, had a more bohemian spirit, and was much younger than her father. Sometimes, Jasmine wondered how they had ended up together. At first, Jasmine had found her father's disapproval of her lifestyle very difficult, but over time, and with the support of Phoebe and Fran, and her mother, she decided that that was his problem, not hers. Over time, Jasmine watched Phoebe and Fran fall in love.

Jasmine decided to take everyone's advice, and take some time off of work. She didn't want to go away at the moment though, she really didn't feel like it. She spent a lot of the time at home, and it was helpful not to see Olivia every day.

When she was back at work, Laura noticed that Jasmine seemed to be a bit more like her old self, the time away had obviously done her some good. She had no idea what had been going on, as she didn't talk about her personal life. At least she seemed better, which was the main thing. One morning, Laura and Olivia were chatting, as Jasmine walked out of her office. Olivia looked up, saying, 'I was just telling Laura that Liam has decided to go back to Cornwall after his contract finishes. He doesn't really get on with London. The good thing is, he gave it a try, so he won't be wondering whether he was missing something.'

Jasmine looked at Olivia, in that way she had, and said softly, 'I think he knew exactly what he was missing.'

She turned and walked back into her office, leaving the words hanging in the air. Laura noticed a look of sadness on Olivia's face, then she turned away, to carry on with her work.

Emma had been trying to get Olivia to go out with her and a few friends from work. 'Come on, you've been moping around recently. You're not with Liam now, so why not?'

'Okay, okay, Friday night it is,' said Olivia.

The girls got home from work on Friday about six, and had something to eat before getting ready for their night out. They tried on some different outfits, asking each other's opinions. In the end, they plumped for skinny jeans with a loose strappy top. Olivia's was cream, and Emma wore a sapphire blue top which looked stunning on her, and complimented her eyes.

When they arrived at the bar, Emma introduced Olivia to everyone, including a guy called Will. They seemed like a nice bunch of people, and Olivia was starting to relax and enjoy herself. Bars and clubs weren't really her thing, but now and again she didn't mind. Emma liked to party every weekend if she could. There were a few of the group on the dance floor, then gradually they went off to get some more drinks. Soon Olivia realised that it was just her and Will still dancing, but what the hell, she was actually starting to have a good time, for the first time in ages. Will began dancing closer, and when the music changed to a slower song, he held her hips as they moved to the music. She put her arms around his neck, and looked into his eyes. He was very handsome, and as she could see he was going to kiss her, she knew that she wasn't going to stop him. He was very gentle, and smelt delicious, clean and salty, as if he'd just walked off the beach. They danced and kissed. Emma, watching from the bar, was thrilled, she had been trying to get Olivia and Will together for a while.

Will and Olivia had been dating for a few weeks. Olivia really enjoyed spending time with him, and now he often made up a foursome with Emma and Matt. Olivia watched Emma and Matt falling in love with each other, although she wasn't sure if they knew it themselves yet. Olivia had had a taste of that with Liam, but there wasn't that same connection there. She and Liam had grown up from teenagers to adults together, and she really cared about him. What she had experienced with Jasmine was something different altogether. They had things in common, they liked being around one another, not necessarily doing anything in particular. Not to mention the phenomenal sex. Olivia had no idea it could feel like that. But she was straight, so how could it work between them. At least things were much easier at work now, particularly after Jasmine had taken some time off. She and Jasmine kept things very professional. It was different to before, and they didn't all go out socially like they had done. Jasmine usually said that she had arrangements, or had to work late, and eventually Laura stopped trying to organise anything. Olivia still babysat Laura's children, and she and Laura regularly had lunch together. One lunchtime, Laura happened to say, 'I'm so glad that Jasmine is more like her old self. I don't know what was going on before, but she seems better now. I think she must have been stressed from over working. It's hard to know, she's such a private person.'

After an evening out together, Will asked Olivia back to his place. Olivia knew what he had in mind, and they had been dating for a while now. Will had taken Olivia's coat, and hung it up. He bent down to kiss her, and she put her arms around his neck and kissed him back. They drew apart, and he took her hand, and led her to his bedroom. He kissed her neck, and started to undo her top. Removing it, he then undid her bra, letting it fall to the floor. He touched her breasts, and leaned in to kiss her, whispering in her ear, 'You are so beautiful.'

She started to unbutton Will's shirt, revealing his chest. Hmm, he had a very nice chest. They took off the rest of their clothes, and climbed onto the bed. Will lay down, and Olivia stroked his body. They kissed, becoming more and more passionate. Will reached across to the bedside cabinet to get a condom. They kissed again, then Olivia sat astride Will, and he ran his fingers down her body, over her breasts and between her legs. Olivia lowered herself onto Will, feeling him inside her. They kissed passionately, and Olivia started moving back and forth, building a rhythm, and building towards a climax. Will came first, with Olivia close behind. As their heartbeats slowed down, Olivia rolled off of Will, and lay beside him.

As Olivia lay there, she was thinking that Will was such a great guy, gentle, handsome and sweet. And also that she had never felt the way she had done when she was with Jasmine.

Now that she had had some time off of work, Jasmine found that plowing herself back into work seemed to be the answer. It was just that work wasn't as much fun as it used to be, and she felt that a part of her was missing. Jasmine knew that Olivia was now seeing a guy called Will, so that was that. She was starting to go out occasionally, usually because Phoebe and Fran practically forced her to. She knew that feeling this way was crazy, that she was responsible for her own happiness, not Olivia, or anyone else for that matter. But that was as it was for the time being. At least she was making an effort now, and things were beginning to get easier.

Today was Olivia's birthday, and it was a fresh spring morning. Emma had made her a birthday breakfast, and a home-made birthday crown to wear, which she had made out of silver card. Olivia laughed, saying, 'Thank you, this is lovely. I really do feel like a birthday princess!'

When Olivia arrived at work, there were cards on her desk from Laura, Jason and Jasmine. Jasmine was out at a meeting all morning. The card from Jasmine read, 'Wishing you a wonderful birthday, with love, Jasmine.' There was also a box wrapped in purple tissue paper, with a beautiful ribbon on it. There was no gift tag to say who it was from, so Olivia began unwrapping the box carefully. It was the vase from the National Gallery, the one of The Fighting Temeraire. Oh Jasmine.

Jasmine returned from her meeting after lunch. 'Happy birthday, Olivia,' she said, and went into her office.

Olivia followed her in, and closed the door behind her. Jasmine looked up. 'Thank you so much for the vase, it's beautiful. And so thoughtful,' she paused. 'Look, I know it's been difficult. I just wanted to say...'

Jasmine interrupted Olivia, 'It's fine. There's nothing to say. Happy birthday.'

Olivia thought about trying to say something again, then thought better of it. She missed how easy things used to be between them. 'Thank you, really,' she said, and left Jasmine's office. Olivia sat at her desk, and a feeling of great sadness swept over her.

That evening, Will was picking up Olivia from work, and they were meeting Emma and Matt at their favourite Mexican restaurant. They ordered a pitcher of margaritas, and they toasted Olivia, wishing her a happy birthday. They had an enjoyable evening together, although Emma thought that Olivia was quieter than usual, and she seemed much more subdued than she had been at breakfast that morning. By the end of the evening, Olivia was a bit tipsy. They headed home, and Will and Emma managed to get Olivia into her pyjamas, and into bed. The next morning, Olivia woke up feeling a bit fragile. She rang Laura to say that she would be a bit late into work, but would work through lunch. Whilst she was lying in bed, she gave herself some time to think about things. Since finishing things with Jasmine, she hadn't really given herself any time. Firstly, she had thrown herself into helping Liam get started in London, and now she was with Will. Olivia did enjoying being with Will. He was good company, although they didn't have much in common. Olivia loved to go to art galleries and discuss books, neither of which interested Will. Still, it was good to have different interests, she told herself. She really wanted things to work with Will. They were so right together in many ways, and she really cared for him. It's just that ever since her birthday, when Jasmine had given her the vase, something had been worrying away at the back of Olivia's mind. She began to face up to the reality that she was in love with Jasmine.

TWELVE

Over the next couple of weeks, Emma noticed that Olivia hadn't really been herself since her birthday. Will had also seen that she had seemed more withdrawn. When they were in bed together, she didn't seem as into it as she had been that first time. It was good, but Will sensed that Olivia was holding herself back. One evening, Will was watching Olivia as she made them drinks in the kitchen. He walked over, putting his arms around her. 'I can't help noticing how distracted you've been recently. You've been getting more and more distant. I don't know what's going on, but I have a suspicion that you're in love with someone else.'

Olivia looked up at him, shocked. 'What?'

'I don't know, but I've grown up with three sisters, and had my share of girlfriends. It's just a feeling I get.'

A tear ran down Olivia's cheek, and Will wiped it away with his thumb. 'But you're so perfect in so many ways, and I really care about you.'

Holding her to him, Will said, 'I really care about you, too, but this will never work if you're in love with someone else. I just hope this guy knows how lucky he is,' and he kissed the top of her head.

Emma appeared in the kitchen to make a drink. 'Where's Will?' she asked.

'He left.'

Emma looked across to see that Olivia had been crying. She walked over to give her a hug. 'Come on, let's sit down and talk about it.' They sat down on the sofa, and Olivia told Emma what had happened.

'Oh, that's such a shame, you and Will were great together. Still, if it's not meant to be. So, are you still in love with Liam?'

Olivia shook her head. She wasn't ready to say anymore yet, she had to figure out some stuff for herself first. Emma hugged her, saying that Olivia could talk to her about it any time.

Olivia wanted to see if she could start to mend her relationship with Jasmine. She missed how comfortable it used to be, working together. Jasmine had practically shut herself off, and hardly came out of her office these days. Olivia decided to take a big step. It was after work one day, and Jason and Laura had already left. Olivia tentatively knocked on Jasmine's door, 'Can I come in? I just wanted to talk to you.'

'Of course, sit down,' Jasmine gestured towards the sofa.

Olivia sat down and looked at Jasmine, who sat back in her chair. 'This is difficult, but I thought we should talk. I know things have been really hard, but I think it's time to move forward now. You can't shut yourself away all of the time.'

Jasmine sighed, 'Look, I just have to deal with things in my own way. I know it's my fault, I should have never told you how I felt about you. That's why I've always kept work completely separate to my personal life.'

Olivia felt for her, 'You can't protect yourself from feeling. You're such a passionate person, that's one of the things I love about you, and you can't let this change who you are.'

Jasmine looked up at Olivia, had she really just said what she thought she had? She looked at Olivia, and Olivia held her gaze. She was so beautiful, and it hurt so much. Jasmine broke the gaze, looking down. Olivia seemed to be dealing with everything so much better than Jasmine. After an interminable silence, Olivia got up to leave. She walked over to Jasmine, and touched her arm. Jasmine felt the electricity race through her body, and she let out a sigh. Olivia said, 'Also, I just wanted to let you know that Will broke up with me. He thinks I'm in love with someone else.'

Jasmine watched as Olivia walked out of the office, closing the door behind her. She stared at the closed door. What was that about? She knew things had been awkward, and she also knew that was partly her fault. She shouldn't have told Olivia how she felt, she used to be good at keeping her feelings to herself. Also, had she rushed Olivia too much? Olivia had never had a relationship with a woman before, was it any surprise that she had freaked out. But Jasmine couldn't shake that last thing Olivia had said, about Will thinking she was in love with someone else. Why would she tell Jasmine that, unless... No, she couldn't go there.

Back at home, Emma sat down next to Olivia on the sofa. 'Livvy, what's up. You haven't been yourself for weeks now.'

Olivia remembered her own words to Jasmine, about not changing who you are. She was slowly coming to terms with the fact that she was in love with Jasmine. So what, it didn't define her. She couldn't deny the feelings that she had for Jasmine any longer. She was a woman who had fallen in love. She knew that the time that she was with Jasmine was the happiest time of her life, why would she throw that away because things had turned out differently to how she had expected they would. Olivia sighed heavily, 'I am in love with someone. Hopelessly, deeply in love. The trouble is, I got scared and broke it off, and I broke their heart, and I don't know what to do.' She looked at Emma with big sad eyes, and began to sob.

Putting her arm around her, Emma said, 'Maybe you should tell this person how you feel. Who is it, is it someone I know?'

'Um, no. Well, yes, actually, you did meet her a couple of times.'

Emma was a bit confused, 'Her?'

Olivia looked up, 'Do you remember the Turner book, with the inscription from J?' Emma nodded. 'J is Jasmine. My boss.'

Emma exclaimed, 'Oh my god, I thought it was Jason you liked. How on earth did that happen?'

Olivia told Emma everything, then paused to wait for Emma's reaction. 'Well, that's got to be one of the most sexy and romantic stories I've ever heard.' She paused, letting this information sink in. 'Oh my god, that day when I came back, and you were both on the sofa, looking as guilty as hell, that makes sense now! You've got to try and get her back. From what you say, she's crazy about you.'

'But I hurt her so badly. I couldn't get my head around it, it all happened so quickly. I feel like she's unleashed a part of me that I never knew existed, and it scares me, and it excites me, and I've never felt more alive than when I'm with her,' sobbed Olivia.

Emma said, 'Look, she'll understand that. All I can say is, that you never looked happier than when you were with Jasmine.'

Olivia looked up through her tears, and smiled, 'Really?' Emma nodded.

The next week at work was strange for Jasmine and Olivia. Olivia was trying to give Jasmine meaningful looks, and kept making excuses to go into her office. Jasmine was wary, and still remained guarded, but she could see that Olivia was behaving differently. She didn't quite know what to make of it. Each evening, Emma would ask Olivia for an update, and by the end of the week, she said it was time to take action.

Jasmine was on her way home on Friday evening. She was tired, as it had been another full on, busy week. Maybe her friends were right, she should ease off a bit. As she walked up the road to her house, Jasmine could see someone sitting on her doorstep. Olivia. Jasmine slowed down as she approached her home. 'Hi,' Olivia said, 'Can I talk to you please?'

Jasmine looked at her quizzically, 'Um, yes. Let me open the door, and we can talk inside.'

Olivia followed Jasmine into the hallway. Jasmine took Olivia's jacket, hanging it up next to her own. 'Come in, I'll put the kettle on.'

Rocky padded over to greet Jasmine, and she bent down to stroke him. Olivia watched as Jasmine put the kettle on, and prepared some food for Rocky. When the drinks were ready, Jasmine turned towards Olivia, and asked, 'So, what did you want to talk to me about?'

Olivia stood and looked at Jasmine, how beautiful she was, those gorgeous dark eyes looking at her enquiringly. She could see that Jasmine was wondering what she was going to say. Olivia was feeling really nervous, and she could feel her heart thumping hard in her chest. Oh well, here goes, she thought. Olivia stated, 'I'm in love with you. Madly, passionately, deeply in love with you. I'm sorry it's taken me this long to realise it. I thought you should know.'

Jasmine's mouth dropped open, and she stared at Olivia. She couldn't believe what she was hearing. Olivia said, 'Can we sit down and talk.'

They moved into the lounge, and sat on the sofa facing one another, as Olivia started to explain. 'As you know, things happened with us so quickly. You really swept me off of my feet, and although I couldn't get my head around it, when I went with my extinct, it did feel right. I just got so overwhelmed. And when Liam came to London, it was so easy spending time with him. After you and I broke up, I did sleep with him once, and I knew immediately it was a mistake. At least we both knew that it really was over.'

Jasmine looked at Olivia, tears in her eyes, 'So what about Will?' she whispered.

Olivia sighed, 'Emma got fed up with me moping around, and made me go out. Will was such a nice guy. The thing is, all of my life, I'd always assumed I'd meet a nice guy, settle down and maybe have kids one day. Being with a woman had never entered my head. I knew that I wasn't meant to be with Liam, and I was hoping that there was someone else for me. Then I realised there was. It was you. You blew me away, and I can't bear the fact that I threw it away.'

As Olivia was talking, tears ran down her face. She continued, 'I know I really hurt you, and I can't tell you how bad I feel about that. Will you give me another chance? Please.'

Jasmine stared at Olivia, so beautiful, so vulnerable. Oh god, how she wanted to kiss her, to hold her. The tears now started down Jasmine's cheeks. 'I can't. I mean, I'm with someone. Her name's Chloe.'

Olivia's face fell, and suddenly everything went muffled, as though her head was in a goldfish bowl. Jasmine could see the shock and hurt in Olivia's eyes. 'Oh shit, I never even thought... shit, I have to go.'

Olivia rushed to the hall to get her coat, and disappeared, closing the door behind her. Jasmine just sat and watched her go, then she started to sob, big heaving sobs, and leaned forward, hugging herself.

Olivia headed straight back home, but could hardly see her way with the tears in her eyes. How could she be so stupid to think that Jasmine wouldn't end up meeting someone. Christ, she had been dating Will, Jasmine would have had no idea how Olivia really felt. When she arrived home, she went straight to her room, and fell on the bed in a heap. It was getting late when Emma came home, and when she saw Olivia's bag on the coffee table and her bedroom door closed, she feared that the evening hadn't gone so well.

In the morning, Olivia was making a coffee. Emma went in to see how she was, and could see by Olivia's tear stained face and smudged mascara that it was not good. She walked over and gave Olivia a hug, and Olivia sobbed in her arms. Once she had calmed down, she explained to Emma what had happened. 'I'm so sorry. At least she knows how you feel about her. If you hadn't told her, you would have always regretted it.'

Olivia knew she was right, but knowing that didn't take away the pain. Emma said that she would run a bath for Olivia, then said they could spend the day together if Olivia would like to. Olivia was very grateful, she didn't want to be on her own today.

Spending time with Emma at the weekend did help Olivia to take her mind off things for a while. They went out for lunch, then went shopping. They had already been to a few shops, and now Olivia was in the changing room trying some clothes on, whilst Emma waited outside. There was music playing in the shop, and Adele's 'Someone Like You' came on over the speakers. The words cut right through Olivia, and tears silently streamed down her face. Then as she gave in to it, she heaved great sobs. She slid down to the floor, her knees up to her chest, and thought that the pain would never end. Emma heard Olivia, and looked around the curtain, about to ask if she was okay. Seeing the state of her, she went in and held Olivia, until her sobs subsided. As she recovered herself, Olivia sniffed, 'Sorry, I will pull myself together. It just hurts so much.'

Emma stroked Olivia's hair, 'I know, I know. When you're ready, we'll go and get something to eat, and maybe a big glass of wine!'

Olivia smiled at Emma, 'Thank you.'

When it came to Monday morning, Olivia was feeling terrible. She decided that she just had to focus on the job, and nothing else. That's what Jasmine had done, she hadn't let her feelings affect work, and Olivia would just have to do the same. When Jasmine arrived, she asked Olivia to come into her office. Olivia's heart was beating so hard, she wondered that Jasmine wouldn't be able to hear it. Jasmine asked Olivia to sit down, which she did, looking at the floor. Jasmine sighed, 'Look, I just wanted to make sure that you're okay.'

Olivia said yes, she was fine. They sat there in silence for a moment, neither knowing what to say. Then Olivia spoke, 'I'm sorry I turned up at your door on Friday.'

Jasmine spoke softly, 'I'm not.'

Olivia looked up and locked eyes with Jasmine. Fuck, this was so hard. Olivia dropped her gaze again.

Olivia wasn't sure how she managed it, but she got through the rest of Monday, and somehow the rest of the week. After work, she would be exhausted, and couldn't focus on anything else at all. Getting through work was taking every ounce of energy that she had. Emma was being very supportive, and had made dinner for Olivia most evenings. It was good that she could talk to Emma, as no one else knew about her and Jasmine. Olivia hated how she was feeling, particularly because she felt that she had brought it on herself. By the middle of the following week, she knew what she had to do.

Jasmine was finding work really difficult. She hated seeing Olivia upset, but they had to keep work as work. For now, she would only call on Olivia when she really needed to. She gave Olivia some work that she could do on her own, and hoped that things would settle down. On Friday afternoon, there was a tap on Jasmine's door. She said to come in, and looked up to see Olivia standing there. 'Hi, would you like to sit down?'

Olivia looked nervous, 'No thank you. I have to give you this,' and she handed an envelope to Jasmine. 'It's my resignation. I have thought about it a lot, and I think that it's for the best.' Olivia looked down at the floor.

A look of horror came over Jasmine's face, 'No, you can't do this, I can't lose you,' she was panicking.

Olivia simply said, 'I've made up my mind. I've spoken to Laura and Jason. They don't know anything about us, I told them that I have to take care of a personal emergency. Jason thinks I just want a bit of time off, and I thought that it would be easier to ask for without raising questions. He and Laura are not expecting me in for the next week or two. I'm sure you'll think of something to tell him, or you can show him my letter.'

Jasmine couldn't believe what she was hearing, and looked pleadingly at Olivia. 'Please, don't do this.'

Olivia looked up, and tried to talk before her voice broke, 'I'm so sorry. I'm not as strong as you, I just can't work here as colleagues after everything that's happened between us. I'm still in love with you, and I need time to get over you. Thank you for everything.

Goodbye, Jasmine.' Olivia turned and walked out of the door, leaving Jasmine dumbstruck.

When Olivia arrived home, she was pleased that Emma wasn't there. She needed time to think, and decided that she wouldn't tell anyone that she had resigned yet, just that she had some holiday booked. Lying on her bed, she started to think about going home for a few days. She rang her mum, saying that she wanted to come home the next day for a break. Ella was delighted. Olivia packed her bag and booked her train ticket. In the morning, she went to find Emma. 'I'm not sure how long I'm going home for. I'll let you know when I know myself.'

'It will be good for you. If you want to talk any time, you will ring me, won't you?'

'Of course,' Olivia replied.

Jasmine hadn't managed to sleep at all on Friday night. She had tried Olivia's number, but it went straight to voicemail. She kept trying over the course of the day, and left a message, asking Olivia to call her. By Sunday evening, she still hadn't heard from her, and decided to go to the flat. Emma answered the door, and was surprised to see Jasmine standing there. 'Hi. Is Olivia in? '

Emma felt a bit awkward. 'Um, no. '

Jasmine looked really worried. 'I really need to talk to her. Please will you ask her to call me. She won't answer her phone or call me back. I can't do anything if she won't speak to me.'

Emma paused, then asked Jasmine to come in. 'Look, she's in Cornwall. She needed some time to think, she's been in a bit of a state recently. She said she doesn't know when she's coming back.'

'Shit, I'm going crazy. I really need to see her. Please will you let me know when you hear from her, and let me know that she's okay. Even if she won't speak to me, I just want to know that she's okay. Please.'

Emma felt sorry for Jasmine, she could see how upset she was. 'Look, I'll let you know when I speak to her. Olivia has to do things in her own way, and she needs this time for herself.'

'I know, thank you, Emma. I can't bear to lose her.'

Emma said, 'It's only a couple of weeks off work, I'm sure things will work themselves out.'

Jasmine's voice broke as she said, 'Olivia handed in her resignation yesterday. I don't know if I'll see her again.'

Emma was shocked, 'Olivia said she had booked some holiday, I didn't know that she'd quit.'

Emma fetched a box of tissues, and handed them to Jasmine. 'Look, I have to ask, if you speak to her, I have to know that you're not going to hurt her.'

'Hurting Olivia is the last thing I want to do. I've been trying to do what I thought was the right thing, but it's just hurting both of us. I just need to talk to her, then it's her call after that.'

Emma said that she would see what she could do, but couldn't make any promises. Emma made Jasmine a cup of tea, and they chatted for a while. Jasmine told Emma how devastated she had been when Olivia had ended things, and hoped that she would change her mind. But over time, Olivia had got together with Liam, then Will, and she had to come to terms with the fact that she had to get on with her own life. So when Olivia had turned up at her home telling Jasmine how she felt, she had really wanted to get back together with her, but at that time she was seeing someone else. Then, when she thought about how difficult things had been at work, and how long it had taken her just to start feeling some semblance of normal after they had broken up, she wasn't sure that she could go there again. Jasmine started crying again, 'I must be stupid, letting her walk away like that. I thought she would want some time, I blamed myself for rushing things with her at the beginning. I never thought that she would leave like that, I thought I was doing the right thing.'

Emma put her arm around Jasmine, 'You weren't to know. I'll talk to Olivia, leave it with me.'

Jasmine wiped her eyes, and looked at Emma, 'Thank you. Sorry I'm in such a state, I didn't mean to get you involved. I've just been so worried.'

'It's fine. You need to go home and get some rest. I'll call you when I've spoken to Olivia.'

Jasmine got up to leave, thanking Emma again. When Jasmine had left, Emma slumped back down on the sofa. Boy, those two needed to get sorted. They were obviously mad about one another, surely they could work something out.

Ella was thrilled to have Olivia back home. She thought that she seemed very quiet, but Olivia had just said that she was tired, and that work had been really busy, which was why she needed a break. She went to bed early on the day she arrived home, and slept heavily well into the next morning. She woke up feeling tired and aching, and Ella told her to stay in bed. She dosed Olivia up with echinacea and vitamin C, and gave her lots of water to drink. 'Darling, you're exhausted. A few days rest in bed is just what you need.'

'Thanks, Mum,' and Olivia drifted off to sleep again.

A couple of days later, Becky went round to see her, taking her some flowers and chocolates for when she felt better. They chatted, and Becky updated Olivia on the gallery, and what she, Dan and Liam had been up to. Olivia told Becky that she was just on holiday. She didn't want to go into everything that was going on at the moment. She needed to decide for herself what she wanted to do, not what other people thought would be best for her.

At work, Jasmine was missing Olivia so much. Laura thought how quiet she was, and when she commented on how it wasn't the same without Olivia, she noticed Jasmine disappear into her office quickly, closing the door. Jasmine hadn't said anything to the others about Olivia resigning yet. If she did, she knew that she would have to tell them what had been happening, and she really couldn't face that at the moment.

Now that Olivia was starting to feel better, she decided to ring Emma. Emma was thrilled to hear from her, and Olivia explained that she would have called sooner, but she hadn't been very well. Emma tentatively asked whether Olivia had heard from Jasmine. Olivia sighed, 'She's left me messages, but I just can't think about her at the moment. To be honest, I've been considering moving back here, while I decide what to do. I think a complete change would be good for me.'

Emma said, 'Look, don't rush into anything. Wait until you're properly better before you decide anything.'

Once she had finished speaking with Olivia, Emma rang Jasmine to let her know that Olivia was okay. Jasmine asked whether she was coming back to London soon, and Emma said that she didn't know yet.

A few days later, Olivia rang Emma to let her know that she was coming back to London, and Emma suggested that they meet at the Mexican restaurant when she finished work on Friday. Emma arrived to see Olivia waiting for her, and they hugged each other. 'It's good to have you back. Do you feel better now?'

Olivia nodded, 'Yes. I really needed to get away. I still haven't decided whether to stay in London or move back to Cornwall.'

Emma looked concerned, 'You can't go back, you have your life here now. Don't make any decisions just yet.'

After their meal, Emma said that she had to go back to the office as she had forgotten something, and said that she would see Olivia back at the flat later. As Olivia was leaving the restaurant, she stopped in her tracks when she saw Jasmine standing a few feet in front of her. Jasmine said, 'I really need to talk to you.' There was a look of desperation in her eyes.

'How did you know I was here?'

'I asked Emma. I said that I had to see you. Please will you come back to my place so that we can talk.'

She looked pleadingly into Olivia's eyes, and Olivia sighed and nodded. Jasmine breathed a sigh of relief. The journey to Jasmine's was awkward, silence hanging in the air oppressively. Jasmine tried to lighten the atmosphere by asking about her trip to Cornwall. She wanted to wait until they were back home before she spoke with Olivia properly. When they arrived at the front door, Jasmine unlocked it, saying, 'Come in, I'll make us some drinks.'

Olivia followed Jasmine into the kitchen, watching the sway of her hips as she walked. She was so beautiful and graceful. If only she could have realised sooner how she felt, she would have spared them both so much pain. Olivia longed to put her arms around Jasmine, to touch her, kiss her neck. Jasmine turned around to see that look in Olivia's eyes, and oh, she knew that look so well. It made her stomach twist and her heart flip. Jasmine started making the drinks, but couldn't concentrate. With her back to Olivia, she simply said, 'I broke it off with Chloe.'

Olivia paused, 'Oh. Why?' She wasn't really sure what to say.

Jasmine turned to look at her, those gorgeous melting brown eyes searching Olivia's face. 'Because from the moment we were together, I knew that I didn't want anyone else, only you. I was trying to move on, but ever since you turned up at my door that evening, I haven't been able to stop thinking about you, about us. I tried to push my feelings away, and I knew that I couldn't bear any more hurt, losing you was the most painful thing I've ever been through. But when you came into my office saying that you were going to leave, I knew that I couldn't let you go. Then when Emma said that you had gone back to Cornwall, I was going spare. I miss you, I want to be with you. I've never loved anyone like I love you.' Jasmine looked at Olivia, and saw a tear run down her face. Jasmine whispered, 'I want to kiss you.'

Olivia nodded, and Jasmine walked over to her, and leaned forward, gently kissing her. As Olivia responded, Jasmine kissed Olivia more urgently, wanting Olivia to feel how much she loved her.

Knowing how Jasmine felt about her, being kissed like this, Olivia felt like she had found water after being lost in the desert, and didn't think that she would ever want to stop drinking. Eventually, they pulled apart, both of them with tears running down their faces. Olivia looked earnestly into Jasmine's eyes, 'I love you.'

'I love you too. I've been in love with you since the day we went to the gallery.'

Jasmine and Olivia sat and talked for a long time. Jasmine said that she had blamed herself for rushing things in the beginning. 'I should have stopped and thought. Obviously you had a lot of change going on, you were starting a new life here.'

Olivia said, 'Admittedly you did freak me out a bit, but you were so passionate, and it was so romantic. I loved spending time with you. I experienced things I'd never felt before. And after we broke up, I realised what I'd given up. Not to mention, sex with you, it's like nothing on earth.' Olivia gave Jasmine a look, which made Jasmine's stomach flip.

Olivia asked about Chloe. Jasmine explained that they had only been dating a few weeks. Jasmine had really thought that she had lost Olivia, and eventually started to go out a bit more, encouraged by Fran and Phoebe. After Olivia had turned up on her doorstep declaring her undying love, she knew it wouldn't be fair to Chloe to keep seeing her, so she ended things with her. She didn't say anything at first because she didn't want to rush anything. But when Olivia came into the office with a letter of resignation, she just knew that she couldn't let her go. Having talked everything out, they both felt they were coming from the same place. Jasmine said that she would talk to Jason, and let him know that Olivia would be back at work on Monday. Olivia said, 'Thank you. As I mentioned, Jason thinks it was a temporary leave of absence anyway, so that should be fine. Also, I might still need a bit of time when we're out with other people.'

Jasmine said, 'Well, I don't tend to be one for public displays of affection, generally. Mostly, I don't think my private life is anyone else's business.'

They decided that they would tell Laura and Jason soon, but not just yet. Jasmine asked, 'Have you told anyone about us?'

Olivia shook her head, 'Only Emma. I wasn't going to say at first, as I wasn't sure how she would react. But I was in such a state, and it was such a relief to talk to someone, and she was so sweet. In fact, it was Emma who told me to try and get you back. She said I'd never been happier than when I was with you.'

'Really? That's so sweet, she's a good friend.'

'Yes, she is, I don't know what I would have done without her.'

Jasmine looked at Olivia, 'I've got a confession. When you didn't call me back after you left work, I called at the flat to find you. Emma invited me in and I told her what a mess I'd made of things. She's very protective of you. But after we talked, she agreed to keep me updated as to how you were.'

'You're a sneaky couple of things, aren't you,' Olivia smiled.

Jasmine looked at Olivia, 'I wasn't going to let you go without a fight,' and leaned forward to kiss her. Then she yawned, and said, 'Well, I don't know about you, but I am so tired. It's been quite an evening. Do you want to stay?'

Olivia nodded, and they got up and headed for the bedroom. They undressed, and climbed under the duvet, and held each other tight. 'I've missed you so much,' whispered Jasmine, tears welling up.

Olivia looked into her eyes, 'I've missed you too. I love you,' and kissed her.

They made love, slowly, sensuously exploring one another tenderly. Jasmine was deliriously happy, and Olivia was overcome that she had nearly lost Jasmine. Afterwards, they held each other close as they drifted off to sleep.

When they awoke on Saturday morning, they were still entwined. Jasmine looked lovingly at Olivia, 'I can't believe you're back in my bed. I'm so happy.'

Olivia leaned over and kissed Jasmine, 'Me too. I can't believe I wasted all of that time searching for something when it was here all along. At least I came to my senses.'

Jasmine looked thoughtful, 'Sometimes it's only when we let go of things that we realise what we had.

You obviously needed that time to get things straight in your head. No pun intended, by the way!'

Olivia laughed, then looked serious. 'I know exactly what I want now, but I was so scared I had lost you for good.'

'Well, you haven't lost me, I'm right here,' and she kissed Olivia.

After breakfast, Olivia said that she would have to pop home to get some clean clothes. 'This time, you can come in with me, no more sneaking around at my place.'

When Olivia let herself in through the front door, Emma looked up, excited. She was just about to ask what had happened last night, when she caught a glimpse of Jasmine behind Olivia. Closing the door, Olivia said, 'Emma, you know Jasmine. I believe that you've become buddies!'

'Of course, how are you?' she asked, smiling.

Jasmine said that she was very well. Olivia laughed, 'Emma, you're like an excited puppy. Okay, let's sit down, and we'll tell you what happened.'

Emma sat on the armchair, and noticed that Jasmine and Olivia were holding hands on the sofa. Jasmine said, 'Well, after you left the restaurant yesterday, I waited for Olivia to leave. She did look rather surprised to see me! I just told her that I needed to talk to her, and asked her back to my place.'

Whilst Jasmine was relating the story, Emma noticed that she and Olivia kept exchanging loving looks. 'I told Olivia that she is the only person in the world for me, that I'm head over heels in love with her, and here we are!'

Emma was hugging herself with glee, 'That's so romantic.'

Jasmine smiled, and said to Emma, 'I owe you thanks, apart from these last few days, Olivia told me that you encouraged her to tell me how she felt about me a few weeks ago.'

Emma replied, 'To be honest, she hadn't been herself for such a long time, it was driving me mad, because she wouldn't talk about it. Then, when she finally told me, everything made sense. You obviously make each other very happy.'

Jasmine and Olivia beamed at each other, then at Emma. 'You're a good friend, I can see why Olivia thinks the world of you.'

That weekend, Jasmine and Olivia decided to go back to the National Gallery. Unlike before, when Olivia had become quiet and distant, now she was animated, and they chatted excitedly about the paintings. Jasmine particularly loved Canaletto's. 'The detail and the architecture are just stunning. I feel that I could walk into the paintings, they're so rich with life.'

Olivia watched Jasmine, she was enthralled. One of the Canaletto paintings was called London: Interior of the Rotunda at Ranelagh. It turned out that the building was in Chelsea, but was demolished in 1805.

Jasmine loved the way that the decor and lights shone out from the painting. After spending a long time looking at each of the paintings, they continued exploring the gallery. They walked through another set of doors, and approached The Fighting Temeraire. Jasmine stood next to Olivia, watching her take in the wonder of the painting, and gently held her hand. Olivia turned, surprised. She smiled at Jasmine, and they stood close together, each feeling that electric connection. Jasmine leaned over to whisper in Olivia's ear, 'I want you. Now.'

Olivia looked up, into Jasmine's eyes. Taking Olivia's hand, which was warm against her palm, Jasmine led Olivia away from the paintings, and through the doors. Leading Olivia down the steps, everything was black marble and white walls and tiles. Jasmine was heading towards the cloakrooms. Olivia couldn't quite believe this, the woman do didn't do public displays of affection, holding her hand, and now this. Jasmine pulled Olivia by the hand, underneath the labyrinthine arches and down the few steps. Fortunately there didn't seem to be anyone else in the washrooms, and Jasmine pulled Olivia into a cubicle with her. Locking the door, immediately her lips were on Olivia. 'Oh my god, I couldn't wait another minute, I want you right now,' she said urgently through her kisses.

Fuck, this is hot, thought Olivia. Jasmine ran her hands over Olivia, kneading her breasts, kissing her neck. She didn't know how on earth she had managed all of those months without Olivia, and now that she had her back, she couldn't keep her hands off of her. She felt as though, if she let go for too long, she might lose her again. She pushed Olivia's denim skirt up to her hips, and slid her hands down her pants, 'Fuck, you're so wet.'

When Jasmine talked like that, it turned Olivia on even more. Olivia kissed Jasmine back, and ran her hands over Jasmine's bottom, then undid her trousers, slipping them down her hips. Being back with Jasmine felt so right, how on earth had she walked away from this. The feel of Jasmine, the excitement that she felt, the overwhelming love was mind blowing. Holding Jasmine with one hand, she slid her other hand down the front of Jasmine's pants. Leaning against the wall of the cubicle, their breathing becoming more erratic, they could feel the excitement, the need, the desperate wanting. They could both feel that sensual build towards release, their breathing becoming more ragged, and a feeling of lightheadedness as the sensations took them higher. As they kissed, their lips felt like they were hot wired to their core, and like an explosion, they came together, panting and feeling their legs weaken. They leaned into one another, breathing heavily, then both laughing. Olivia was hoping that no one had heard them. 'You are so fucking hot,' Jasmine kissed Olivia again.

After readjusting their clothes, Jasmine stepped out of the cubicle, followed by Olivia. Jasmine looked very cool, and Olivia was bright faced, and looking as guilty as hell. A lady washing her hands did a double take as she saw the two women coming out of the same cubicle, in the reflection of the mirror. Jasmine smiled very sweetly at her, and as the woman left, Olivia burst out laughing. 'You are so naughty,' she said to Jasmine.

Jasmine gave her a wicked smile, and said, 'Let's go and get some lunch.'

Back at Olivia's on Sunday evening, she and Jasmine had had a wonderful weekend. Olivia was so happy. Emma arrived home, smiling at the two of them snuggled up on the sofa. She commented on how cosy and happy they looked. Olivia and Jasmine smiled at each other, and then at Emma. Jasmine said that she would have to leave soon, to get organised for work in the morning. They hadn't really discussed when they were going to tell the others at work. They decided to wait and see how it went for now. They kissed goodbye at the door. After Jasmine had left, Emma sat down beside Olivia, 'Okay, I want the details!'

Olivia told her about the gallery, and how they had visited it before. 'Jasmine said that's when she knew she had fallen in love with me.'

Emma said, 'Aw, that's so romantic. And what else happened?'

Olivia blushed. Emma said, 'Come on, you've got to tell me, you have a very naughty look on your face!'

So Olivia told her how Jasmine had touched her hand, and that Jasmine had wanted her there and then. 'Wow, that is so hot, what happened next?'

'Well, Jasmine took me by the hand, led me to the toilets, and pulled me into a cubicle, saying that she had to have me right now. And we fucked, and it was amazing. In public, Jasmine may seem sophisticated and refined, but behind closed doors, she is the freest and sexiest person I've ever met. Not to mention, she has a filthy mouth!' Emma looked flabbergasted. 'And then Jasmine walks out, cool as anything, and smiles at this woman who was washing her hands!'

Emma laughed, 'You two are a right horny pair! You obviously drive each other wild. It's great to see you so happy.'

Olivia walked into the office on Monday morning, feeling very happy. She said good morning to Laura, who was really pleased to see her back. Olivia asked if Jasmine was in yet. Laura said no, this was the first day in weeks that she had arrived before Jasmine. 'Hopefully she's at last taken my advice, and is going to slow down a bit, she's been working way too hard,' explained Laura.

Jason arrived, smiling cheerily. He always seemed very relaxed, Olivia didn't think she had ever seen him in a bad mood. Jasmine arrived, smiling and looking gorgeous. 'Good morning all,' she said as she breezed into her office.

Laura looked at Olivia, 'Well, someone's looking better. To tell you the truth, Jason and I have been so worried about Jasmine recently. Jason tried to talk to her, but we couldn't get anywhere.'

Olivia replied, 'She probably just got bogged down with work.'

Jason and Laura noticed how much lighter the office felt now that Jasmine was back to her old self. She usually left the office at the same time as the others, and seemed so happy now. Whatever had happened before, they were pleased it was over. They started to socialise again. If they went out for lunch together, Laura would sometimes catch a glance between Olivia and Jasmine, like she had seen when they'd played rounders that time. Maybe they had had a falling out, she wondered. Anyway, it all seemed good now.

THIRTEEN

Spring was turning into summer, and Laura arranged another game of rounders and football. Everyone met in Regent's Park as before, but as it was June now, it was much warmer than when they had last got together. Felicity and Harry ran over to Olivia, and gave her a hug. They split the teams, with Laura, Olivia, Felicity and Jason against Peter, Jasmine and Harry. Leaving their picnic rugs and food bundled up, they started kicking the ball around. It was very friendly and fun, and the kids were having a whale of a time. Gradually, the adults became more competitive, and the game started becoming more of a rugby match, with them picking the ball up and running with it. At one point, Jasmine tackled Olivia, and they both fell to the floor. They were laughing so much, that they couldn't get up. Looking down at Olivia, Jasmine leaned forward to kiss her, then remembered where she was. Felicity came running up to them and threw herself on top of them, and they all laughed helplessly. Laura and Jason went over to help them up, and they all decided that it was time for lunch. Whilst they were eating, Peter said, 'It's great that you all get on so well together. I suppose that's the advantage of working in a small company, especially when it's your own business. At our work, we have a Christmas meal and an occasional party, and that's about it.'

After chatting for a while, they decided it was time for another game of rounders. The children seemed to have an inexhaustible supply of energy, and played all afternoon. Laura was so pleased that they were all socialising again.

Back at work a couple of weeks later, Laura was getting ready to leave for lunch. Just as she was about to go, she realised she had forgotten to give Jasmine a message. Olivia wasn't at her desk, she must have gone for lunch already. Laura thought she had better go and tell Jasmine now, whilst she remembered it. She went straight to Jasmine's office, and put her head around the door, 'Jasmine, I forgot to tell you...' and stopped abruptly when she saw Jasmine and Olivia in the middle of a very passionate kiss, their hands all over one another. Jasmine and Olivia jumped back from each other, Olivia's face flushing beetroot red. They looked at Laura, wide eyed. Laura just stood there for a moment, not sure what to say. 'Um, I'm so sorry, I should have knocked,' she blushed profusely.

Jasmine was very calm, 'Please don't apologise. Shut the door and come and sit down. I'm so sorry about this. I should have spoken to you before now, I didn't want you to find out like this.' Once Laura had sat down, Jasmine continued, 'It's not how it looks.

Actually, I'm really not sure how it does look! Anyway, Olivia and I are dating.'

Laura was still pretty shocked, 'How long has this been going on?'

Jasmine looked at Olivia, then at Laura. 'We dated for a few months, then stopped. We've been together since the spring.'

As Laura let this information sink in, things started to make more sense to her. She remembered the stolen glances when they'd all gone out. And she noticed at the park that they seemed very close. But she would have never imagined, not in a million years. Olivia had been going out with guys. Then she realised why Jasmine had been so withdrawn all that time, it made sense now, that things had been so strained between the two of them. 'Does Jason know?' she asked.

Jasmine replied, 'No, not yet, but I'm going to have a chat with him this week.'

Olivia said, 'I'm so sorry. Also, I'm so relieved that you know.'

Olivia and Jasmine exchanged a look, and Laura couldn't help laughing. 'You two are like a couple of teenagers. As long as you know what you're doing.'

A couple of days later, it was nearing six o'clock, and Jasmine went into Jason's office. 'Hi, can I have a chat with you?'

Jason looked up, 'Of course. Here, take a seat,' Jason said, moving some books out of the way. Jasmine sat down, wondering how to start. Jason spoke first, 'Can I just say, it's so great now you're back to your old self. I was so worried about you. I'm guessing that whatever it was is sorted out now?'

Jasmine looked at Jason, she was very fond of her friend. 'That's what I wanted to talk to you about. Basically, I've met someone, and I've fallen in love,' she said matter of factly.

Jason was surprised, Jasmine never usually spoke of her personal relationships. He assumed that she wasn't really interested. Jason smiled, 'That's wonderful. Who's the lucky guy?'

Jasmine hesitated, 'Well, actually, um, it's not a guy. It's a woman. It's Olivia.' She sat there, looking at Jason.

'Oh,' Jason wasn't sure what to say.

Jasmine continued, 'I've only ever been interested in women, and as it's no one's business but mine, I don't usually talk about it. But in this case, I think you need to know.'

Jason looked at her, still not sure what to say. 'Well, thank you for telling me. I assume it won't affect anything here at work, will it?'

Jasmine shook her head, 'Of course not. And Laura knows, by the way. At lunchtime the other day, you were out and Laura came back unexpectedly. She saw us kissing in my office. We had been meaning to tell both of you,' Jasmine looked so serious and embarrassed.

Jason couldn't help laughing, his face creasing and his blue eyes twinkling. 'Well, well. As long as you're happy, I'm happy,' and he laughed again.

Jasmine breathed a sigh of relief, 'Phew, I was so nervous about telling you. Thanks for being so understanding.'

It was Friday, and Jasmine was going home with Olivia after work. Jasmine said, 'Well, Jason and Laura know, so we can relax about work. We should still keep things professional in the office, but out of work will be much easier now we don't have to pretend there's nothing between us.'

Olivia unlocked the door, and Jasmine followed her inside. Over dinner that evening, Jasmine said, 'I'd love to visit Cornwall some time, and see where you grew up. It sounds lovely. Also I'd love to meet Becky and see her gallery.'

Olivia looked at her, 'I'd love that too. I'll be going back soon, why don't you come with me? It would make more sense us both being away at the same time. You and Jason cover for each other anyway, and if you're away with me, Laura won't have so much extra work to do.'

Jasmine thought about it, 'I guess it does make sense.'

The more Jasmine thought about it, the more excited she became. 'Yes, let's do it. I will obviously run it by Jason, but I know he'll be fine with it. Before we hired you, most of the time we only had Laura.'

Olivia explained that she hadn't yet told her friends and family about their relationship. 'If you're okay with it, I would just say we're friends initially, I want them to get to know you first. Also, I don't yet know how I'm going to tell them.'

Jasmine understood, and there was no way that she was going to rush anything, she had learned that the hard way. Olivia asked Jasmine how old she was when she came out. 'It was about ten years ago, when I was twenty. I was madly in love with this girl, and couldn't hide it any more. My mum had already guessed, and she was very supportive. My dad, on the other hand, had a really hard time with it. He wouldn't have my girlfriend in the house, and if I tried to talk about her, he would either change the subject or leave the room. It wasn't long after that, that I moved out, which helped relieve some of the tension. He's better than he was, but I just don't talk about my personal life with him, and he doesn't ask. Mum has tried talking to him over the years, but he's very old fashioned. He's fifteen years older than mum, too, and has different ideas about how things should be.'

Olivia looked at Jasmine, 'That's such a shame, you poor thing. I hope my parents are okay when I do eventually tell them. My mum and dad are great, you'll love them. And I think you and Becky will get along really well.'

Jasmine smiled, and leaned over to kiss Olivia.

Work was so much easier now that Jasmine and Olivia could talk openly about their plans and their weekends. Laura and Jason were pleased that they were both so happy. Jasmine had a chat with Jason about going away with Olivia, and it was all agreed. Olivia spoke to her mum, who was delighted that she was bringing a friend. 'Mum says you can stay in Ben's old room. He's been living with Tina for quite a while now. We reckon that they'll tie the knot soon, the way they've been talking.'

FOURTEEN

Olivia and Jasmine were all packed, and ready to set off for Cornwall. Emma and Matt took them to the station, and helped them with their cases. 'Have a great time guys,' Emma hugged each of them in turn, and they boarded the train.

Jasmine said, 'I'm excited, but also quite nervous. Also, I've been thinking, when we get back, I'd like you to meet my mum. I was thinking we could go out for dinner, maybe.'

Olivia looked at her, 'Yes, I'd like that. And don't be nervous, everyone is really friendly, you're going to love it.'

On the long journey, Olivia talked about growing up in Cornwall. She didn't remember Middlesex at all, as she was only two when her parents moved them all. Olivia talked lovingly about long summers at the beach, and how lovely the people were where she grew up. She adored the beach at St Ives, and her favourite part of the train journey was that of the ride from St Erth to St Ives, when she would get her first glimpse of the beach. Olivia so wanted Jasmine to experience this, so had asked Ella to pick them up from St Ives, even though it meant lugging their cases onto another train.

As the train approached St Ives, Jasmine agreed that the view was enchanting, and watched Olivia as she looked excitedly out of the window. Olivia saw Jasmine watching her in the reflection of the window, and turned to smile at her. Jasmine looked deep into Olivia's eyes, 'I love you so much.'

Olivia smiled back at Jasmine, feeling a surge of love for her. 'I love you, too.'

As the train pulled into the station, Jasmine and Olivia stood up, and collected their cases. Getting off of the train, Olivia saw Ella waving, and walking towards them, with arms outstretched. 'Darling, it's so good to have you back.' She hugged Olivia, then smiled at Jasmine. 'You must be Jasmine, Olivia's told me so much about you. It's lovely to meet you.'

'It's lovely to meet you too. Thank you for letting me stay, it's so kind of you.'

They headed to the car, Ella chatting away, updating Olivia on what had been going on. They still spoke regularly on the phone, but where Ella lived, everyone seemed to know everyone else's business, so there was always some news. When they arrived back at the cottage, Jasmine was enchanted, 'Oh, this is so beautiful.'

Olivia's dad came to greet them. Ella said, 'Steve, this is Jasmine.'

They shook hands, Jasmine saying how pleased she was to meet him, and thanking them again for letting her stay with them. Steve said that he would take the cases upstairs, saying that Olivia would show Jasmine her room later. He told them to have a sit down after their long journey. Jasmine loved Olivia's parents, they were so welcoming, and Olivia was thrilled that Jasmine was with her.

Ella and Steve had prepared a lovely meal, and they sat down together to eat. They chatted away, and Jasmine was saying how she was looking forward to seeing Becky's gallery. After dinner, over coffee, Olivia said she would help clear up. Her parents were having none of it, and said to go and unpack. Olivia led Jasmine upstairs to Ben's room, which was next to hers. 'And this is my room.'

Jasmine walked into the blue and white bedroom, with its pretty blue and white check curtains and duvet, and sat down on the bed. She ran her hands gently over the cotton duvet cover, taking everything in. Olivia walked over to the window, and held her hand out to Jasmine, who stood and walked over to her, taking her hand, their fingers interlocking. The cottage was on a hill, and Olivia's room had a view over the rooftops of the beach in the distance. Jasmine looked out at the view, the blue sky kissing the water in the distance. Wistfully, she said, 'Why would you want to leave this behind, it's beautiful.'

'Something was calling me, and I had to discover what it was. I think it was you.'

Jasmine turned to Olivia, tears welling in her eyes. That was one of the most beautiful and romantic things she had ever heard in her life. Olivia kissed Jasmine, and she could feel the love, that connection that had brought them together. They stood for a long time, in each other's arms, looking at the view.

In the morning, Olivia knocked on Jasmine's door. She heard mumbling, and opened the door. 'Good morning, sleepy head!' Jasmine was just waking up. 'Did you sleep well?'

Jasmine rubbed her eyes, and sat up, 'Yes, very well thank you. I think I was asleep the minute my head hit the pillow.'

'It's the sea air, very therapeutic.'

They went down to breakfast in their pyjamas, and Jasmine felt like a little girl again, having a sleepover. Ella greeted them, 'Morning girls, what would you like? We've got cereal and toast, juice, tea and coffee.'

'Oh, coffee for me please, Mum. I expect Jasmine will have tea.'

As Ella made the drinks, she asked, 'So what are you two up to today?'

'We're going to meet up with Liam, Becky and Dan at the cafe later.'

They had a leisurely breakfast, and Ella asked Jasmine more about London, and her publishing company. Jasmine felt so comfortable here, it was so different when she was with her own parents.

At the cafe, Olivia asked what Jasmine would like to drink, telling her that the milkshakes were the best that she had ever tasted. Jasmine said, 'It's years since I've had a milkshake. Which flavour do you recommend?'

'I love the coffee one, and the banana one is gorgeous if you fancy something fruity,' she raised her eyebrows at Jasmine.

Laughing, Jasmine said, 'Oh, definitely fruity!'

Olivia ordered the shakes and they sat down. When the drinks arrived, Olivia watched Jasmine expectantly. Jasmine said, 'Mmm, yes, it's delicious. It tastes almost as delicious as you,' and she gave Olivia a cheeky look.

Olivia looked at Jasmine, but before she could say anything, she looked up as she heard her friends coming into the cafe. It was all hugs and kisses, and then Olivia introduced Jasmine. 'Liam, you've already met, and this is Becky, and her boyfriend Dan.'

They all shook hands, saying how pleased they were to meet one another. Becky wanted to know all about Jasmine, and Jasmine wanted to hear about the gallery. Becky said, 'Pop into the gallery, and I'll show you around.'

'Thank you, I would love that. Olivia's told me so much about it.'

Olivia asked, 'How is your new assistant getting on?'

'Really well, but it's not the same without you.' Jasmine smiled at Olivia. Becky continued, 'Her name is Lucy, and I think she has a bit of a thing for Liam. She's always asking what we've been up to, and fishing for information about him!'

'Don't be daft,' laughed Liam, embarrassed.

Olivia said, 'Well, you're a good catch, I can see why she'd like you.' Liam looked at Olivia sadly, and Olivia felt awkward, and changed the subject.

Dan asked, 'So, do you have any plans for the week?'

'Yes. Jasmine has never been to Cornwall before, so there's loads to show her, and she really wants to go to the Eden Project.'

'You'll love it there,' said Becky.

They spent a few hours catching up, then said their goodbyes. Olivia said, 'Let's go to the beach, I want you to see it close up. Also, we have to go for a walk along the beach at dusk, it's magical.'

As they walked along, Olivia wanted to know what Jasmine thought of her friends. 'They're really nice, and they obviously think a lot of you. They miss you, too.'

Olivia was thoughtful, 'You know, when I came back last time, after I gave you my resignation, I was seriously thinking of staying here.'

Jasmine looked at her, a heavy feeling in her stomach. She really didn't want to think about what might have happened. 'I'm so glad you didn't.'

'Emma kept telling me not to rush into anything. Of course, I didn't know that you and she had been scheming!'

'Well, I did turn up on her doorstep in a bit of a state! Emma didn't know that you'd tried to resign.'

Olivia sighed, 'I didn't want to tell anyone anything, until I knew myself what I wanted to do.'

They walked down the steps, onto the sand, and sat down. Now it was the end of June, and the weather was improving. There were lots of people around, families having picnics, and children laughing and building sandcastles. They took off their shoes, and having rolled up their jeans, pushed their feet into the sand. Olivia loved the feeling of the grains between her toes, the sand dusting her feet. Jasmine said, 'You're so lucky to have grown up here, it's idyllic.'

Looking across to Jasmine, Olivia said, 'I love that I get to share it with you.'

They sat on the beach all afternoon, sometimes chatting, and much of the time in companionable silence, watching everything going on around them. Jasmine found the sound of the sea washing up on the shore very relaxing. Although there were a lot of people around, there was so much wide open space here. Every now and again, Jasmine and Olivia's hands would touch in the sand, and they would look at each other and smile. They went for a paddle, feeling the salty water splashing around their legs, and trickling sun beaded droplets to their ankles. Jasmine loved hearing the seagulls, and the sounds of laughter from the children on the beach. Everything felt so fresh and spacious here, it was wonderful.

Late that afternoon, they were ready to eat. Olivia's favourite place was a small cafe on the Wharf, and they walked up the beach towards it. After eating in the tiny restaurant, Jasmine agreed that the food was excellent. Dusk was approaching, and Olivia took Jasmine for a walk along the beach, as promised. They walked slowly, watching the sky change colour, and how as it reflected in the sand, it appeared to change at their feet. It was quiet now, with just a couple of people walking their dogs.

Olivia said, 'I love this time of day on the beach.' She held out her arms, face up to the sky, and started to spin around. Jasmine laughed, watching Olivia spinning around freely, laughing. 'Come and dance with me,' Olivia grabbed Jasmine's hands, and they span around at arms length. Then they fell in a heap on the sand, laughing. They lay side by side, looking up at the sky, with sand in their hair. Olivia reached across for Jasmine's hand, and there they lay, until it started getting colder. Then they sat up, shaking the sand from their hair. Jasmine looked at Olivia, so happy. They were both covered with grains of sand, and Jasmine loved the smell of the sea on her skin. Jasmine said, 'Thank you for today, I've had a wonderful time.'

Somehow, being here on the beach, Jasmine felt a new freedom, like the normal rules didn't apply, and she embraced Olivia, kissing her deeply, passionately. When they arrived back at home, Ella greeted them, 'My word, you two look like children who have been playing in the sand all day! Why don't you go and get showered, and I'll make you some hot chocolate.'

Olivia and Jasmine headed upstairs to shower. After putting on their pyjamas, they made their way back downstairs to the cosy lounge. Ella brought in hot chocolates and biscuits for them. 'Thanks, Mum.'

'Thank you, Ella, this is lovely.'

They sat down together and chatted about their day. Ella said that Ben and Tina were coming over the following day. After Olivia and Jasmine had gone to bed, Ella was saying to Steve how pleased she was that Olivia had made such a good friend in London, and how happy she seemed to be. Steve agreed, 'It's like when she was younger, and every day was an adventure, she always had something to be excited about.'

Ben and Tina arrived the following afternoon, and Olivia introduced them to Jasmine. They were sitting in the lounge chatting, when Ben said, 'We've got some news for you. Tina and I have just got engaged!'

Tina held out her hand, showing a fine platinum band with a single diamond in the centre.

'It's beautiful,' exclaimed Olivia, and jumped up to hug Tina, and then her brother.

Their parents were thrilled, and Steve said that they would go out tonight to celebrate. They all asked lots of questions, and Ben and Tina said that they planned to get married in the spring, although they hadn't set the actual date yet. It would be a fairly small wedding, and they would like to have a marquee in the garden at her parents place for the party afterwards. Jasmine saw how happy they were, and thought that they made a lovely couple. Although this was the first time that she had met Olivia's family, she felt really included. Olivia's family was so different to hers, and they all seemed much closer to one another. Jasmine watched Olivia chatting with Tina, asking about what kind of dress she was going to have, and thought how lucky she was to have met her. She loved her so much, it felt like her heart was going to burst.

Ben had noticed Jasmine watching Olivia, and he went over to talk to Jasmine. Jasmine asked him about the wedding, and Ben asked how she was enjoying Cornwall. 'I understand you're Olivia's boss?'

Jasmine nodded, 'Well, my partner Jason and I own the business, and Olivia is my assistant. She's really good, an amazing colleague. She practically organised a book launch on her own, I was very lucky to find her.'

Ben looked at Jasmine, 'Yes, I think Livvy could probably do anything she wants to. That's if she wants to do it, of course! She's very strong minded, although most people don't see that side of her. She's a very sweet person, and always wants to help people, she wouldn't hurt a fly.'

That evening at dinner, Ben was chatting with his sister. Olivia was telling him how much she loved working at the publishing company. Ben said, 'I'm so pleased for you. I was talking to Jasmine earlier, and she thinks the world of you. You're very lucky to have a boss like her.'

Olivia smiled, 'I know,' and looked over to Jasmine, who caught her eye and smiled back. Olivia's heart flipped.

Olivia took Jasmine to Becky's gallery. It was a white stone wash building, with cottage windows. There were glass decorations hanging in the window which caught the light, and reflected beautiful colours onto the walls. They walked in through the open door, and Becky looked up. She said hello, and walked over to hug Olivia and Jasmine. The gallery had two rooms. The first one had the desk with the till, and that room led through to a slightly bigger room. Practically every space on the walls was filled with artwork. Becky accepted artwork from many different artists, so there were all different styles, including drawings, oils and watercolours. Jasmine was drawn to one particular picture. It was of the beach at St Ives, and its colours were soft and almost abstract. It captured the essence of St Ives, and reminded Jasmine of their day on the beach, and Olivia twirling around in the sand. 'Becky, I love this painting, I'd like to buy it, please. Who is the artist?'

Olivia was beaming, 'It's Becky. She's an amazing artist, I'm always telling her so.' Becky blushed, and smiled, delighted.

Jasmine looked at her, 'You didn't say that you were an artist yourself. With a talent like this, you should be shouting from the rooftops.'

Becky took the picture down, and said that she would go and wrap it up. After chatting a bit more, and being introduced to Lucy, Jasmine paid for her painting, and they took it back to Olivia's.

The following day, they were heading for the Eden Project. It was raining, but as a lot of the Eden Project was covered, that wasn't going to be a problem. Olivia borrowed her Mum's car. Jasmine didn't realise that she could drive, and Olivia explained that in London, she didn't really want to, or need to with the public transport. In Cornwall, however, having a car was pretty essential. The drive would take the best part of an hour, and on the way Olivia pointed out some of her favourite places, as Jasmine took in the stunning scenery. Even in the rain, the rugged scenery was beautiful. Jasmine was really excited to be visiting the Eden Project. When they arrived, Jasmine's eye was caught by the sculpture of the horse near the entrance. 'It's beautiful,' she exclaimed, walking over to it.

Olivia watched her, thinking, yes, beautiful is certainly the word. Jasmine turned and smiled, and Olivia took a photo of Jasmine next to the horse. It was busy as usual, and they queued for their tickets.

The man at the desk explained that the tickets were valid for a year, so they could come back as much as they liked within that time. They headed for the Rainforest biome first. Olivia loved it, it was like going on an adventure. They walked past an old truck that had been painted in many bright colours, with birds and flowers. Olivia said that if she got her own car, that's how she would like it painted! When they arrived at the baobab bar, Olivia said, 'You've got to try one of these smoothies, they're amazing.'

Jasmine sipped at the pale yellow drink, which was made with coconut milk, banana and baobab. 'Ooh, it's lovely. Unusual, and very refreshing too!'

Jasmine's favourite area was the Mediterranean biome, as she found it very peaceful. Near the entrance, paella was being cooked in massive pans. The smell was divine, and they decided to eat lunch there, at one of the little round tables. The paella tasted as good as it smelled. After they had eaten, Jasmine looked at Olivia, smiling. 'I'm having such a wonderful time. I adore Cornwall, and your friends and family are wonderful. I'm still not sure why you wanted to come to London, and I can see why Liam found the pace too much.'

Olivia said, 'I do love it here, it is a magical place. Also, I knew that there is a lot more life out there. I'd had a longing to go to London since I was quite young, and sometimes you have to follow what feels important. I've always got home to come back to, although London is also home now. If I hadn't made the move, a part of me would have always been wondering whether I had missed something. Now I can know which suits me more. And as I said before, I would never have met you if I hadn't followed my heart.'

Olivia smiled lovingly at Jasmine, who gave her that look, that look that said Olivia was the only person in the world to her, and her stomach did its familiar flip. It was time to explore outside, and they zipped up their waterproofs in readiness for the weather. There was so much to see, and Jasmine wanted to see all of it. After a very full day, they visited the shop, which was full of lots of interesting things. Jasmine spotted a beautiful necklace made from tagua seeds, which had been dyed an amazing array of bright colours. Jasmine bought some gifts for Laura and Jason, and Olivia bought some of her favourite organic chocolate. Jasmine also bought a small lemon tree, which she decided she would put in a pot by a sunny window at home. They chatted away happily on the drive home, and Olivia said that they would stop off to get a meal at one of the local pubs. Olivia knew about this great pub, tucked away along a long, winding road. The food there was home cooked, and fabulous. Arriving inside, the pub was cosy, with lots of nooks and crannies. There were wall lights with little lamp shades on, which created an orangey glow around them. The pub was very busy, but Olivia found a small table in the corner. Over dinner, Olivia passed a gift bag to Jasmine. 'What's this?' she asked, opening the bag. Inside was the beautiful necklace that Jasmine had admired. 'Thank you, I love it.' She held Olivia's hand across the table.

Jasmine put the necklace on, and against her olive skin and dark hair, it looked stunning. 'Beautiful,' Olivia smiled.

Becky was thrilled that Jasmine had bought her painting. She thought that Jasmine was very nice, and she was glad that Olivia was happy in London. It's just that she felt she was hardly getting any time with Olivia. Before when Olivia had visited, they had got together most days, even if they didn't meet until the evening. She was talking to Dan about it, and he said that as Jasmine had never been here before, Olivia was just showing her around. He said it was natural that she would be out more than usual. Also, Jasmine didn't know anyone, and it was nice that Olivia wanted to her to have a really good time. Dan looked at her, 'Honey, nothing will change the fact that you grew up together, and are best friends,' and he kissed her.

Yes, she knew Dan was right, but Becky had really missed her friend since she had moved away.

It was nearing the end of the week, and Olivia was really looking forward to taking Jasmine on her favourite walk. She explained that it was a coastal walk, about five miles, from Looe to Polperro. Olivia parked the car on the road leading up to the start of the walk.

Thankfully, the weather had cleared up, and it was a beautiful day. Olivia opened the gate, and she and Jasmine walked across the field towards the coastal path. Olivia was right, Jasmine thought it was beautiful. The path was quite rugged, with hills to climb up and down. The coast was to their left, with the sea stretching for miles. About half way through, Olivia led Jasmine to some rocks that were slightly off of the path, and looked right over the sea. They sat down, holding hands as they looked at the view. They drew close, and as they kissed, nothing else existed for them, except each other. After resting for a while, they continued the walk, passing by Talland Bay, and onto Polperro. As they began the descent, Jasmine looked at the rocks rising out of the water, the boats in the bay, and the little cottages, painted in various colours. 'It's so beautiful, so quaint.'

Olivia was thrilled that Jasmine loved it, Polperro was very special to her. They walked along the road, and Olivia took Jasmine to her favourite restaurant, which was run by a local family. It was a quaint restaurant, with cottage windows, and a stream outside. The food was delicious, and Jasmine was very glad of the rest. Although she was used to walking a lot around London, she wasn't used to all these hills. They walked around the village, and stopped to get an ice cream, taking a long time to decide as there were so many flavours to choose from. Olivia chose a coconut one, and Jasmine eventually plumped for mango. They walked towards the harbour to eat them, whilst watching the boats bobbing around.

After spending a couple of hours there, it was time to head back. They walked at a leisurely pace, stopping for rests along the way, and savouring the view. It was getting quite late when they returned home, and Olivia suggested a last evening walk on the beach at St Ives before they had to go back to London. There were very few people around, and it was starting to get dark. As they walked back up the beach, along the harbour wall, Olivia pulled Jasmine underneath one of the arches, where it was dark. She held Jasmine close, kissing her passionately, Jasmine responding eagerly. Jasmine had been going mad, not being able to touch Olivia, except occasionally holding her hand or the odd stolen kiss. This week they had had hardly any time alone, as they were either with other people, or in public. As things heated up between them, a part of them knew that it was too open. They reluctantly pulled back, breathing heavily. 'We can't do this here, it's too risky.'

They straightened themselves up, and wandered back onto the beach. Liam had been making his way home, when he recognised Olivia, coming out from under one of the arches. He stopped, seeing Jasmine following her out. It looked like... No, it can't be, he must be imagining things. If he didn't know better, though. He shook his head, and headed on home. A few days later, he mentioned it to Ben, who told him,

'No, Jasmine has a partner, Jason. Look mate, I think you were imagining it, I know you still have feelings for Olivia.'

It was time to leave, and Olivia and Jasmine packed their cases into the car, and also the wrapped painting, which they gently laid on the parcel shelf. Jasmine had already decided that she would hang it in her bedroom, opposite her bed. It would be the last thing that she would see before she went to sleep, and the first thing when she woke up. Ella dropped them at the station, and they said their goodbyes. Jasmine gave Ella a hug, 'Thank you so much for this week, you've made me feel so welcome.'

Olivia hugged her mum, and they said goodbye. When Ella returned home, she saw a gift on the kitchen table. It was from Jasmine, an exquisite handmade vase in the most beautiful shades of blue and turquoise. The note read, 'Thank you so much, I felt like one of the family, you made me feel so welcome. Olivia is very lucky to have such a beautiful family. Love from Jasmine.' Ella was very touched, and put the vase in pride of place in the lounge.

FIFTEEN

Jasmine and Olivia arrived back at Jasmine's house. Leaving their cases in the hall, Jasmine gently put the wrapped painting on the table. Walking over to Olivia, Jasmine took her in her arms and kissed her. Through her kisses, she said, 'I can't wait a minute longer, I have to have you now.'

Olivia felt the same, she had that familiar twist in her stomach, and her body was hot with desire. As they made their way upstairs to the bedroom, they discarded their clothes along the way. Olivia fell back onto the bed, and Jasmine leaned over, kissing her forehead, down her face, softly kissing the contours of her neck. Olivia was writhing at the sensation of her touch, as she felt Jasmine's mouth moving down her body. The muscles in her stomach tightened, and she felt Jasmine's mouth between her legs. 'Oh my god, that feels so good, aah, aah...'

Having waited a week, and been desperate to be with Jasmine, Olivia was so highly aroused, and she came quickly, crying out with pleasure. She ran her hands down Jasmine's back, then rolled over, so she was now on top. Jasmine had the most beautiful soft skin. She kissed Jasmine's breasts, then sucked on them. Jasmine's dark eyes watched her sensuously, and she arched her head back in pleasure. Olivia trailed down, her hands sliding down Jasmine's hips, and then pushing her thighs apart. As her tongue explored Jasmine intimately, Jasmine breathed, 'Yes, oh fucking yes,' and she grabbed hold of the sheets. Olivia could make Jasmine feel like no one else could. She came hard, orgasm following orgasm. Olivia slid up the bed, smiling at Jasmine, and they kissed. Jasmine whispered, 'What are you doing to me, you drive me wild.'

Olivia laughed, 'I could say the same. I've never felt so free as when I'm with you.'

Lying in bed, Jasmine said, 'I had the most wonderful week, thank you.'

'Thank you for coming, and sharing it with me. Everyone loved you.'

'Your family and friends are lovely. Do you think they would like me as much if they knew I was your girlfriend?'

Olivia giggled. Jasmine asked, 'What's so funny? '

'I hadn't really thought about it like that, I mean that you're my girlfriend. I think that's the first time you've called me that.'

'Do you think you'll tell them?'

Olivia thought for a moment, 'I will tell them at some time, I'm just not sure when. It will probably be a bit of a shock to them. It came as quite a shock to me!'

Jasmine propped her head on her hand, looking at Olivia, 'So what changed for you? I mean, after I had kissed you and freaked you out, when I turned up at your door a few days later, it was you who kissed me first.'

Olivia smiled at Jasmine, 'I *was* completely freaked out. I was also incredibly turned on, which freaked me out even more!' Jasmine laughed, and Olivia continued, 'I had experienced this amazing connection with you, and I'd never felt anything like it in my life. I tried to convince myself that you had caught me off guard, that it was a romantic gesture. I tried to distract myself, not think about it. But whenever I did think of it, I couldn't shake the feeling, and when you appeared at my door, saying those lovely things, my instincts just took over.' She paused, 'Now we've got to talking about it, why did you make a move in the first place, didn't you think I was straight?'

Jasmine paused, 'Well, you can never be completely sure. I was immediately attracted to you, that much I do know. I've never fallen for someone so quickly. I did try sending you signals, and sometimes the way you looked at me, and the things you said, I thought that you may be attracted to me. Then, when we were working together on the book launch, we were spending so much time together. I felt very close to you, and you talked a lot about Becky and Emma. Also, there was that photo of you and Becky on the beach together. I don't know, personally, I think that you don't fall in love with someone because of their gender, I think that you fall in love with the person as an individual.'

Olivia thought about that for a moment, 'Well, I've never been attracted to a woman before, but I know that I'm crazy about you,' and kissed Jasmine.

Back at work on Monday, Laura greeted Jasmine and Olivia, asking if they had had a good time in Cornwall. Jasmine replied, 'It was wonderful, and such a different pace to London, although Olivia kept us very busy sightseeing and walking. Have we missed much here?'

'Not really, I think Jason and I held the fort very well.'

Jason arrived, and they chatted about the holiday. Later that day, Jason and Laura commented on how happy and relaxed Olivia and Jasmine were. Being in Cornwall, Jasmine had felt a freedom that she hadn't experienced here in London. Although she and Olivia had been careful around others, that day on the beach when she had watched Olivia spinning around, face up to the sky, and they had danced and then lay on the sand together, she had felt so free. Jasmine hoped that soon Olivia would tell her parents about them. At least in London, it was so much easier now that their friends knew.

After work, Olivia and Jasmine were heading home. Jasmine said that she wanted Olivia to meet her mother at the weekend, and would it be okay if she booked a table for them. 'Yes, of course. Will you invite your dad?'

Jasmine sighed, 'Not this time. I don't think I could stand the tension, and I wouldn't want to put you through it. I'm sure that you'll meet him eventually.'

Olivia turned to look at Jasmine, and felt for her. She took Jasmine's hand in hers, and gave it a gentle squeeze as they walked along. Jasmine looked up, surprised. Olivia smiled, 'Is this okay? You are my girlfriend!' and they both laughed.

This small gesture was a big step for both of them. Olivia wanted to be able to be relaxed with Jasmine in public. Having had the week together in Cornwall, she realised how desperately she wanted it. Being in London was easier as she didn't know many people, and their friends now knew about them. For Olivia, this was a part of building up to being more open with other people, although she was still very worried about how her friends and family back home would be. For Jasmine's part, she loved the freedom that she had experienced in Cornwall, and holding Olivia's hand now, walking along the road, felt so good. Ever since Olivia had made that comment about not changing who you are, it had really struck a nerve.

Jasmine arrived at Olivia's on Saturday evening to pick her up for the meal with her mum. Olivia opened the door, and Jasmine was standing there smiling. She was wearing a black tailored trouser suit, with a short jacket, which accentuated her long legs. Under the jacket she wore a fine cream camisole. As she walked inside, Olivia said, 'You look gorgeous,' and kissed her.

Whilst they were embracing, Emma walked across the lounge, and laughed. 'Hey, you two, how about closing the door!'

Olivia and Jasmine pulled apart, laughing. Olivia closed the door, and Emma said, 'I see you're becoming exhibitionists now then!'

Emma looked at the two of them, grinning like idiots. She said, 'You know, you make such a gorgeous couple, you both look stunning.'

They said thank you, and Olivia blushed. Olivia was wearing her dark red dress, the one she wore for Phoebe and Fran's party. She didn't have much in the way of dressy clothes, as she had never really needed them before. She usually wore smart casual clothes for the office. Olivia said, 'I could do with a couple more outfits for going out, maybe we can all go shopping together?'

Jasmine said that she would love to, 'Mmm, watching you getting dressed and undressed all day, sounds good!'

Emma pulled a face of mock horror, 'Okay, I'm in as long as I'm not the third wheel, and you two can keep it in your pants.'

Olivia and Jasmine exchanged a look between them, like naughty children, and they all laughed. As they were leaving, Emma said, 'Have a good time. I would say don't do anything I wouldn't do, but I know what you two are like!'

As the taxi drove along Regent Street, Olivia asked, 'Does your mum know about us?'

Jasmine replied, 'Yes, of course,' and leaned across to kiss her.

Arriving at the Cafe Royal, Olivia was glad that she had dressed up, she thought that it was very smart, not the kind of place she would usually go to. Jasmine gave the name of their booking, and they were shown to their table. The carpets were a rich navy blue, and the tables had deep burgundy tablecloths on. The whole place reeked of class. They had just sat down, when Jasmine looked up to see her mum arriving. Jasmine stood to greet her, 'Mum, I would like to introduce you to Olivia. Olivia, this is Grace.'

Olivia was feeling really nervous. They shook hands, Olivia saying how nice it was to meet her, and hoped that Grace didn't notice how sweaty her hands were. Grace was of medium height, and her shoulder length grey wavy hair was pulled back off of her kindly face with a hair clip. The waiter came over to take their drinks order, then disappeared. Jasmine asked, 'So how are you, how is dad?'

'I am very well, thank you. Your father is well, the same as usual, you know how he is. So, tell me what you've been up to.'

Olivia thought that Grace was very nice, but she also felt a bit like she was there for an interview. She knew that was because she was so nervous, and she really wanted this to go well. Jasmine spoke about how well the business was doing, which was one of the reasons that they had needed to hire another assistant, which in turn was how she had met Olivia. Jasmine looked at Olivia, smiling. They also talked about the book launch that she and Olivia had organised. Grace then asked Olivia about growing up in Cornwall. She was very interested to hear about St Ives and Becky's gallery. Jasmine told Grace all about their recent visit, and the beautiful painting that she had bought at the gallery. Grace was particularly interested to hear about the Eden Project, as she was very interested in plants and flowers.

The meal was delicious, and as the evening wore on, Olivia began to relax. Every now and again, Jasmine would touch Olivia's hand under the table, which she found reassuring. Towards the end of the evening, they had all just ordered a coffee to finish with, and Olivia felt Jasmine's hand slide up her thigh, and she let out a little squeal, which she hoped she covered with a cough. When Jasmine touched her unexpectedly like that, it sent a feeling through her body that took her breath away. Olivia excused herself, and went to the ladies room. She was feeling hot and bothered, and splashed some cold water onto her face. Olivia was leaning on the sink, regaining herself. The door opened, and Jasmine was behind her, hands around her front, stroking her breasts. Jasmine's hand started to move towards the hem of Olivia's dress. Olivia breathed heavily, 'We can't do this here...' but Jasmine had an effect on her that she couldn't explain, and all reason went out of the window.

Jasmine's hand slid into Olivia's lacy pants, and Jasmine kissed her neck, breathing in her ear, 'You are so gorgeous, I can't keep my hands off you,' and Olivia just gave into it...

Olivia followed Jasmine back to the table, knowing that her face was as red as her dress. Fuck, how was she going to carry on talking to Jasmine's mum as if nothing had happened, surely she would guess. Jasmine sat down, as cool as a cucumber, adding cream to her coffee, which had since arrived. She carried on the conversation effortlessly. Olivia wanted to know how she could do that so easily, and wondered whether she could learn to do it, too. Olivia busied herself putting sugar into her coffee, and then cream, and kept sipping it, hoping that her face was returning to its normal colour. After they had all finished, Grace got up to leave. 'Dinner is my treat, I took care of it whilst you were... otherwise engaged.'

Olivia was sure that she gave a knowing smile. She felt her face go red again, wishing that the ground would swallow her up. As embarrassed as she was, it was at this point that Olivia realised how much she liked Grace. Grace continued, 'Olivia, it was lovely to meet you. I can see that you make Jasmine very happy.'

Olivia replied that it was lovely to meet her too, and thanked her very much for dinner. They watched her leave, then Olivia sat back down. 'I am so embarrassed, your mum knew, did you see her face?'

Jasmine laughed, 'My mother thinks that you're charming, she said so when you'd left for the bathroom. Also, she was a bit of a girl, too. Maybe I'll tell you one day.'

They walked out onto Regent Street, and decided to walk for a while to get some fresh air, heading towards Oxford Circus. As they walked, Jasmine asked whether she had enjoyed herself this evening. Olivia said, 'Yes, I did. Your mum is really nice. I was really nervous to start with, but I had a good time. That is, until the end of the evening, when I could have died with embarrassment!'

Jasmine laughed, 'I told you, my mum is fine. As I said before, she's open minded, and was very supportive when I came out.'

'You once mentioned that you had fallen madly in love when you were twenty, and came out to your parents. What was her name?'

As they walked along the road, Jasmine looked down, and when she raised her head, she looked worried, 'Phoebe.' She looked sideways at Olivia, who now slowed her pace.

'Phoebe. Not your best friend Phoebe?' The answer was in the look on Jasmine's face. 'Shit, when were you going to tell me. I can't believe you.'

'Look, it was a long time ago. We were together for about six months, that's all. It was all over years ago.'

Olivia felt humiliated. They walked the rest of the way in silence, and as they approached Olivia's flat, Jasmine went to follow her up the steps. As Olivia turned, Jasmine could see tears in her eyes. Jasmine desperately wanted to hold Olivia, and make everything better again. Olivia said, 'I think it's best that you go now,' and went inside the flat, shutting the door behind her.

Emma was in the kitchen, and heard the front door open. She was about to go and ask if Olivia and Jasmine had had a good evening, when she caught the back of Olivia going to her room, and slamming the door. Oh dear, she thought, trouble in paradise.

Jasmine stood outside, weighing up what to do. She knew from before, that Olivia was better if she was left alone to start with, so she could get her head around things. She walked back around the corner, and called a taxi. When she arrived back home, she tried ringing Olivia. Predictably, it went straight to voicemail, and Jasmine left a message saying that she would call her again in the morning. It was getting late now, so Jasmine decided to go to bed. She lay there for a long time, thinking about Olivia, and willing herself to go to sleep.

Olivia threw herself down on the bed, crying. She couldn't believe it, she felt so stupid. It wouldn't be so bad if Jasmine had told her. She heard a tap on the door, then Emma's voice, asking if she would like a drink. 'No thanks, but you can come in.'

Emma opened the door, and Olivia sat up. She was still wearing her dress, but looked all dishevelled. Emma sat down on the bed next to Olivia. 'Want to talk about it?'

Emma was the one person that Olivia could talk to about Jasmine, and she nodded, and told her what had happened, then she started crying again. Emma put her arm around Olivia. 'Unfortunately, things like this are going to happen sometimes. I don't suppose Jasmine was thrilled when Liam turned up out of the blue.'

Olivia looked at Emma. Okay, she had a point there. 'But I told Jasmine everything, she knew about Liam.'

Emma squeezed Olivia's shoulder, 'Yes I know, but, I'm trying to put this delicately. Jasmine is thirty, there are going to be some exes around, and I think that you're going to have to come to terms with that eventually. She was hardly going to introduce you to Phoebe as her ex.'

Olivia said, 'Yes, I know, but she could have told me sooner.'

Emma looked at Olivia, 'I think you need to talk to Jasmine, shutting her out won't help. And remember, she is crazy about you, I don't think I've ever seen two people more potty about each other.'

Emma smiled, then asked Olivia how the meal had been, and about Jasmine's mum. She said it had been a very nice evening, then Emma noticed her blushing. 'Oh my god, what happened?'

Olivia told her about Jasmine following her to the bathroom, and what had happened. Emma was incredulous. 'I can't get over you, I never dreamed what you would get up to, the quiet girl from college.'

Olivia smiled, 'Jasmine brings out something in me, I've never felt so free in all my life.'

Emma got up, saying, 'Call Jasmine,' and left the room.

Jasmine had drifted off to sleep when she heard her phone ringing. She came to, and seeing that Olivia was calling her, picked it up. 'Olivia, I'm so glad you called. I'm so sorry.'

'Me too, do you want to come over in the morning, and we'll talk.'

'We can talk now, I can come over.'

Olivia said no, that she needed some sleep. She said goodnight, and hung up the phone. Jasmine lay in bed, looking up at the ceiling. Eventually, in the early hours, she drifted off to sleep.

Bright and early the next day, there was a knock at the door. Emma opened it, and let Jasmine in. She said that Olivia was still in bed, so to go and knock on her door. Jasmine tapped the door gently. Olivia was expecting to see Emma, so was surprised when it was Jasmine at her door. 'Can I come in?' Olivia nodded, and Jasmine sat herself on the bed.

Jasmine said, 'I'm really sorry I didn't tell you about me and Phoebe. Look, it was nearly ten years ago. It was a short relationship, and it finished because Phoebe wanted to be with Fran. You've seen how they are together, how happy they are. Phoebe is a good friend, and as I say, she helped me deal with coming out, especially when my dad was being such a bastard. It's like with you and Liam, you don't want to be with him in that way, but he was a big part of your life, and nothing is going to change that.'

Olivia looked at Jasmine, 'Yes, but you knew about Liam all along. I've never kept anything secret from you. If you had told me before, I don't know...'

Jasmine lifted Olivia's chin, and wiped her tears. Looking her straight in the eye, she said, 'Olivia, I am really sorry that I didn't tell you sooner. I have no idea when would ever be a good time for a conversation like that. But I do know that I am head over heels, completely in love with you. You make me feel like no one has ever done, when I'm with you, I feel I can do anything. I can't stand to hurt you, and I also don't know what to do now. Please, tell me what to do.'

Jasmine looked so distraught, Olivia couldn't bear it. 'Kiss me,' Olivia said, as she looked at Jasmine's beautiful, dark eyes.

Jasmine leaned in, and kissed Olivia as if she were at sea, and Olivia were her life raft.

SIXTEEN

As August began, Olivia asked Jasmine what she would like to do for her birthday, which was on the fifth. Jasmine said that a meal out together would be good, but she really didn't mind what they did. Olivia booked a table at the restaurant in Covent Garden where they'd had their first date. Leaving the office together, they headed towards the restaurant. Olivia had reserved a table on the veranda again. In this hot weather, it was perfect. Once they were seated, Jasmine looked at Olivia across the table, 'Do you know, it's nearly a year since we first came here.'

Olivia smiled, blushing, 'Yes, it's not a day I'll ever forget! You really did turn my world upside down.'

'Do you think I shouldn't have told you how I felt?'

Olivia looked down, 'No, of course not. I know we've had some ups and downs, but I wouldn't swap any of it for how I feel now. I didn't realise it at the time, but I think you freed me.'

Jasmine looked deeply into Olivia's eyes, 'I think it was you who freed me,' and she held Olivia's hand across the table.

Olivia looked back at Jasmine, overwhelmed with feelings of love for her. The waiter came over to take their order, and Jasmine let go of Olivia's hand. Once they had ordered, Olivia handed a gift to Jasmine, 'Happy birthday.'

It was a shiny pink gift bag, and inside was a blue velvet covered box. Jasmine opened it to see a beautiful platinum necklace with an abstract pendant, which was both delicate and stunning. Depending on how you looked at it, it could possibly be a bird or an angel. 'It's beautiful, thank you so much,' Jasmine smiled at Olivia.

She put it on, and it sat perfectly at the opening on her blouse. Olivia looked at Jasmine, 'It looks perfect on you. Also, I have booked us tickets to see Hamlet at the Barbican on Saturday evening.'

'That's fabulous, I really wanted to see it. Thank you, you're spoiling me.'

As the meal came to an end, Olivia settled the bill and they walked down the stairs, and back into Covent Garden. Deciding to go for a walk before they headed back, Olivia asked whether Jasmine would like to stay with her that night. They walked along The Strand, then over Waterloo Bridge to the South Bank. As they walked alongside the river, Jasmine took Olivia's hand, and she looked up, surprised. 'More public displays of affection!'

Jasmine simply said, 'I don't want to hide anymore.'

Olivia stopped and turned to face Jasmine, gently ran her hand down the side of her face, and leaned in to kiss her.

On Saturday evening, Jasmine and Olivia arrived at the theatre to see Hamlet. It was one of Jasmine's favourite plays, but Olivia had never seen it before. The theatre was packed full. Having taken their seats, it was only a few minutes until the house lights dimmed, and the audience quieted down. Jasmine found the play mesmerising. After the house lights had come up at the end of the play, and the audience were beginning to leave, Jasmine turned to ask Olivia whether she had enjoyed it. 'Yes, it was excellent. What did you think of it?'

'I loved it. It's quite different to other versions that I've seen. It's also a visually stunning production. I love how they did the dinner party scene. When Hamlet was speaking his soliloquy, with everyone in the background moving in slow motion, it was quite beautiful.'

They left the theatre and headed back to Jasmine's place. Jasmine unlocked the door, and Olivia followed her inside. 'Thank you so much for tonight, I loved the play.'

Jasmine was in the kitchen, pouring them both a glass of wine. Olivia walked up behind her, sliding her hands around Jasmine's hips, and kissing the side of her neck. Olivia whispered, 'You're so beautiful.'

She kissed softly down Jasmine's neck, and along her shoulder. Jasmine's body responded to Olivia's caresses, and she thought that she'd better put down the bottle of wine before she dropped it. With Olivia whispering in her ear, kissing her like that, and the touch of her hands on her hips, she felt that she didn't have any control over her body. It was as if Olivia had put a spell on her, and it felt divine. She felt a tingle down to her core, and then Olivia began to slowly slide Jasmine's skirt up her thighs, revealing the lacy tops of her stockings. Jasmine was breathing more heavily, and Olivia was kissing Jasmine's back, whilst also running her hands along Jasmine's thighs. Olivia undid Jasmine's top and discarded it, then unzipped her skirt and let it fall to the floor. Then she slipped Jasmine's panties down her legs and Jasmine stepped out of them. Now Jasmine was wearing just her black lacy bra and stockings.

Olivia whispered, 'You look so gorgeous, I think I'm just going to have to make love to you right now.'

Jasmine sighed with pleasure, melting at Olivia's touch, 'Oh, yes.' She felt that delicious build, and Olivia massaged her breasts with one hand, whilst slowly exploring Jasmine with the other. Jasmine closed her eyes, leaning her head back on Olivia's shoulder, and gave in to the sensations. She was close to coming, then Olivia turned her around, and dropped to her knees. Jasmine felt Olivia's tongue where her need was greatest, and oh, it felt so good. Jasmine was all sensation, and it wasn't long before she came hard, supporting herself with her hands behind her on the table. Olivia was relentless, and the spasms continued, orgasm following orgasm. As Jasmine came back down to earth, her legs weak, Olivia held her, and kissed her passionately. Jasmine threw her arms around Olivia, kissing her fervently. Eventually, she said, 'Fuck, that was mind blowing.'

It was a hot summer, and JJ Publishing were very busy with two book launches. They were all doing long hours, but knew things would slow down again afterwards. One evening after work, Jasmine said that Phoebe and Fran were having a barbecue on Saturday. She thought that it would be a good chance for them to relax as work had been so busy. At Phoebe's name, Olivia's stomach turned over, and she told herself not to be silly. Jasmine had explained everything, and Phoebe was a part of her life, whether she liked it or not. Jasmine had never said anything about her still being friends with Liam. As Jasmine had said, their relationship was over many years ago, long before Olivia was on the scene.

Saturday was another hot day, and Jasmine wore pale lemon capri trousers with a white strappy top. Olivia thought how Jasmine always looked so elegant, whatever she was wearing. Olivia was wearing frayed, cut-off denim shorts with a white tank top, and a straw hat. The barbecue was from noon, and would go on for as long as people stayed. Jasmine and Olivia arrived a little after one o'clock, and greeted Fran at the door. They all said their hellos, and Olivia gave Fran the bottles of wine and snacks that they had brought with them. They walked through to the garden, and Olivia was glad of her straw hat, as it was such a hot day. She recognised people from the last party, and they greeted her warmly. Olivia was thinking that such a lot had happened since that party. She had broken up with Jasmine, and a few months later they'd got back together, and been away to Cornwall. Jasmine's friends were so pleased they were back together, as Jasmine had been in such a state after they'd broken up. There were a couple of women who had hoped they might have a chance with Jasmine, but she hadn't been in a place to be with someone else. Then suddenly Jasmine had met Chloe, although that had been pretty short lived, once Olivia was back in her life.

The garden was beautiful, with a big lawn, and a large patio where the barbecue was set up. There was a long table with check table cloths, which had bowls of salad, fruit, cream and an array of drinks. There was also a big jug of Pimm's and lemonade, and another of fruit punch. Jasmine and Olivia had a very relaxed day, idly chatting, and lying in the sun. Jasmine was catching up with a group of friends, and Phoebe walked over to talk to Olivia. 'I hear Jasmine had a fabulous time with you in Cornwall. I've never seen her so happy.'

Olivia smiled, 'Yes, it was really lovely. We didn't get much time to ourselves, though, as we stayed at my parents. I didn't have my own place until I moved to London.'

'Does your family know that you and Jasmine are an item?'

'Not yet. I need to speak with them. I'll have to go down there, tell them in person. I'm not sure how to broach it, really. I've never had a relationship with a woman before, this is all so new to me. I'm not sure what to do,' Olivia looked concerned.

Phoebe smiled, 'Well, there isn't a manual unfortunately! It's always best to be yourself. If you are true to yourself, you can't go wrong. I'm not saying it's not difficult, but sometimes the best things are worth fighting for. When the time comes, you'll know what to do.'

Olivia looked at Phoebe, 'Thank you.'

'Any time. Now, go and help yourself to some more food.' Olivia got up to look for Jasmine.

Jasmine was talking to Susan, over by the table where the food and drinks were laid out. Susan noticed that Jasmine kept looking over to where Olivia was sitting, chatting with Phoebe. They had been talking about work, as Olivia walked over to join them. 'Hi,' said Jasmine, kissing Olivia. 'Olivia, this is Susan, I don't think you've met. Susan, meet Olivia.'

They shook hands. Susan thought that it was so sweet, how Jasmine couldn't take her eyes off Olivia. She thought to herself how lucky Olivia was, and what she wouldn't give to be with Jasmine. She wondered whether Olivia realised how lucky she was. The three of them chatted for a while, before refilling their plates with food. They sat on the grass to eat, and when Susan saw a friend arrive, she excused herself. Jasmine noticed Olivia smiling as she walked away. Jasmine asked her what she was thinking. 'Have you known Susan long?'

Jasmine thought for a moment, 'I'm not sure, maybe a year or so, I met her here at one of Phoebe and Fran's parties. Why?'

Olivia laughed, 'I think she wants in your pants!'

Jasmine laughed, 'No way.'

'Yep, she was so flirty with you, fluttering her eyelashes,' Olivia nudged Jasmine playfully.

'Well, maybe she had something in her eye. I'm yours and yours alone.'

Jasmine leaned forward to kiss Olivia, who kissed her back eagerly, until someone said that they'd throw water over them. More people were arriving, and Jasmine said that she'd go and get them another drink. Olivia stayed where she was, watching as Jasmine walked over to the table, collected a couple of glasses, and reached for the fruit punch. Whilst she was pouring the drinks, Jasmine heard a couple of women talking. They were wondering who was the girl in the denim shorts and straw hat, sitting on the grass on her own, as they had not seen her before. 'She is gorgeous, and those legs, they go all the way up! I wish she'd move her hat so I could see her eyes.'

Jasmine smiled to herself, and as she walked past the women, she said, 'They're green, and they're gorgeous!' and headed back over to Olivia with their drinks.

The women looked at each other, embarrassed, and laughed. Jasmine told Olivia what she had just heard. Olivia said, no way, they can't have done. Jasmine replied, 'You may have not realised it, but you are a beautiful person. Also, you are sweet, kind and passionate. Not to mention you have fabulous tits!'

Olivia laughed out loud. Again, she thought about how outrageous Jasmine could be.

It was now after ten, and most people had left. Those who remained had moved some chairs into a circle near the remaining warmth from the barbecue. Olivia was teasing Jasmine about Susan flirting with her, and Jasmine brushed it off again. Phoebe said, 'Actually, she does fancy you something rotten, but everyone knows you only have eyes for Olivia. She realised that it's a lost cause, and is dating Samantha now. Probably best not to mention that to Samantha, by the way!'

Olivia was feeling tired now. It had been really hot, and at the end of a busy week, she was ready to go home. She and Jasmine said their goodbyes and headed home. On the way, she said that she'd really enjoyed herself, and also had a good chat with Phoebe. Olivia said that she knew she was going to have to have a chat with her family, and Phoebe had been helpful, telling her to just be herself. She decided that she would speak to them soon, although the thought of it gave her butterflies and a heavy feeling at the same time.

SEVENTEEN

Once work had quietened down, Olivia arranged to go and visit her parents for a few days in September. She thought that it would be best to go alone, and said that she would call Jasmine when she arrived. Olivia was feeling really nervous, but now that she had made the decision, she just wanted to get things out in the open, and tell everyone about her and Jasmine. She decided she would talk to her parents first, alone. She arrived home on the Saturday, and had just had dinner with her parents. Ella had noticed that her daughter didn't quite seem herself, and asked whether she was alright. Olivia took a deep breath, 'Mum, Dad, there's something I need to talk to you about. I'm not quite sure the best way, so I guess I'll just start. As you know, I met Jasmine when I got the job in London. We all get on really well at work, as you know. Well, um, I don't really know how to tell you...' Olivia's heart was beating so fast and hard, and her palms were sweating profusely.

Ella touched Olivia's arm, 'Darling, you know you can talk to us about anything,' and smiled, although she was getting concerned, wondering if something had gone wrong at work.

Olivia breathed in a shaky breath, and continued, 'Well, the thing is, Jasmine and I became very close.'

Ella said, 'Yes, I know when you were both here, you seemed to be very good friends.'

Olivia took another deep breath, 'Well, we became very, very close,' she paused, this was really hard. Her heart was banging in her ears. 'Well, we, we've become rather more than friends, actually.'

Ella looked at her daughter, not sure if she was following where the conversation was going.

'Well, um, she's my girlfriend.'

Phew, at last. Olivia felt so relieved to say the words out loud, and she now felt really worried about her parents' reaction. Ella and Steve looked at her, then each other. They didn't know what to say. Eventually, Steve said, 'But you were with Liam. Do you like women now?'

Olivia paused, then said, 'I like Jasmine.'

Ella looked at Olivia, 'Are you happy?'

Olivia beamed, 'Yes, happier than I've ever been. I love her, and she loves me.'

Ella and Steve looked at each other again. Olivia said, 'Look, I know this is a bit of a shock. It came as a shock to me too, actually. We went out for a few months and I broke it off, because I couldn't quite come to terms with it. At that time, Liam was in London, and we were spending lots of time together. I wanted it to work with Liam, but it just didn't. I did date this really cute guy, Will. He broke it off with me because he knew I was in love with someone else. Then finally, I had to admit it to myself, I was in love with Jasmine. We got back together not long after my birthday.' Olivia sat back in her chair.

Ella looked at her daughter, 'So you were together when she came here to stay?' Olivia looked wide eyed at her mum, wondering what she was going to say. 'Why didn't you say something at the time?'

'I didn't know how to. And I wasn't ready to tell anyone, to be honest.'

Ella smiled, 'Well, that is about the last thing that I thought you'd ever say, but I know when you were here together in the summer, you were both very happy, running around like children! If you're happy, then that's all that matters.'

'Oh, Mum.' Olivia got up and hugged Ella, and a tear ran down her face.

She looked at her dad, and he said, 'I feel the same as your mum, if you're happy... Jasmine is a lovely girl.'

Olivia hugged them tightly, telling them how much she loved them. She said that tomorrow she would talk to her friends and Ben, but that now she was so tired, she was going ring Jasmine, then have a bath and go to bed.

Jasmine had been thinking about Olivia all day, although she knew that she wouldn't arrive at her parents until the afternoon. Olivia had sent a text saying that she was nearly there, and that she'd ring when she had spoken to her parents. Jasmine popped out in the morning to go food shopping, to keep herself busy. In the afternoon, there was a Doris Day film on television, which she watched with Rocky curled up on her lap, purring contentedly. After dinner, she was relieved when the phone rang, and she heard Olivia's voice. Olivia sounded excited and relieved, and until now, Jasmine hadn't realised how tense she had been. She let out her breath slowly, letting her lungs fill with air again. Olivia was saying that her parents were surprised, but very supportive. Jasmine loved hearing how happy Olivia was, and felt a tear run down her face. After chatting for a while, Olivia said she was going to have a bath and go to bed, as she was exhausted. Jasmine put the phone down, and gave Rocky a big hug. She couldn't wait for Olivia to come home, and didn't know how she would manage to wait a whole week without seeing her.

Olivia awoke on Sunday morning to the smell of a cooked breakfast. She walked into the kitchen, rubbing her eyes. Ella said, 'Good morning darling, I was just about to wake you, it's gone eleven.'

'Really? Well, I was so tired, physically and emotionally. I was so worried about telling you and dad about me and Jasmine yesterday,' Olivia sat down at the table to eat.

Ella sat down opposite her daughter, 'Well, as I say, as long as you're happy, I'm happy. But I am a bit curious as to how it happened.'

Olivia smiled, 'It was all rather romantic. It turned out that Jasmine had liked me for ages, and wasn't going to say anything, then one day it just happened. I was very surprised to say the least, and I was also confused. But I couldn't deny how I felt about her. Like I said yesterday, I spent some time with Liam, then dated Will, but I just knew it was Jasmine that I wanted to be with.'

Ella said that Ben was going to pop in that morning, and Olivia's nerves returned like a boomerang. Ella said she was sure he would be fine about it. When Ben arrived about an hour later, he kissed and hugged Olivia. The conversation was very similar to the previous night, and just like Ella had said, it was all good. After they had a general catch up about work and Ben and Tina's wedding plans, Ben said, 'Huh, I've just remembered something Liam said to me when you were down here with Jasmine. He told me that he had seen you and Jasmine on the beach, and it looked like... but I told him he was imagining things.'

Olivia felt her cheeks go bright red, 'But we didn't do anything, he can't have seen anything.'

Ben said, 'Don't worry about it, he didn't see anything. He had an impression of something, and I said no, he must have got it wrong. He was still carrying a torch for you.'

Olivia calmed down, telling her brother that she was going to be speaking to her friends later on.

Olivia walked into the cafe, and her nerves had bubbled to the surface again. Becky leaped up when she saw Olivia, and they hugged. Becky was really pleased that Olivia was on her own this time, so they would get more time together. Dan went and ordered their drinks and they all sat down again. Liam asked whether Olivia was okay, he thought that she seemed a bit worried. Ah well, moment of truth, she thought.

Okay, deep breath. 'There's something I need to talk to you about. It's about me and Jasmine. We've been working together since last summer, as you know. As you also probably know, we've become very close friends.' Olivia hesitated, she was feeling so nervous, and her heart was thumping so hard in her chest. Okay, do it quickly, like pulling off a plaster. 'I don't really know how to say this, other than to just come out and say it. We spent a lot of time together, and became very close. Over time, things developed. And, um, well, we started a relationship. Jasmine is my girlfriend. I just thought you all should know.'

Liam looked flabbergasted, 'Bloody hell, I wasn't imagining things.'

Becky said, 'What do you mean? Did you know something about this?'

Liam said, 'Back in the summer, I saw them on the beach, and it looked like, I don't know, I didn't actually see anything.'

Becky looked shocked, 'I don't believe it, Jasmine. Since when are you gay? What the fuck.'

241

Olivia said, 'Look, I didn't plan it, it just kind of happened.'

Becky's voice was hard, 'Oh, so if I had said to you, I fancy you, you and I would be together would we?'

Olivia sighed, 'No, of course not. When you met Dan, you just knew that you wanted to be with him. Jasmine is amazing, and although it took me a while to get my head around it, I am in love with her, it's as simple as that. I just wanted you guys to know, I didn't want it to be a secret anymore.'

Becky looked hurt, 'So, when you were both here in the summer, you were already together?'

Olivia hesitated as she looked at Becky, 'Yes.'

Becky got up, 'I need some fresh air,' and she left.

Dan got up too, saying, 'She'll come around. She found it hard in the summer when she didn't get to spend much time with you. Look, I'm going to go and find her, I'll see you later.'

Olivia couldn't believe it, she really hadn't expected Becky to act like that. Becky knew how Olivia felt about Liam, so that wasn't the issue. Olivia looked at Liam, and he seemed lost for words. Eventually, Olivia said, 'I'm sorry about this, but I had to tell you guys. We've had some ups and downs, but Jasmine and I are together now.'

Liam looked at Olivia, and smiled, 'Jasmine is one lucky girl.'

Olivia smiled back, and they started chatting. Olivia asked about Lucy, from the gallery. Liam said that

Becky had been trying to get them together. He thought she was very nice, and he was thinking about asking her out. Olivia was thrilled for him, and asked lots of questions. He said that he didn't want to rush into anything, after being with Olivia for such a long time. They spent about an hour together, and Olivia was relieved that things seemed to be okay between them. Olivia thanked Liam for staying and chatting with her, then they went their separate ways.

When Olivia arrived back home, she rang Jasmine. She was thrilled to hear from her, and asked how it was all going. Olivia explained that her family were very supportive, and happy for her. Her friends were a different matter, though. Becky in particular was struggling with the news. 'I've tried calling her, but she won't answer. Dan said to give her some time. I guess it was a bit of a shock, but I expected if there was going to be a problem, it would have been with my parents if anything.'

Jasmine said, 'Oh, you poor thing. I wish I was there with you. I'm sure that Becky will come around. When I came out, I had some issues with friends too. People often don't like it when you change, they seem to see it as a threat somehow.'

Olivia asked what had happened with her friends. Jasmine said, 'Well, I was meeting new people a lot anyway, so I guess my circle of friends did change over time. Some friends couldn't accept my lifestyle, so over time I moved on. If they didn't like my lifestyle choices, there wasn't anything I could do about it. Not that it was a choice, it's just that until I came out, they just didn't know.'

Olivia said, 'But I haven't changed, I'm still the same person, surely Becky can see that.'

Jasmine really felt for Olivia. From her vantage point and experience, she could see that Becky was struggling with jealousy and also the changes that had been happening. Becky's best friend had moved a long way away, and now she had fallen in love. Becky probably felt like she was losing Olivia, and she knew how that felt. Jasmine was sure that Becky would come around in time. After chatting for a while longer, they said their goodbyes. Olivia said, 'I love you.'

'I love you too. Ring me any time,' said Jasmine, and they hung up their phones.

Ella came home to see Olivia sitting morosely at the table. She asked her what was the matter, and Olivia told her mum how Becky had responded to her news. Ella gave her daughter a hug, saying that she was sure Becky would get over it sooner or later. 'Becky does come over quite a bit to chat with me and your dad. She has been like a sister to you, and she misses you so much. Give her some time, it's just been a bit of a shock, that's all.'

Olivia hugged her mum, 'Thanks Mum, you're so great.'

It had now been three days since Olivia had spoken to Becky. She hadn't returned any of her calls, so

Olivia decided to go to the gallery. When Becky saw Olivia, she asked Lucy to take over, and they went out the back, to the staff area. Olivia said, 'I'm going home tomorrow, so I just wanted to say goodbye. I really wanted to be able to talk to you, and I know my news was a bit of a shock.'

'That's putting it mildly,' Becky said sulkily.

Olivia looked at Becky, 'You're my best friend, nothing will change that. I'm going to go now, but you know you can call me any time.'

Olivia hugged Becky awkwardly, then left the gallery. She decided to go for a walk on the beach, it was always a good place to go when she needed to clear her head. She thought about when she had brought Jasmine here, and the two of them dancing and laughing on the sand. In that moment, she missed Jasmine so much. Taking her phone out of her pocket, she dialled Jasmine's number. 'Hey you, how are you doing?'

'I'm missing you so much. I'm at the beach at the moment, I can't wait to come home.'

Jasmine sighed, 'I wish I was there with you. Still, you'll be back tomorrow, it's not long now.'

EIGHTEEN

Olivia's train arrived at Paddington, and she made her way onto the concourse. She saw Jasmine waving, and headed towards her. As she approached, she put down her case, and they hugged each other tightly. Jasmine whispered in her ear, 'I've missed you so much.'

Olivia responded, 'I missed you too,' and kissed Jasmine full on the mouth.

Their embrace became passionate, and in that moment, no one else existed for them. 'Let's go home,' said Jasmine, picking up Olivia's case.

They arrived back at Emma's flat so that Olivia could drop her case off. Emma and Matt were there, and asked how the week was. Olivia gave her friend a hug, and said, 'It was good to see mum and dad, but Becky is being weird with me. After telling her about me and Jasmine, she disappeared and wouldn't talk to me. I went into the gallery to say goodbye yesterday, and that was that. Liam and Dan were okay, although surprised. I'll try calling Becky soon, I guess it was a shock for her.'

Emma gave Olivia a hug, saying, 'I'm sure she'll come around. In the meantime, you've got us.'

Olivia smiled, 'Thank you, you're so great. Matt, look after her!'

'Oh, he does!' Emma winked.

Olivia said that they were going back to Jasmine's for the rest of the weekend, so she would see her on Monday evening.

By the time Olivia and Jasmine had arrived back home, it was early evening. Jasmine told Olivia to go and sit down whilst she cooked dinner for them. The smells coming from the kitchen were divine. Olivia noticed that Jasmine had laid the table beautifully, and in the centre was a single stem vase, with a red rose in it. Jasmine cooked salmon with a pesto and crumb topping, with dauphinois potatoes and salad. 'This tastes delicious,' Olivia exclaimed as she took her first mouthful. 'It has such a gorgeous flavour. If you like, you can cook for me every day!' Olivia laughed.

Jasmine simply said, 'Okay,' and Olivia looked up to see Jasmine looking at her seriously.

Jasmine reached her hand across the table to Olivia, 'Move in with me.' It wasn't so much a question.

Olivia looked at her, 'Stop kidding me.'

'I'm serious. Move in with me. I thought about it a lot while you were away. I love you so much, and I can't bear it when we're apart. You practically live here at weekends anyway.'

Olivia was completely taken by surprise. She wasn't sure what to say. Jasmine was thinking, oh no, please don't say I've rushed it again. She hadn't intended on asking Olivia just yet, but it had just slipped out. 'You don't have to decide now. Please say you'll at least think about it.'

Olivia smiled, and Jasmine was relieved. 'I will think about it. You are crazy, and I love you!'

After dinner, Jasmine sent Olivia to rest on the sofa, saying that she would clear up. After a long day travelling, Olivia was really tired. It wasn't long before she had drifted off to sleep on the sofa. When she opened her eyes sometime later, Rocky was curled up by her feet, purring contentedly. Olivia looked around to see where Jasmine was. 'Hey, sleepy head.' Jasmine was sitting in the armchair, reading, and smiled at her.

'Sorry, did I fall asleep?' As Olivia sat herself upright, Rocky moved onto the sofa and stretched his paws out. Once Olivia was settled again, he climbed onto her lap, and curled up again.

Jasmine smiled, 'You two look very cosy there, Rocky loves you.'

Olivia stroked Rocky, and he purred loudly. They chatted about what they would do the following day, deciding that a day at home would be perfect. Olivia said, 'After my week back home, I'd just really like to relax, and not have to talk to anyone about anything!'

Jasmine looked at Olivia with dark eyes, 'Well, if you don't want to talk, I can think of a thing or two we can do...'

When Olivia and Jasmine arrived for work on Monday morning, Laura said, 'Hello, good to have you back, Olivia. Did you have a good time?'

Olivia said yes, and suggested they have lunch together so that they could catch up properly. Jason arrived, and they all had a chat before they started work, and soon Olivia was back in the swing of things. She still kept thinking about Becky, deciding that she would call her soon. She didn't like leaving things the way they were. It was probably the first time that they'd had any kind of falling out, and Olivia hated how it felt.

After work one evening, Emma and Olivia were in the lounge chatting over a glass of wine. Emma said, 'It's good to catch up with you, I don't see much of you these days. I take it things are going well?'

Olivia nodded, 'Jasmine is wonderful, we have a great time together. When I got back from Cornwall, she asked me to move in with her.'

'Really. What did you say?'

'I said I would think about it. I'm mad about her, but we haven't been together that long. I don't want to rush into it.'

'Well, you guys are so cute together, and Jasmine is obviously crazy about you.'

Olivia smiled, and Emma noticed the soppy look on her face. Emma was wondering whether to ask her what she wanted to. Before she had a chance to say anything, Olivia asked her what she was thinking.

'Well, I don't think there's a delicate way of asking this, but I can't help wondering what it's like to be with a woman. Not that I want to myself, I do love guys! But for you, don't you miss it?'

Olivia laughed, blushing, 'To be honest, I don't. Jasmine makes me feel like no one else has ever done. She's tender, sensuous, and so fucking hot in bed. Well, not just in bed! She just seems to intuitively know what I want, even if I don't realise it myself. I've never had orgasms like it. You know, I'm so much more confident too, she makes me feel so safe. And we have so much in common. So, how about you and Matt?'

Emma grinned, 'Really good. Matt is so sweet, and so gorgeous. And like you, the sex is great!'

Laughing, they clinked their glasses together. Olivia asked, 'Do you fancy going on that girl's shopping trip we talked about. I thought maybe we could go this Saturday, and have lunch out.'

'Ooh, yes, that would be great.'

When Jasmine arrived on Saturday morning, Emma let her in, giving her a hug. Olivia came out of her room, and went over to kiss Jasmine, saying, 'You look gorgeous.' Jasmine was wearing dark blue skinny jeans, long black boots with high heels, and a single breasted black jacket over her white shirt.

'You look so fucking hot,' said Jasmine, admiring Olivia's washed out jeans and tight blue t shirt. Olivia knew that look so well, and if they had been alone,

Olivia knew what would have followed. As it was, Emma smiled at Olivia, and she blushed in response. Once they were all ready, they set off towards the shops. As Emma's flat was near Bond Street tube station, she was in a prime position for shopping. Emma had decided that when she moved to London, she wanted to be in the centre, in the middle of the action. She had a good job, and once she had been promoted she could afford to move more centrally. It was one of her colleagues who told her that a friend of his, a journalist, was looking for someone to flat share.

They walked onto Oxford Street, which was a typical, bustling Saturday morning. Olivia was after getting a couple of dressier outfits, perhaps a dress and a trouser suit. Usually she would wear jeans and t shirts or shirts, and smart trousers for the office. Although her red dress was lovely, she wanted to have a bit more choice if she did want to dress up. After wandering around the shops for a couple of hours, they decided it was time to get a drink. Jasmine had her usual tea, Olivia a latte, and Emma ordered a hot chocolate. So far, Emma had bought some jeans and a pair of blue shoes with a little heel, and Olivia had bought some brown knee high boots, which went well with her biker jacket. After their little break, they carried on down Regent Street, and then towards Covent Garden. Olivia caught sight of a dress shop which had the most beautiful dress in the window. 'Ooh, Jasmine, that would look gorgeous on you, you have to try it on.'

The dress was shoulder-less, in a deep plum colour. It was slim fitting, with a detail on the left hip which made it slightly asymmetrical. Jasmine asked to try the dress on, whilst Emma and Olivia took a seat. When Jasmine walked out, they both said, 'Wow.' Jasmine looked absolutely stunning. Looking at Olivia's face, Jasmine didn't need to ask what she thought of it, she knew that look, and felt a longing and a throb between her legs.

Jasmine smiled sweetly at the assistant, a woman probably in her twenties, 'I'll take it, thank you.'

Olivia said, 'Shall I come and give you a hand with the zip?'

Jasmine nodded, and Olivia got up, following Jasmine to the changing room. As soon as she pulled the curtain across, Olivia's lips were on Jasmine, kissing her lips, then her bare shoulders. Jasmine turned around, and Olivia unzipped the back of the dress, kissing down her back as with each inch, she exposed more flesh. Olivia slipped the dress down, and Jasmine stepped out of it. She was now only wearing her pants and high heeled boots. Fuck, Olivia wanted her so much. With Jasmine still facing away from her, she ran her hands across her chest, massaging her breasts, then down her body, around her fabulous round backside. Holding Jasmine's breasts with her left hand, Olivia ran her right hand down her stomach, continuing lower and lower. Jasmine groaned with pleasure as she felt Olivia inside her, then slipped her left hand behind her, and down the waistband of Olivia's jeans. Jasmine breathed, 'You're so wet, oh my god,' and they started a rhythm, sending sensations through their bodies that made them feel lightheaded. Jasmine's breathing was becoming more and more ragged, and she came, shuddering and groaning with pleasure. Olivia was close behind her, and her legs went weak as her orgasm tore through her. Olivia wrapped her arms around Jasmine, as they came down from orgasm together. Her desire for Jasmine still overwhelmed her sometimes. Jasmine turned around, and they kissed, with Olivia giggling at her own audacity. 'What are you doing to me, woman!'

Jasmine laughed, 'I could say the same about you.'

Olivia walked back out to towards Emma, and sat down. Emma, seeing the look on her face, laughed, 'I don't believe you two! I really can't take you anywhere!'

Olivia flushed, 'What? Was it really that obvious?'

Emma nodded, 'Yep, you may as well have had a neon sign! Don't ever take up poker!'

Olivia felt her face go even redder. Jasmine walked out of the changing room, with the dress over her arm. She looked so cool and collected, and this made Emma laugh even more. Olivia waited with Emma whilst the dress was beautifully wrapped up, and Jasmine paid for it. As they left, they said goodbye, with Olivia avoiding eye contact with the assistant.

Jasmine said, 'Well, I don't know about you guys, but I think it's time for lunch.'

Emma smiled, saying 'Yes, I expect that you two have worked up quite an appetite!'

Jasmine and Olivia looked at each other, then Emma, and laughed. They headed towards New Row, where there was this lovely little sandwich bar that Jasmine had recommended, just around the corner from Covent Garden. There was a great choice of sandwiches and paninis, and you could make up your own combo if you wished. They chatted over lunch, and watched people rushing by outside, through the large windows. Lunch was delicious, and having had a rest, they were all ready to get shopping again.

After a few more shops, Olivia spotted a dress that she really liked. It was a deep green, and Jasmine said it complemented her eyes perfectly. She went to try it on, and came out to show the others. The dress was quite short and sleeveless, with a plunging v neck. 'So what do you think?'

Jasmine smiled, and quietly said, 'It's perfect, and your tits look amazing in it.'

Olivia laughed, 'I think I'll get it then!' and disappeared back into the changing cubicle.

After a couple more shops, Olivia found a gorgeous pair of navy trousers. They were made of fine material, hanging beautifully from her hips, and tapered at the ankle. She found a navy sleeveless top which looked fabulous with the trousers, and bought them both.

After a fun and successful shopping trip, the three of them headed back to Emma's to drop their shopping off. Emma suggested that they go out dancing tonight, and Jasmine and Olivia agreed. They decided to have dinner first, choosing their regular Mexican. Having ordered their drinks, Emma was telling Jasmine how she had brought Olivia here to celebrate her getting the job. 'You had just called, and Olivia was ecstatic.'

Jasmine smiled at Olivia, 'The day I walked into the office and saw Olivia sitting there, I will never forget. I knew that she was special, and I knew that I was in trouble!'

Emma laughed, then said to Olivia, 'There was another time a few months later, that you rang me after work to meet you here, and you were in a very peculiar mood. I never did know what was going on that day.'

Olivia blushed, and hesitated, 'I, um, it was the day of the book launch. Jasmine had just told me how she felt about me. She had kissed me, and I freaked out. The thing that really freaked me out, was that the kiss had really turned me on. I was so confused.'

Jasmine touched Olivia's hand. Emma asked, 'If Jasmine had told you how she felt, but not kissed you, do you think you would still have got together?'

Olivia was thoughtful for a moment, 'It's hard to say. Maybe not, because I would never have known how that kiss would have made me feel. I certainly would have never guessed how things were going to turn out!'

Jasmine looked at Olivia, 'From my point of view, although I was trying really hard not say anything, I think it was inevitable. I had wanted to kiss you from the moment I first saw you.'

Olivia and Jasmine exchanged a loving glance. The waitress came over to take their order, and it wasn't long before the food arrived. The three of them chatted away happily, and discussed where they were going to go that evening. Jasmine said she knew of a bar and club not far away, if they fancied it. Emma was always up for trying somewhere new, so after dinner, they put on their jackets and headed off.

The club was a smart place, with deep blue walls and coloured lighting around the bar. It was thronging with people, and whilst Jasmine checked their jackets into the cloakroom, Emma and Olivia went to order some drinks. Emma finished her drink quickly, and was itching to get onto the dance floor.

They were having a wonderful time, and Emma thought that Jasmine was a great dancer. Olivia said that she was going to get another drink, and would watch them dancing for a while. She had been sitting at a table near the bar, when a woman came over and asked if she could join her. Olivia said yes, the seat was free. The woman had short dark hair, and the most beautiful, piercing blue eyes. She was a slight build, about five foot four. She wore black jeans and a black waistcoat. Around her neck was long black corded necklace, with a silver pendant on the end of it. 'Phew, it's good to sit down. I've been dancing for ages.' Olivia smiled, and sipped her drink. 'I've not seen you in here before,' the woman said.

Olivia replied, 'I don't usually go to clubs, I'm here with my friends, they're still dancing. I like your necklace.'

'Thank you, it's a feather. To me, it symbolises freedom,' she leaned in closely so that Olivia could look at her necklace, and looked at Olivia with those piercing blue eyes. She really is very attractive, thought Olivia. Jasmine could see from the dance floor that someone had joined Olivia's table. She continued dancing with Emma. The woman put her drink down on the table, still looking at Olivia intently. 'Would you like to dance?'

'No thank you, I'm happy sitting here, thanks.'

The woman tried to make a bit more small talk, but wasn't getting anywhere. She got up to leave, and held her hand out, 'It was nice to meet you...'

'Olivia,' she said as she shook the woman's hand.

'Lovely to meet you, Olivia. If you change your mind, I'm Chloe.'

NINETEEN

Chloe sauntered off and sat back down at the bar. She couldn't help looking at Olivia. There was something about her, a girl next door, but so much more. Oh, how she would love to kiss those lips. Chloe had thought that Olivia looked a bit lost sitting at the table alone. Well, she thought, I did try. I would love to dance with her, though. In a moment of spontaneity, she grabbed a pen from the bar and scribbled her phone number on a piece of paper. Her heart beating fast, she approached the table. Olivia looked up, to see Chloe's blue eyes looking into her green ones. 'Look, I know you're not interested now, but if you change your mind, here's my number. Call me.'

Olivia looked surprised, and before she could say anything, she saw Jasmine walking over. Chloe turned around, and now it was her turn to be surprised. 'Jasmine, what are you doing here?'

It suddenly dawned on Olivia who this was. Chloe. After they had broken up, when Olivia had turned up on Jasmine's doorstep, she said she was seeing someone. Chloe. Jasmine replied to Chloe, 'Hi, I'm here with my friends. I see that you've met Olivia. How are you?'

'Well, thank you,' and felt awkward as Jasmine sat down next to Olivia, and squeezed her leg.

'Good to see you, enjoy your night,' Chloe said, and disappeared. As she walked away, she thought, so that was Olivia, the girl who broke Jasmine's heart. Well, it looks like she mended it again. And I can certainly see the attraction.

Jasmine said, 'I see you have an admirer.'

Olivia said, 'She asked me to dance, and I said no. So that was Chloe, then. She's very attractive.'

Emma saw the tension from Olivia, and also cottoned on to what was going on. 'I'm just off to the ladies,' she said, and left the table.

Jasmine said, 'Well, I can't say I blame her for trying.'

Olivia looked at Jasmine, 'You seem very relaxed about it.'

'Well, what am I supposed to say? She was hitting on you, and I know you're not interested.'

'I mean, about the fact that you two were an item.'

Jasmine shook her head, 'We only went out for a few weeks. She's really nice, but I was still heartbroken over you leaving me.' Jasmine looked at Olivia, then down at the floor.

Olivia felt a pain shoot through her body, she hated that she had hurt Jasmine so much. Olivia took Jasmine's hand, and squeezed it. As she looked up,

Olivia leaned across and kissed her. Emma came back from the bathroom to see Jasmine and Olivia holding hands. Well, that seems to have gone okay, she thought, relieved.

It was after midnight, and Olivia and Jasmine were ready to go home. They waited for Emma to come back from the dance floor, and collected their jackets.

When they arrived home, Emma said goodnight and went to her room. Jasmine followed Olivia into her bedroom, and they started to get undressed. Since Olivia had met Chloe, she was feeling unsettled. After she had brushed her teeth, she slipped under the covers. Jasmine climbed in beside her, and cuddled up to her back. Olivia said, 'Chloe was stunning. She has amazing eyes.'

Jasmine murmured, 'Uh huh.'

She felt Olivia take a deep breath. 'Did you sleep with her?'

Jasmine held her breath for a moment, she really did not want to be going there. Olivia continued, 'I know it's none of my business, really, but I can't get the thought out of my head, I just want to know.'

Jasmine simply said, 'Yes,' and felt Olivia's body stiffen. Jasmine's heart sank. Hesitantly, Jasmine started, 'After you ended things with Liam, I was hopeful that we might have another chance. Then, when you started seeing Will... I thought I had lost you.'

Olivia turned over to face Jasmine, tears in her eyes, 'Sometimes I just don't get why you're with me, you could have anyone you want.'

Jasmine looked into Olivia's eyes, 'I want you. No one else. You. You seem to be forgetting that Chloe was hitting on you. I think that is one of the many things that I love about you. You don't realise just how fucking sexy you are, and it's quite disarming.'

Olivia smiled in spite of herself. Jasmine continued, 'You are sweet, thoughtful, kind, and you have a freedom in the way you express yourself that moves me. You inspire me, and you continually take my breath away.'

A tear ran down Olivia's face, and she kissed Jasmine, very gently and slowly, trying to convey how much Jasmine meant to her. They held one another, and became entwined, and made sweet, slow love into the early hours.

When Olivia and Jasmine got up mid-morning, they went into the kitchen to get a drink. Emma was having her breakfast, and she watched the two of them, the way they were with each other, how they moved around with one another. 'You two are the cutest couple. What are you going to do today?'

Olivia looked at Jasmine, and smiled. Then she looked at Emma, 'Not a lot, we're a bit tired after last night. We'll probably go for a walk. How about you, are you seeing Matt today?'

'No, he's playing football with his mates today.'

'You can come out with us if you fancy it,' Jasmine offered.

Emma said thank you, but that she would leave the lovebirds to themselves today!

Over the next few weeks, Olivia was still trying to get to talk with Becky. When Olivia rang her mum, she would get updates, and she knew that Becky would stop by to chat to Ella. 'Mum, it's so hard. I can't do anything if she won't answer the phone.'

Her mum said that Becky was still struggling to come to terms with everything. 'You have to remember, that you're off doing this exciting new thing, working in London, and you've fallen in love, and you're happy. Becky is still here, her best friend has moved away and she feels that she's losing you to Jasmine. You've been friends since you were so young, and I'm afraid it really is a case of time, you can't rush her.'

Those last few words really struck a chord. Olivia remembered how she had felt when Jasmine had declared how she felt about her. Ultimately, she had needed some time and headspace to realise on her own what she wanted. 'Thanks, Mum.'

Olivia did keep trying to speak with Becky. Eventually, one day Becky answered her phone. 'Hi Becky, how are you?'

'I'm okay, how are you?'

Olivia tried making small talk, but it was pretty hard going. Olivia hated how things felt between them, and the stilted conversation. Olivia said, 'Look, I really want to be able to talk to you. I miss you. I'm still the same person I was, nothing has changed.'

Then it all came out. Becky told Olivia how she had felt when Olivia had moved away, how she missed her, and their life, hanging out with Dan and Liam. 'I think it's great that you knew what you wanted to do, and good that you did it. It's just that I thought you would get it out of your system, and you would come home, get back with Liam, and things could go back to the way they were. But you've been gone over a year now, and you're with Jasmine, and I'm just finding it really hard. I know I sound selfish, but that's how I feel,' Becky sobbed.

'Oh Becky. I didn't know myself whether I would like London, but I knew I had to try it. I didn't have a long term plan, and I certainly would never have imagined in a million years what would happen with Jasmine. But things do change, life changes, and we have to go with that. As it is, I'm loving my life here, but that doesn't change the fact that you're my best friend, and I miss you.'

Once they had cleared the air, they talked like they used to, and Olivia was relieved. She asked how Lucy was getting on at the gallery, and Becky told her that she and Liam had started dating. Olivia was really pleased for him. Becky said, 'So am I, I was fed up of his moping about. Also, Lucy was going all soppy every time he came by the gallery. They're very sweet together.'

A couple of evenings later, over dinner, Olivia told Jasmine her about her conversation with her mum, and also how she had eventually got to talk with Becky. Jasmine was thrilled for her. Olivia wondered whether her mum had had a chat with Becky, and encouraged her to talk to Olivia. Becky was like another daughter to Ella, they were very close. Whatever had happened, Olivia was so happy about it.

Jasmine said, 'While we're on the subject of family, I was thinking about inviting mum out for dinner. I wondered how you'd feel about me inviting my dad too. '

'It would be nice to meet him.'

'I wouldn't introduce you as my girlfriend, but as my colleague, if you would be okay with that? As I mentioned before, my dad is old school and stubborn, but I do want him to meet you.'

'I can't pretend I won't be a bit nervous, but let's do it.'

'Okay, I'll arrange it with mum.'

Olivia was getting dressed, ready to go out for dinner. She decided to wear her new green dress. She was putting her earrings on, and in the reflection of the mirror, she could see Jasmine walking up behind her. Olivia smiled, and Jasmine stood behind her, wrapping her arms around her. Kissing her neck, she said, 'You look gorgeous.'

'Thank you, so do you. I'm feeling really nervous about meeting your dad, why did I agree to this?'

'You'll be fine. You've already met my mum, and she loves you.'

Olivia turned and kissed Jasmine. They were ready to go, and the cab had arrived. When they arrived at the restaurant, their coats were taken to be hung up. They were shown to their table, and Jasmine's parents were already seated. Grace caught sight of them, and they rose as Jasmine approached with Olivia. 'Hello darling, how are you? Olivia, lovely to see you again.'

They each kissed one another on the cheek, and then Jasmine introduced Olivia to her father. 'Pleased to meet you, Mr Carter,' Olivia shook hands with him.

'Pleased to meet you, too. And call me Henry.'

Henry was about six foot tall, with steely grey hair swept back, and parted at the side. He was stocky, and his face had strong features, as though it was carved from granite. Olivia supposed he was quite handsome, but she also found him rather intimidating. They took their seats, and ordered drinks. 'So, how are you, Dad?' asked Jasmine.

'Well, thank you. And yourself?'

Henry wasn't a man to use more words than he needed to. After a few more short exchanges, Grace saved them by talking about a charity that she was beginning to become involved with. With Grace and

Jasmine keeping the conversation going, Olivia was able to relax a bit. As Jasmine had already told her what her father was like, she was prepared for the lack of small talk. Still, Henry was polite towards her.

As it was now November, the conversation turned to Christmas. Grace asked whether Olivia had any plans. 'I was planning on going to go back to Cornwall for Christmas, but I haven't discussed it with Jasmine yet. I was going to ask her if she'd like to come with me.'

As soon as the words had left her mouth, she thought, Shit. Jasmine looked round at Olivia, surprised and pleased. Henry asked, 'What does Jasmine have to do with your holiday arrangements?' and seeing the look on Olivia's face, said, 'I see.'

Jasmine looked at him, then at Grace. Henry's face went dark, and he stood up, 'Excuse me, I need some air,' and he walked out into the foyer of the restaurant.

Jasmine was furious, 'Oh, for Christ's sake, this is ridiculous. He is impossible.'

Olivia excused herself, and rushed to the toilets, shutting herself in a cubicle. Jasmine followed after her, and tapped on the door. Olivia said, 'I'm fine. I'll be out in a minute.'

But Jasmine could hear the sob in her voice. 'Hey, come out and we can talk.'

Olivia sniffed, 'It was going so well, why did I have to mention going to Cornwall.'

Jasmine sighed, 'He's always been like this. You didn't do anything. He's pompous and rude. Please come out.'

Reluctantly, Olivia opened the door, and walked out to Jasmine. Jasmine put her arms around her and held her. Once Olivia had regained herself, she wiped her eyes and they went back out to the table. They saw that Grace was talking with Henry in the foyer, with lots of gesticulating between them. Grace returned, saying, 'Sorry about that, your father has a headache and is going home.'

Jasmine looked at her mother, 'I don't know who you think you're kidding, he is so fucking rude. I don't know how you put up with him.'

Grace looked lovingly at her daughter, 'Don't let him ruin the evening. Now, tell me more about your plans for Christmas,' and she touched Olivia's arm.

Olivia was grateful for Grace being so sweet, and said she was going to ask Jasmine to come back with her for Christmas. Jasmine was delighted, and saying that she would love to. Grace really liked Olivia, and appreciated how happy she made Jasmine. In the past, if something like tonight had happened with Henry, Jasmine would have made a scene, and it wouldn't have ended well. Now, the three of them could enjoy the rest of the evening in a much more relaxed atmosphere. As the evening wore on, and the wine was flowing, Olivia plucked up the courage to ask Grace how she and Henry had met. Grace smiled, 'Well, I was at an event thrown by a colleague of mine. I was nearly thirty, and at that time I had just recently come out of a rather volatile relationship, and was nursing a broken heart. Then along came Henry, suave, charming and decidedly straight forward. He was dependable and direct, and it was a nice change for me. Being quite a lot older than me, he seemed confident and sorted, and after an emotional rollercoaster of a relationship of the previous couple of years, I was ready for some stability. I did want to have a baby, and then when I became pregnant rather quickly, he insisted that we got married, he wouldn't hear of me having a baby unwed. I did love him, though.'

Olivia asked, 'But he wasn't the love of your life?'

Grace looked at Jasmine, 'I'll always love him because we have Jasmine. But the love of my life was the person I was with before I met Henry.'

'Did you ever see him again?' Grace shook her head.

Jasmine said, 'I don't think you ever told me this. Would it never have worked with you two?'

Grace looked down, 'No, we were great when things were good, but we clashed, and when you are with an amazing artist who has massive periods of self-doubt and could be very moody and destructive, it was hard. I said I needed some time apart, and it was just after that, that I met your father.'

Jasmine said, 'I know what he's like, and for me that's one thing, but I don't want him to take it out on Olivia.'

Grace smiled at her, 'I know, darling. That you and Olivia have each other, even when things can be really difficult for you, is what is really important. I see the way you look at each other, and how you are together. Don't let convention get in the way, like I did.'

Jasmine looked puzzled, 'What do you mean?'

'The person I was with before your father, the love of my life, she was called Jasmine, and you were named after her.'

TWENTY

Jasmine just sat staring, trying to take in what she had just heard. Olivia held her hand, worried. Eventually, she stuttered, 'Wh, what are you talking about, why have you never told me this before?'

Grace said gently, 'I had told you before that I was in love with someone before I met your father. I also told you that we stopped seeing one another because I wanted to have a baby and they didn't. Also, even if she had wanted to, it was more a case of it not being easy to have a child in a same sex relationship. It's easier nowadays than it was thirty years ago, not to say that it's plain sailing. And like I said, our relationship had been rather a rollercoaster, so not the best environment to bring a child into the world.'

Jasmine looked at Grace, 'Why are you telling me this now?'

Grace looked into her daughter's eyes, 'Your father is a good man. I wish he was more accepting of your relationships, but you know how old fashioned he is. I'm telling you this because I see how happy you are together, and when you thought you had lost Olivia, I hated seeing you like that,' she turned to Olivia, 'Sorry, but I have to say this. Now that you know what you

270

have together, and how happy you are, hold onto it. I know what it's like, and how it feels. Jasmine, I've never seen you so happy, and I don't want anything to get in the way of that. I've always admired how strong you are, how passionate you are about your convictions. I wouldn't change anything about my life, because I have you, and I love you more than anything.'

'Oh, Mum,' Jasmine and Grace hugged each other.

Then Jasmine turned to Olivia and held her hand. She wiped her eyes, 'Does dad know about your previous relationship?'

Grace shook her head, 'No, only that it had been difficult and that it had ended. At the time, I didn't want to talk about it, and he didn't ask, so that was that.'

'Were there other women?' Jasmine wanted to know, her mind was filling with so many questions.

'No, only her.'

'Why didn't you tell me this when I came out?'

Grace sighed, 'It was a difficult time, and after the way your father reacted, I knew that I couldn't say anything. Also, I was scared to talk about it. It took me a long time to get over her, and eventually I had shut those feelings away. I couldn't bear to open that up again, I'm not as strong as you are.'

When Olivia and Jasmine were back at home that evening, Jasmine was in a contemplative mood. As they were getting undressed, Olivia unzipped Jasmine's dress, lowering it off of her shoulders, and kissing the back of her neck. Olivia asked whether Jasmine was okay. 'Yes I am. I was pretty shocked about what my mum said, obviously. You know, she talked about my convictions and strength, but I'm wondering about that. I do keep a part of myself shut away. When we were in Cornwall, I did feel freer, and it felt good,' Jasmine sighed.

Olivia looked Jasmine in the eye, 'You are a strong person. Just because you don't tell everyone your business doesn't mean you're not strong. It's like you've always said, your business is your business, no one else's.'

Jasmine smiled at Olivia, and touched her face gently. 'I think it's sad that my mother didn't go for what she wanted to.'

'She did. She wanted you. And she had already said that her relationship with Jasmine wasn't working. She's happy with your dad, and accepts him as he is.'

'I guess you're right. Thank you. It certainly explains why she was so cool and supportive when I came out,' and she kissed Olivia.

They were putting their pyjamas on whilst they were talking, and Jasmine asked, 'Is it really okay to come home with you for Christmas?'

'Yes, I've spoken to mum. Also, I've asked that you share my room with me, if they would be alright with that. I explained that I practically live with you at weekends anyway.'

Jasmine looked astounded, 'What did she say?'

'She said yes!' Jasmine hugged Olivia, she was so excited.

'Talking of living together, move in with me, please. I love you so much, and I hate it when you go home,' Jasmine made puppy eyes at Olivia.

Olivia laughed, 'Okay, yes.'

Jasmine was ecstatic, 'Really?'

'Yes, really!' Jasmine kissed Olivia, holding her close.

Then she started to slowly remove Olivia's top, kissing from her neck, downwards. As Jasmine ran her hands down Olivia's body, she felt that familiar twist and want in her stomach, and melted as she felt Jasmine's lips on her breasts. She lay back on the bed, closed her eyes, and gave in to the ecstasy.

They decided that Olivia would move in with Jasmine when they returned from Cornwall. Firstly, Olivia needed to tell Emma. After work one evening, as they were chatting, Emma asked how things were going. Olivia said, 'Really good. Jasmine is coming to Cornwall with me for Christmas. Also, do you remember me saying that she asked me to move in with her not long ago?'

'Yes I do. From the look on your face, I'm guessing you said yes?' Olivia nodded, beaming from ear to ear. 'I'm really pleased for you. I'm going to miss you living here, though.'

Olivia said that they would still hang out together. 'Emma, I want to thank you. You really helped me to get settled in London, it was so much easier than if I'd done it on my own. Also, you've been so supportive of me and Jasmine, I can't tell you what that means to me.' She hugged Emma tightly, and as they drew apart, she asked, 'So how are things with you and the lovely Matt?'

Emma smiled, 'Very good, we're really happy. This is my longest relationship, and it feels good. I certainly don't feel ready to settle down yet, though.'

'I'm really happy for you,' Olivia smiled at her friend.

Just before the office was closing for Christmas, Jasmine and Jason took Laura and Olivia out to dinner, to celebrate another successful year at JJ Publishing. They went back to the restaurant in Covent Garden, where they had taken Olivia when she had first started working there. Sitting at the table with their drinks, Jason said, 'Well, it's been another great year, thank you Laura and Olivia for all your hard work,' and they raised their glasses.

Jasmine was thinking of what a rollercoaster of a year it had been. After the start of the year, when she had been heartbroken, she would have never believed how happy she could be again. Olivia couldn't believe that she had nearly lost Jasmine, and they looked at each other, feeling what the other was thinking. Jason cleared his throat, and Jasmine and Olivia blinked and turned towards the others. 'Sorry, I got a bit lost in thought,' said Jasmine, and Olivia blushed.

Laura said, 'I think you two are very sweet together!'

Jasmine smiled, and said, 'Actually, there's something we wanted to tell you both. You obviously know that we've been together for quite a while now. Well, Olivia is going to be moving in with me after Christmas.'

Laura and Jason both congratulated them.

Olivia and Jasmine arrived at St Erth station, to see Ella waiting for them. They all kissed and hugged one another, and started chatting, catching up on each other's news. When they arrived at the cottage, Olivia took the bags up to her room. Ella said that she would put the kettle on, and make them some drinks. Whilst they were sitting around the kitchen table, Olivia said, 'Mum, I've got some news for you. As you know, Jasmine and I have been together quite a long time now, and I usually stay with her at the weekends. Well, I'm going to be moving in with her when we get back to London.'

Ella smiled at her daughter, she could see how happy she was, and Olivia hugged her. She was also thinking that it seemed a bit quick, it wasn't long ago that Olivia had told her that she and Jasmine were together. Of course, she wasn't sure how long they had been together before Olivia had told her about the two of them. 'Well, if you're happy, I'm happy. Where will you be living?'

Jasmine explained that she had a house in Chelsea. 'You and Steve must come and visit us, I have a guest bedroom. You can come and see the office too, and we can take you to the theatre, it would be great.'

Ella smiled, 'That would be lovely, thank you.'

Jasmine said that she would sort out some dates and they would arrange something. Olivia said she wanted to go and see Becky, and Jasmine suggested that she go on her own, as she thought Becky would be more comfortable with that. Jasmine said that she'd go for a walk, then Ella suggested that she stay there for a chat instead.

Olivia set off towards the gallery. As she arrived, Becky looked up, beaming when she saw her friend, 'Olivia, I'm so pleased to see you,' and she rushed over and hugged her. Becky told Lucy that she was going to pop out to get a drink with Olivia, and would be back soon. They set off, arm in arm towards the cafe. Olivia was thrilled, it felt like old times again.

Jasmine sat at the table with Ella, looking out of the window. 'It's so beautiful here. Olivia was very lucky growing up in this environment. She has such a lovely family and great friends, I sometimes wonder why she ever wanted to go to London.'

Ella asked, 'Did you grow up in London?'

Jasmine looked at Ella, she found that she was very easy to talk to. 'Yes. I had a very good upbringing, a good education, trips to the theatre, dinner parties. But it often felt a bit superficial, like I had to be on my best behaviour. I get on well with my mum. My dad is fifteen years older than my mum, and, I don't know, I don't feel I really know him. He didn't take kindly to learning that I was gay. Actually, he was horrible about it, and I don't feel that I can ever be myself around him,' Jasmine sighed, then continued, 'I moved out when I was twenty, into the house where I am now, and I loved it, I felt that I had a lot more freedom. But when I met Olivia, she was the most natural and free person I think I've ever met. I just loved being around her. I obviously don't have to tell you how special she is. She gives me the inspiration to be myself, and I love her more than I've loved anyone else in my life, and sometimes I just can't believe how lucky I am.' Jasmine's eyes welled up with tears, and she looked down, saying, 'Sorry, I didn't mean to say so much, I...' and she looked up to see a tear run down Ella's face.

Ella put her hand on Jasmine's, 'Olivia is lucky to have met you.'

Ella talked about Olivia's childhood, and family holidays. She fetched the photo albums, and Jasmine loved seeing the pictures of Olivia when she was little. Ella talked so lovingly about her family, Jasmine was moved. Again she thought about how different Olivia's family was, compared to her own.

Ella had been surprised, to say the least, when Olivia had told her about herself and Jasmine. Now she knew though, she thought back to the summer when Jasmine had stayed, and how happy they were together. The memory of them coming home with sand in their hair and giggling like children made her smile. And after the way Jasmine had spoken this morning, she had no doubt of Jasmine's love for Olivia.

When Olivia returned from seeing Becky, she walked into the lounge to see Jasmine and Ella sitting together on the sofa, chatting. 'You two look very cosy,' she smiled.

Jasmine said, 'Hi, how was it with Becky?'

'It was good, we talked through things a bit more, and apart from that, it was like old times again. It was so good to see her.'

Jasmine looked at Olivia, and Ella saw the look between them, how they adored each other. Ella got up to put the kettle on, and Olivia sat down next to Jasmine. They held hands, and Olivia asked, 'Did you go for a walk?'

'No, I stayed here and chatted with your mum. She showed me some photos of you when you were little. You were so cute!'

'Oh no, how embarrassing! Mum!'

Ella returned with some drinks, laughing, 'Well, you were cute!'

That evening, when Jasmine and Olivia were getting ready for bed, Jasmine said, 'I love your mum, I really feel that I can talk to her. I found myself telling her things that I wouldn't usually talk about, other than to you, that is.'

Olivia smiled at Jasmine, 'Yes, she is the best.'

'Thank you for inviting me here, there's nowhere else I'd rather be.'

Olivia took Jasmine in her arms, and kissed her.

The next morning, Jasmine awoke, and rubbed her eyes. Olivia was already sitting up in bed, with a big grin on her face, 'Happy Christmas Jasmine,' and leaned down to kiss her.

Jasmine smiled up at Olivia, 'Happy Christmas to you too.'

'Look, we've got stockings!' Olivia was really excited.

Olivia climbed to the end of the bed to retrieve the stockings, and passed one of them to Jasmine. Jasmine was thrilled, she felt like a little girl again. They unwrapped the presents inside, and pulled out a satsuma from the end of the stocking. Olivia unpeeled hers, and started to eat it. The smell always took her back to past Christmases, and Jasmine laughed to see her so happy. 'I love you so much,' she said, and kissed Olivia, tasting the citrus juice in her mouth.

She pulled Olivia towards her, and Olivia eagerly kissed her back, and ran her hands under Jasmine's top, kneading her breasts. Then she felt Olivia's hand slide down the waistband of her pyjamas, and she whispered, 'We can't do this here...'

Olivia cut her words short when she slid her fingers into Jasmine, and breathily said, 'Yes we can.'

Jasmine arched her back and sighed, and gave into the feelings coursing through her body, Oh yes, that felt so good.

Olivia went downstairs, pulling Jasmine by the hand. She led Jasmine over to stand by the Christmas tree, putting her arms around her waist, and kissing her. Jasmine kissed her back, until they heard footsteps on the stairs, and pulled back. Ella and Steve appeared in the lounge, and they all wished each other a happy Christmas. They ate breakfast around the table, before getting showered and dressed. When they were back downstairs, there was a knock at the door, and Ben and Tina were standing there with bags of presents in each hand. As they wished everyone a 'Happy Christmas', the condensation swirled around the words in the crisp morning air. There were hugs and kisses all around, and Olivia said, 'Come on in and warm up. You remember Jasmine.'

Ben and Tina said, 'Of course, happy Christmas,' and they hugged her.

Once that they had all got settled, they began to open their presents. Ella unwrapped a beautiful silk scarf, in various shades of pink. 'Oh Jasmine, thank you, it's so beautiful.'

Jasmine was thrilled that Ella liked it, and Olivia smiled as she watched Jasmine. Jasmine unwrapped her present from Olivia. It was a painting of the beach at St Ives, which Olivia had had painted from a photograph that she'd taken back in the summer, when Jasmine had first come to Cornwall. 'I love it, thank you so much. It reminds me of our week here in the summer,' and she looked lovingly at Olivia.

Olivia opened Jasmine's gift to her. It was a small box, and Olivia opened it to see an exquisite platinum ring, made up of three entwined strands, two of which were shiny, and the third had a matt finish. 'Oh, it's beautiful. Thank you so much,' and Olivia hugged Jasmine. She placed the ring on the ring finger of her right hand, and held her arm out to admire it.

Whilst Steve and Ella cooked the lunch, they told the others to go off to catch up with each other. Olivia told Ben and Tina that she was going to move in with Jasmine once they returned to London, and Ben loved seeing how happy his sister was. Then she asked them how the wedding arrangements were coming along. They explained that it would be quite a small wedding, and they had set the date for next May. They were going to get married in the local church, and would have a marquee in the garden at Tina's parents' home. 'Will you be my bridesmaid, Olivia?' asked Tina.

'Yes, I would love to!' Olivia hugged Tina.

They said that Jasmine was obviously invited, and she said that she would love to be there.

Lunch was a real feast, with the traditional turkey, stuffing, and all the trimmings. There were mounds of vegetables and roast potatoes. They all chatted excitedly whilst eating, and toasted Steve and Ella for the meal. After such a big lunch, no one had room for the Christmas pudding, so they decided that they would eat it later. They thought that it would be good to go for a walk for some fresh air, and also walk off the lunch. It was a lovely bright day, and very cold, so they wrapped up with scarves and gloves. Ella wore her new pink silk scarf, which suited her pale colouring perfectly. When they were starting to head back home, Olivia called Jasmine over to the beach, telling the others that they would catch up with them. Olivia looked into Jasmine's eyes, 'I just wanted to thank you again for my present, I love it.'

Jasmine looked back at Olivia, that look that seemed to touch her soul, and said softly, 'I think that two of the strands are you and me, and that the third one is the love that connects us. I was wondering whether you might like to wear it on your left hand?'

Olivia looked at Jasmine, 'What are you saying?'

Jasmine moved closer, whispering, 'I'm saying that I love you, and I want to spend the rest of my life with you.'

Olivia looked up, into Jasmine's eyes. Jasmine smiled, and took Olivia's right hand, sliding the ring off, and then onto the ring finger of her left hand. Olivia kissed Jasmine, and the two of them became entwined in one another, kissing deeply and passionately, and at that moment there was no one else in the world but them.

When Olivia and Jasmine returned to the cottage, Ben and Tina were setting up a game of Monopoly. Olivia hung up their coats, and Ella noticed them whispering and giggling together. Everyone sat down to play. Olivia and Ben became really competitive, which Tina and Jasmine thought was hilarious. Tina also later commented to Ben that she had noticed that Olivia was now wearing the ring from Jasmine on her left hand. As the game was taking a long time, they decided to have a break for Christmas pudding, and to watch the Dr Who special on television.

Later that evening, after Ben and Tina had left, Steve and Ella said goodnight, leaving Olivia and Jasmine snuggled up on the sofa together. Jasmine squeezed Olivia's hand, 'I've had such a wonderful day, thank you.'

Olivia looked up at her, 'It's been brilliant spending Christmas with you.'

'I can't wait for you to move in with me,' Jasmine kissed Olivia, and they cuddled up together contentedly.

A couple of days later, Olivia and Jasmine went to Becky's to meet up with her, Dan and Liam. Jasmine was a bit nervous, and Olivia told her that she would be fine. When they arrived, Becky hugged Olivia and Jasmine, and they went to greet the others. Liam was already sitting down with Dan. Liam got up to give Olivia a hug, and Jasmine noticed the way that he still looked at Olivia. Poor guy, she thought, I know just how that feels. When they had all said their hellos, they sat down with a drink each. They chatted about their Christmases, and the presents that they had received. Becky noticed the ring on Olivia's left hand, 'It's beautiful, was it a Christmas present?'

Olivia looked at Jasmine, then at Becky. She nodded, 'It's my gift from Jasmine.'

Becky exchanged a look with Dan, then smiled at Olivia, 'So, what else did you have?'

A while later, as Jasmine was returning from the bathroom, she walked past the kitchen and caught a bit of whispered conversation between Becky and Dan. Becky looked concerned, '... are they engaged now? The ring is on her wedding finger, it just seems so quick.'

Dan said, 'Look, I don't know, but they seem really happy together.'

Jasmine cleared her throat, and Becky jumped, turned around and smiled. Jasmine could see that her cheeks were very red. 'Hi Jasmine, would you like another drink?'

'Yes please. You have a lovely home, thank you for inviting me. I love being in Cornwall, it's so relaxing compared to London.'

Dan asked whether she would move away from London sometime. Jasmine thought for a moment, 'I don't know, London has always been my home. I've never really considered it before.'

They took the drinks through to the lounge. Jasmine wanted to mention to Olivia what she had heard, but before she had an opportunity to say anything, Olivia said, 'I've got something I wanted to tell you all. I'm moving in with Jasmine when we get back to London. When I'm settled in, I'll give you the address.'

They all congratulated them, but Jasmine could see that Becky didn't look too happy about it.

When they were walking back home, Jasmine told Olivia about the conversation she had accidentally overheard, 'I wanted to say something to you, I thought it might be best to delay telling them about you moving in with me.'

Olivia replied, 'I've spoken to Becky about us, and I said I spend my weekends at your place anyway. I just want it out in the open now.'

Ella and Steve were preparing tea when Jasmine and Olivia arrived home. Ella asked whether they had a good time catching up with the others. Olivia said yes, and that she had told them about her moving in with Jasmine. Ella asked, 'Was Becky okay with you about it?'

Olivia replied, 'She seemed to be, but Jasmine heard her talking to Dan, and she thinks that were rushing into it. Of course, we were together for a few months before we had a break,' Olivia looked awkwardly at Jasmine, then continued, 'Since we got back together, it's been another eight months.'

Ella looked at Olivia, 'Did you break up for long?'

'It felt like too long. It was a big mistake. I got scared and confused, and I had this crazy idea that I needed to be on my own to get my head around what had happened. That was at the time when Liam came to London. The good thing is, that I knew for sure what I did want, but I thought that I had lost Jasmine in the process.'

Olivia looked at Jasmine, and she smiled back at her. 'Anyway, we've known each other for a year and a half now, and it's what we both want.'

Steve and Ella smiled at the two of them, and they sat down to eat together.

When it was time for Olivia and Jasmine to head back to London, Ella dropped them back at the station to catch their train. Ella hugged Jasmine, saying 'Look after my girl.'

Jasmine replied, 'I will. Thank you so much for having me to stay, I've had the most wonderful time.'

Ella hugged Olivia, 'I love you. Call me when you're home safely.'

'I love you too, Mum. Thank you for everything.'

They boarded the train, and waved out of the window as the train pulled out of St Erth station. Olivia sat down next to Jasmine, and held her hand. 'My mum loves you,' she grinned.

'I love your mum! I feel like I've got a second home here.' Olivia kissed Jasmine briefly on the lips, and sat back against the seat, still holding her hand.

'Tomorrow, we can start moving your things in properly. We can take the car, it'll be easier. I've already emptied out some wardrobe space and drawers for you.'

Over the long train journey, they excitedly discussed moving in together.

TWENTY ONE

Back in London, Olivia was hanging her clothes up in the wardrobe in Jasmine's bedroom. Jasmine came in to see if she needed any help. 'I'm okay, thanks. I'm just finishing now.' Jasmine sat on the bed, watching Olivia putting away the last of her things. 'Wow, we're really doing this!' said Olivia.

Jasmine smiled, she couldn't be happier, 'Yes, and I get to wake up with you every day. I can't think of anything more perfect.'

Olivia walked over to Jasmine, and kissed her. 'I've got something for you. Close your eyes.'

Jasmine closed her eyes, smiling, wondering what Olivia was going to do. She felt Olivia take her left hand, and slide something onto her ring finger. 'You can open your eyes now.'

Jasmine looked down at her hand, to see a platinum ring with two bands, and a pale pink stone in the middle.

Olivia said, 'I bought this ring in Cornwall to celebrate getting my job in London, and now I want you to have it.'

'I love it, thank you,' Jasmine kissed Olivia, pulling her down onto the bed.

Olivia laughed, and Jasmine rolled over so that she was on top of Olivia. 'I love you so much. Now, I think we should celebrate you moving in, and I have something in mind.'

She began undoing Olivia's top very slowly, as if she was unwrapping a gift, kissing gently down Olivia's body. Olivia was already tingling with anticipation, and arched her back as she felt Jasmine's fingers running down her body.

It was an hour or so later when Jasmine looked over at the clock. They had drifted off to sleep, and Jasmine stroked the side of Olivia's face. 'Hey you, wake up, we've got to get ready. We've got Phoebe and Fran's new year party this evening,' and she kissed Olivia.

They got up, showered and dressed. Jasmine wore her long black satin halter neck dress, with stunning blue glass drop earrings and a matching necklace. Olivia wore her green dress, which Jasmine loved on her.

Arriving at Phoebe and Fran's, they hugged and kissed each other welcome. Jasmine took the bottles of wine they'd brought with them through to the kitchen. Making their way into the lounge, they saw fairy lights strung around, with soft lighting, and music playing. The table with the buffet on had been pushed to one side, to make space for people to dance. Jasmine and Olivia recognised a few people from the barbecue in the summer, and said hello. Then Jasmine noticed the woman who had been eyeing up Olivia at the barbecue, wondering what colour her eyes were. Jasmine introduced herself, and the woman shook her hand, 'Hi, I'm Sylvie. This is Jenna.' Jasmine introduced Olivia, who smiled and shook hands with Jenna and Sylvie. Sylvie said, 'I love your dress, Olivia.'

Olivia blushed, and thanked her. Jasmine smiled cheekily, 'It brings out her eyes, don't you think?' and looked at Sylvie, giving her a wink. Sylvie blushed.

Jasmine and Olivia went to dance, and on one of the slower numbers, Phoebe noticed the rings on their left hands. She nudged Fran, who raised her eyebrows. When they walked over to get a drink, Phoebe asked, 'Is there something you wanted to tell us?' Jasmine looked nonplussed.

'The rings?' said Phoebe.

Jasmine smiled, 'Oh, yes. I bought it for Olivia as a Christmas present. And Olivia gave this one to me. She's moved in with me.'

'Congratulations,' Phoebe hugged them both.

As midnight approached, everyone started the countdown, and then cheered, kissed and hugged each other. Jasmine whispered in Olivia's ear, 'Happy new year, I love you.'

'I love you too,' and they kissed, getting lost in one another, and danced into the early hours.

Jasmine loved living with Olivia, and waking up with her every morning was divine. She couldn't remember ever being this happy. Olivia was equally blissfully happy, Jasmine was wonderful to live with. Going back to work, Jasmine and Olivia happily walked along side by side, smiling at each other. Arriving at work, Jasmine went to her office, and Olivia sat at her desk. When Laura arrived, they chatted about their Christmas and new year celebrations. Then Olivia told Laura that she had moved in with Jasmine, and Laura congratulated her. At lunch that day, Laura was admiring the ring Jasmine had bought her. Laura started to say something, then stopped. Olivia asked her what she was going to say. 'Well, it's a bit of a personal question, and really none of my business.'

'You can ask, and if it's too personal, I can always not answer!'

Laura hesitated, 'Well, I can't help wondering how you ended up with Jasmine.'

Olivia smiled, 'I wonder that myself sometimes! It was after the first book launch that I helped with. You had just gone home, and Jasmine told me how she felt about me. I was completely gob-smacked. I had never been involved with a woman before, it had never entered my head. We kissed, and then I freaked out and bolted. I was in a bit of a mess that weekend. Partly it was because of the way I felt after that kiss. It was so sexy, and that really confused me. Anyway, I tried to forget about it. Jasmine had been going mad with worry, and kept ringing me, trying to apologise, saying it would never happen again. I just avoided her, until she turned up at home to say sorry. Well seeing her, I don't know, I was just so drawn to her, and I walked over and kissed her.'

Laura was listening, rapt in the story. 'She is quite different away from the office, I had no idea. And the way she makes me feel...' Olivia blushed. 'I found it difficult to get my head around, though, and that's why I broke things off. I felt terrible, but I needed some space. Then I realised what a huge mistake I had made. I thought I had lost her.'

Laura looked at her friend, 'Well, you certainly make each other very happy. I must confess I did wonder about Jasmine, she's so private about her personal life.'

'Well, even if you hadn't walked in on us, she was going to tell you and Jason.'

Laura was blushing, 'I felt awful when I walked in on you both. I could not have been more surprised!'

'You and me both, we're usually well behaved at work! We thought we were alone. It was a relief once you knew, to be honest.'

One evening after work, Jasmine and Olivia were chatting over dinner. Jasmine was saying she thought it was about time that she had a talk with her dad. 'I don't know that it will get me anywhere, but I'm going to tell him that we're living together. I'm so sick of him dismissing what's going on, pretending it's not happening. Once I've told him, it's up to him what he does with that information.'

Olivia could see the look of determination in Jasmine's eyes. She realised how lucky she had been with the way her parents had handled her coming out.

That weekend, Jasmine went to visit her parents. Grace opened the door, and hugged Jasmine. She asked after Olivia, and Jasmine said that she was well. Jasmine took off her jacket and went into the lounge, where her dad was sitting, reading the newspaper. 'Hi Dad, how are you?' she walked over to give him a kiss on the cheek.

He said that he was well, and asked how she was. Grace came into the lounge with some drinks, and they sat down. They made some small talk, but Jasmine couldn't really concentrate, she wanted to get this conversation over with. Jasmine took a deep breath, then said, 'I've got something that I wanted to tell you both. You know that Olivia and I have been together for quite a long time now, well, she's moved in with me. We're living together.'

Henry made a huffing noise, threw his paper to the floor, and went to get up. Jasmine glared at him, and stood up, saying, 'Sit down, I haven't finished talking.'

Henry was so shocked, that he did just that. Grace just looked at them both, wondering what on earth was going to happen. Henry's face looked like thunder. Jasmine had never spoken to him in that way before, and now it was like the flood gates opening. 'I'm so fed up of you treating me like an itinerant teenager. Just pretending something isn't happening doesn't make it okay. I've been gay for as long as I can remember, it's not something I can put in a box, and nor can you. It's not a choice I made, either. It's who I am. I thought that by keeping my sexuality secret from everyone except my close friends, it was because it was no one else's business, which is true to a point. What I hadn't realised, is that by playing along with your ridiculous game, I was denying myself who I am. Meeting Olivia, she's such a truthful, free person, that I realised that I was putting myself in a box. Not because of my privacy, but because I was trying to hide that part of me. I'm not going to do that anymore. Olivia is the most honest, open, beautiful person I've ever met. Through knowing her, I'm learning to be myself. I'm madly in love with her, I'm happier than I've ever been, and I want to spend the rest of my life with her. If you don't accept me for that, that's your choice.'

Jasmine sat down, breathing heavily. It felt so good to at last express what had been building up inside her for so many years. Grace was still watching wide eyed. She admired her daughter, and had no idea how Henry would react. Jasmine had never faced up to him like that before. Henry looked at Jasmine with steely eyes. 'You have made yourself very clear. Now, I wish to go to my study, please excuse me.'

He got up, walked across the room, and left, closing the door behind him. Grace went over to sit next to

Jasmine, putting her arm around her. 'Well, do you feel better for that?' she laughed.

Jasmine turned towards Grace, 'Mum, I just had to say something. What he does with it is up to him. At least I've said my bit.'

Grace hugged her daughter, 'Congratulations on moving in together. Olivia is a lovely girl.'

'Thanks, Mum.' Jasmine said that she was going to leave, she was eager to get back home.

Olivia heard the key in the front door, and looked up as Jasmine arrived home. She was anxious to hear about what had happened. 'How was it?'

Jasmine took off her coat, and sat down next to Olivia, 'A bit brutal.'

'Who for, you or your dad?'

Jasmine smiled, and told Olivia everything that had happened. When she had finished, Olivia said, 'Well, good for you.'

Jasmine admitted she felt so much better for getting her feelings off her chest. She had expected that her dad wouldn't take the news well, but at least he had stayed long enough for her to say what she had wanted to, for the first time in her life. 'It was very cathartic. I've decided that I'm not going to hide who I am anymore, from anyone.' Looking at Olivia, she said, 'I wanted to thank you. You've given me the confidence to be myself.'

Olivia replied, 'I always thought that you were a very confident person. You've always seemed so bold and in control.'

'In control isn't confidence, though. To be honest, it's probably the opposite. Letting go, although it feels a bit scary, is also exhilarating. I feel that now, I can truly be me, and it's though you, living your own truth, that I've been able to see that.'

Olivia didn't know what to say. She looked at the earnest expression on Jasmine's face, and leaned in to kiss her.

Jasmine and Olivia had settled in together very well. They got together regularly with Emma and Matt. Emma said that she missed Olivia, but was glad that she was happy. Emma said, 'Matt and I have been thinking about him moving in with me, but we haven't decided for sure yet.'

'Well, that sounds great. You two are so good together, and I can highly recommend it.'

'I know, I can see how happy you are.'

One evening, Olivia was chatting with Jasmine about going to Cornwall for a long weekend to get fitted for her bridesmaids dress. Ben and Tina's wedding was now only a few weeks away. She said that if she went on a Friday, she could be back home on a Monday, ready for work on Tuesday. Olivia arranged the date, and booked her train ticket.

When it was time for Olivia to catch her train, Jasmine hugged her, saying, 'I'll miss you, call me when you get there. Send my love to everyone.'

Olivia kissed her, 'I'll miss you too.'

Jasmine waved Olivia off, and set off to work. Tomorrow would be Saturday, and Jasmine had planned to spend the day with Phoebe. Fran was going to be out for the day, and with Olivia away, they decided to get together, something they didn't do very often these days.

Saturday arrived, and Jasmine and Phoebe decided to go shopping, and have lunch out. In the afternoon, they went to Camden Lock market, somewhere that they used to go a lot when they were dating all those years ago. It was such a vibrant place, full of colour, interesting stalls, and wonderful smells from everything from candles to the food being cooked in the open air. Phoebe asked whether Jasmine had brought Olivia to Camden Lock. 'No, I haven't yet, although I'm sure that she'd love it here.'

'You two seem very happy. Are you enjoying living together?' Phoebe asked.

'Oh yes, it's wonderful.'

Phoebe smiled at her friend, and Jasmine noticed a look in her eyes, almost of sadness.

Back at Jasmine's after dinner, they were drinking coffee, and Phoebe said, 'Oh, you were telling about the painting that you bought in Cornwall, on your first visit. I'd love to see it.'

'Yes, it's in our bedroom, come and have a look.'

Phoebe followed Jasmine upstairs, and they stood back to admire the painting. Jasmine said, 'It's beautiful, isn't it. It really captures the spirit of the place.'

Phoebe turned around, kissing Jasmine full on the mouth. Jasmine pulled back, shocked, 'Shit, what the hell are you doing?'

'I've been wanting to kiss you all day. I hardly get to spend any time with you alone. I can't stop thinking about you.'

'What the hell are you talking about? What about Fran?'

'I do love Fran, but I think I'm in love with you.'

Jasmine sat back on the bed, trying to take this in. Phoebe made a move towards her, and Jasmine pushed her away. 'No, no way. What the fuck is going on?'

Jasmine couldn't believe what was happening. Phoebe looked at Jasmine, 'I don't think I should have let you go all those years ago. You were madly in love with me, I don't know what happened.'

Jasmine replied, 'I do. You fell in love with Fran. You two are meant to be together.'

'Most of the time, things are good, and other times, I don't know what I'm doing, I don't feel the same as I did. But when I see you, I think of what could have been. I had to tell you how I feel about you.'

Jasmine put her head in her hands, then looked up at Phoebe, 'Shit, you've really got to talk to Fran. Relationships do change over time, it's natural. You need to sort out whether you want to be with Fran or not, but you won't do that by jumping into another relationship, and certainly not with me. I love you as a friend, but that's all. We were together over ten years ago, we're long finished. And I love Olivia, and I've never been happier.'

Phoebe looked at Jasmine, then started to laugh. Jasmine looked confused, then Phoebe started to cry, and sat down on the bed next to Jasmine. 'I'm sorry, I don't know what I was thinking. Please forgive me.'

Jasmine put her arm around Phoebe, 'It's okay, just forget about it.'

Phoebe turned to hug Jasmine, crying into her shoulder. Then she looked up at Jasmine, and went to kiss her again. Jasmine jumped up, 'I think you ought to leave.'

She stood up and went downstairs to get Phoebe's coat. Phoebe walked slowly down the stairs, and put her coat on, without saying anything. As she opened the front door, Jasmine said, 'I don't want to talk about this again.'

Phoebe simply said, 'Sorry,' and she left.

Jasmine watched her walk down the road, then closed the front door, and leaned against it, breathing a sigh of relief. Fuck, where the hell did that come from. Jasmine walked back into the lounge to finish her coffee, and sat down in the armchair. She replayed what had just happened in her head, and still couldn't believe it. Why now, after all these years. Poor Fran, she thought, I wonder if she knows anything. Should she tell Olivia? Jasmine thought back to how Olivia had reacted when she had found out that she used to date Phoebe, she had been very upset about it. Jasmine decided that she would wait and see, and if there was an appropriate moment, she might broach it. Jasmine had no interest in Phoebe whatsoever, and Olivia didn't see Phoebe and Fran unless she was with Jasmine, so that shouldn't be a problem.

Phoebe made her way back home, feeling upset and frustrated. She didn't know why she had acted like she had, she should have spoken to Jasmine, explained her feelings. Not that it would have made any difference, Jasmine only wanted to be with Olivia, that much was clear. Since Jasmine had been with Olivia, it had reminded Phoebe of what she was like when they were first together. They had been so happy, so in love. Then Phoebe fell for Fran, and for years she had been happy staying friends with Jasmine. She did love Fran, but being around Jasmine in love, seeing the glow in her face, it had reminded Phoebe of what it was like when they were together. Phoebe unlocked the front door, and after hanging up her coat, she walked into the lounge, and saw Fran. 'Oh, hi. I didn't realise you'd be back yet.'

Fran smiled, 'Well, it's well past eleven now. Did you have a good day with Jasmine?'

'Yes thanks. I'm really tired, I'm going to go to bed now.'

Phoebe disappeared, and Fran thought that she didn't seem quite herself. About half an hour later, Fran went to get changed for bed. She brushed her teeth, and as she got into bed next to Phoebe, she could hear Phoebe crying.

Fran leaned over, touching Phoebe's shoulder, 'Hey, what's up?' Phoebe just shook her head, she didn't want to talk.

Jasmine met Olivia at the station on Monday afternoon. 'I'm so pleased you're home, did you have a good journey?'

'Yes thanks, I really missed you. Mum and dad send their love.'

'Would you like to eat out this evening or at home?'

Olivia looked at Jasmine, with yearning in her eyes, 'Home, please. I don't think that I can wait though a whole meal before I get my hands on you!'

Jasmine's stomach clenched with anticipation, and they headed home. As they got inside and closed the door, Olivia dropped her bags and grabbed Jasmine, kissing her long and full on the mouth. Jasmine responded eagerly, and they hastily pulled off their coats and shoes, and Jasmine led Olivia upstairs. Olivia undid Jasmine's blouse, and slid it off. She kissed her bare shoulders, and up her neck, whilst running her fingers all over Jasmine's body. Jasmine's skin tingled in response to Olivia's touch, she wanted her so badly. she unbuttoned Olivia's jeans, and slid them down her hips. Then she undid her own trousers and stepped out of them, whilst Olivia took off her jumper and bra. Jasmine whispered in Olivia's ear, 'I'm so wet for you.'

Olivia ran her hands down Jasmine's body, then dropped down to her knees and kissed her just where she yearned for it the most. 'Oh my god, that feels so good, ah.'

Olivia ran her hands over Jasmine's stomach and bottom, whilst she expertly built up the pressure and made Jasmine come, her legs weakening as she let go. She fell back on the bed, and Olivia leaned over her, kissing her passionately. Jasmine began kissing down Olivia's body, and those fabulous tits that she couldn't get enough of. Jasmine said hoarsely, 'Fuck, you are so sexy,' and rolled Olivia onto her side, so that she was behind her. Then she slid her hand under her bottom, stroking her gently, then Olivia could feel Jasmine's fingers inside her. She closed her eyes as she gave in to the sensuous feelings, and Jasmine kissed Olivia's back whilst working her magic, causing her to sigh and groan with pleasure. Oh, yes, it was good to be home.

A couple of days later, Fran finally got Phoebe to talk. 'I'm so sorry, I'm so sorry,' Phoebe was crying.

Fran was worried, 'Sorry about what. I know something is wrong, but I have no idea what it is. You were upset when you came home Saturday night. Is it something to do with Jasmine?'

Phoebe began crying even harder, and Fran put her arm around her until she calmed down a bit. 'Is something the matter with Jasmine?'

Phoebe shook her head. Eventually, through her sobs, Phoebe told Fran what had happened. Fran sat back, shocked. Once Phoebe had explained everything to Fran, she started to calm down. Fran couldn't believe it. She felt numb all over, and said that she would move into the spare bedroom whilst they decided what they were going to do.

In the office, Laura was asking Olivia about her visit home to Cornwall. Olivia explained that she'd had her fitting for her bridesmaids dress, and that Tina looked gorgeous in her wedding dress. 'Although it was only a short visit, it was good to see everyone. Becky, my best friend, is also a bridesmaid, so we all had a lot of fun trying dresses on.'

Jasmine walked into the outer office as they were chatting, and said, 'I can't wait to see you in your dress. I think you'd look amazing in a wedding dress, too,' and looked at Olivia in a way that made her insides melt.

Laura felt a bit like a third wheel, and said, 'I think I'll pop out and get some drinks, what would you like?'

Olivia turned around, her cheeks flushed, 'I'll pop out, I think I could do with some fresh air.'

Laura smirked, and Olivia grabbed her jacket and bag, and headed for the cafe. As she was walking up the road towards the cafe, she saw Fran. 'Hi, how are you?'

'Um, okay I guess,' Fran replied, 'We're trying to work things out.'

Olivia was a bit confused, 'Sorry, is everything okay with you and Phoebe?'

Fran shook her head, 'Not really. I didn't know how she had been feeling, and after what happened, I'm just not sure that I can stay with her.'

Olivia asked if she wanted to talk, and they went into the cafe together. Sitting down with their drinks, Fran started telling Olivia what was happening. She said that she loved Phoebe, but just didn't know that it could work, knowing how she felt. She explained that Phoebe had been distant and acting strangely, and how she wouldn't talk to Fran about it at first. Then she started talking about Jasmine, saying how a few of their friends really fancied her. 'Well, you know how it is. People notice Jasmine, men and women. She's very beautiful. She told me it was a mistake, but I can't get the thought of them together out of my head, there's too much history between them.'

Olivia felt the colour rush from her face, and she felt as though everything was going in slow motion. 'What are you talking about?'

'Oh my god, you didn't know? I'm so sorry.'

Fran had presumed that Jasmine would have told Olivia. Olivia felt sick, and said, 'I have to go,' and rushed off before Fran could stop her.

TWENTY TWO

Jasmine was thinking that Olivia had been gone a long time. She checked her phone, and saw that she had a missed call. Olivia's probably forgotten which drink I asked for, she smiled to herself.

She dialled her voicemail and heard Fran's voice, 'Jasmine, it's Fran. I just bumped into Olivia. She asked how I was. I thought she knew what happened. She seemed pretty upset, I'm really sorry.'

'Shit.' Jasmine put the phone down.

Olivia walked along the road, tears in her eyes. She kept replaying Fran's words over and over again in her head, 'She told me it was a mistake, but I can't get the thought of them together out of my head.' Did that mean what she thought it did? Her head hurt at the thought of it, and she still felt sick. Olivia heard her phone ringing, and saw that it was Jasmine. She couldn't talk to her now, not walking along the road. She let it go to voicemail.

Jasmine walked out of her office to speak with Laura. She explained that something had come up, and Olivia wouldn't be coming back to the office this afternoon. Laura saw the strain on Jasmine's face, and realised that there must be some problem between her and Olivia. Laura hoped that whatever it was would be sorted out soon. Jasmine finished up what she was doing as soon as she could, and started packing her bag up to go home.

Olivia didn't want to go home just yet. She knew that Jasmine would be leaving work soon, and she needed some space to calm down before she could talk to her. Olivia still had a key for Emma's flat, so she headed there. She sent Emma a text to let her know, so that she wouldn't surprise her. When she arrived at the flat, Olivia headed straight for her old room. She threw herself onto the bed, convulsing with sobs, the tears flowing down her face. Sometime later, Olivia heard a tap on the door, and Emma looked in. Seeing the state of Olivia, she went over to hug her. Olivia started crying again, and Emma waited for her to calm down, before asking what was going on. 'I think Jasmine might be having an affair.'

Emma looked shocked, 'No way. She's crazy about you.'

Olivia told her about bumping into Fran. She said that something must have happened if Fran might be leaving Phoebe, they had been together for years.

Emma said, 'I just can't believe it. What does Jasmine say?'

'I haven't spoken to her yet, I've only just found out.'

'You've really got to talk to Jasmine.'

Jasmine made her way home, calling Olivia's number again, and leaving a message, 'Please, Olivia, we need to talk. I don't know what Fran said, but nothing happened. I really need to talk to you.'

When she arrived home, she called out to Olivia, and went to look for her. She wasn't at home, shit, where was she. There was only one place that she could think of.

There was a knock at the door, and Emma opened it to see Jasmine standing there, looking upset. 'Is she here?' she asked Emma.

'She is, but she's in a right state.'

'I have to see her, I have to explain. Please.'

Emma could see how desperate Jasmine was. She stood back to let Jasmine in, and closed the door. Jasmine went to the bedroom, and opened the door to see Olivia on the bed. She looked terrible. Jasmine wanted to hold her, but knew that she would have to tread carefully. Jasmine started to move towards Olivia. 'No, don't,' Olivia warned.

Jasmine stopped. 'Can I sit down? '

'No.' Olivia glared at Jasmine.

Jasmine was flustered and frustrated. She was also kicking herself for not telling Olivia what had happened herself. 'I don't know what Fran told you, but I promise you that nothing happened. I love you, it's that simple.'

Olivia sobbed, 'The minute I go away, Phoebe is there. Did you fuck her?'

'No, I didn't do anything, I swear to you. We spent the day together. Phoebe came back home for a coffee, and she tried to kiss me. I stopped her, and told her to leave. That's it.'

'Why didn't you tell me?' Tears were streaming down Olivia's face.

Jasmine was dearly wishing that she had, but it was too late now. She was going to have to deal with it as it was. If only she could hold Olivia, and she would know how she felt. Jasmine let out a long breath, 'Nothing happened, and after the way you reacted when you found out Phoebe was my ex, I wasn't sure whether to tell you. I had missed you, and when you got home, I really wasn't thinking about it. I should have told you, I'm sorry.'

Olivia was hurting so badly, and as she looked at Jasmine, a hard expression crossed her face, 'Fran says lots of their friends fancy you. I suppose it was just a matter of time.'

Jasmine stared at Olivia, feeling like she had put a knife through her heart. 'Fuck you.'

Jasmine left the room, and headed for the front door, slamming it behind her as she left.

Jasmine couldn't believe that Olivia had said that. Christ, did she think that she was that shallow, or that easy for that matter. When would she get it into her head that Jasmine only wanted Olivia, and no one else. Maybe she was better off without her. In her heart she knew that wasn't true, but in this moment, her heart felt like it was breaking into little pieces.

The next day, Jasmine arrived at work early. She didn't know what she was going to do, but for now, she was going to bury herself in work.

Olivia knew that Jasmine had meetings all day, and took advantage to go back home and collect a few things to take back to Emma's. She was just going to stay a couple of nights, so that she and Jasmine could both cool down. Then, they could talk. After Jasmine had left Emma's yesterday, she hadn't tried calling Olivia again. Olivia couldn't forget the look of shock and hurt on Jasmine's face. She knew that what she had said was below the belt, but she was still very upset with Jasmine. Olivia arrived in the office a little later than usual, but Laura was pleased to see her. She didn't know why Olivia hadn't come back to the office yesterday afternoon, and decided from the look on Olivia's face, that it was best not to ask. Laura let Olivia know that Jasmine was in her first meeting already. Olivia got stuck in with work, and managed to avoid seeing Jasmine all day. The next few days were very much the same, with both women keeping busy and avoiding each other. On the couple of occasions when they did have to talk, it was very strained.

Back at home, Jasmine was feeling miserable. She hated that she could feel so bad over someone else. At least when she was single, things were more straight forward. But who was she kidding, she wouldn't trade any of the time that she had spent with Olivia. Although it had been unbelievably painful at times, they had shared so much love, so much fun and companionship. Not to mention, the phenomenal sex. She missed her so much. But how could they be together if Olivia didn't trust her. She was young, maybe that was part of the problem. She had only had one serious relationship before Jasmine. Well, she wasn't going to do the chasing this time. If Olivia was going to run off, she would leave her to it. Jasmine decided that tonight, she just needed to forget for a bit, and numb the pain. She wanted to go to a club, have some drinks, and dance.

When she arrived at the club, Jasmine checked her jacket and went straight to the bar to order herself a rum and cola. After her third drink, she made her way to the dance floor. She didn't notice how people watched her walking over to dance, thinking how they would love to dance with her. It was dark and noisy at the club, with flashing disco lights and a thumping beat. It was Friday night, the music was loud, and it was packed with people dancing closely together. Once she had been dancing for a while, a good looking guy starting dancing with her. She didn't care, she just wanted to get lost in the rhythm, and let go of her thoughts for a few hours. They danced for a long time, Jasmine sometimes with her hands on his shoulders, and his on her hips. He really liked this woman, she was so sensual. He watched her lips, really wanting to kiss them. Jasmine was aware of him starting to lean in, and she excused herself, and started to walk away, back towards the bar. The guy followed her, offering to buy her a drink. 'That's very kind, but no thanks. I'm with someone.'

'I can't see anyone. You've been dancing with me for the last hour.'

'Look, you're really cute, but you're not my type.'

He smiled, his best cute smile, 'What is your type, then?'

'Well, for starters, you would need to have tits.'

'Oh.' The guy couldn't help but laugh, and deciding that it was a lost cause, wandered back to the dance floor.

Just then, Jasmine then heard a voice behind her, 'I can help you there!' and turned around to see Susan smiling at her.

They hugged, and Jasmine asked where Samantha was. Susan explained that they weren't together now. 'I'm surprised to see you here. I didn't think this was really your scene.'

'Well, tonight it is. I don't want to talk, I just want to drink and dance.'

They sat at the bar together, Susan drinking wine, and Jasmine nursing another rum and cola. They got up to dance, and the cute guy watched the two of them together, realising that tonight was not going to be his lucky night, as he had thought earlier. Susan danced closely with Jasmine, thanking her lucky stars that she'd come out tonight. This was the first time that she'd been alone with Jasmine. That was, if you could call being in a packed full nightclub alone. Susan wondered whether Jasmine was still with Olivia, but as she didn't want to talk, she wasn't going to ask. Well, she would see where the evening would take her. Susan danced as close to Jasmine as she could dare get. Jasmine was oblivious to this, her head was muzzy, and all she could feel was the throb of the music beating through her.

At two in the morning, Susan knew that it was time to take Jasmine home. Jasmine was too far gone to tell Susan where she lived. She found out that Jasmine had checked her jacket, and was trying to ask Jasmine where the receipt was. Susan slid her hand into the back pocket of Jasmine's jeans. No receipt. As she tried the second back pocket, Susan couldn't help feeling a rush of excitement as she touched Jasmine. She pulled out the receipt. After she had collected their jackets, she led Jasmine outside into the crisp, cool air to get a cab. Back at her place, Susan got Jasmine onto the bed, took off her jacket, and removed her jeans. She pulled the covers over Jasmine, and left her to sleep. Leaving a glass of water on the bedside table, she went to bed.

On Saturday morning, Olivia's phone rang, and it was Fran. She asked if they could meet up, and Olivia agreed. They arranged to meet at a cafe near Oxford Circus at midday. Olivia arrived to see Fran already at a table. 'Thank you for coming. I just wanted to talk to you, I felt awful about the other day.'

Olivia replied, 'Sorry I ran off. If Jasmine had told me, I wouldn't have reacted like I did. How are you?'

Fran said that she wasn't great. She still didn't know what she was going to do. Phoebe wanted them to stay together, but how could she when she was making a move on Jasmine. She can't be happy or she wouldn't have done it. Fran looked at Olivia, 'For what it's worth, Phoebe said that Jasmine was shocked at her behaviour, and made her leave. Jasmine only has eyes for you, you need to know that.'

Olivia replied, 'The day I saw you, Jasmine tried to explain. I was really upset, and I said something really horrible. We haven't spoken since, except for at work. I think I've really screwed it up this time.'

Then Olivia asked Fran what she thought she was going to do. She didn't envy her situation, and she realised how lucky she was in comparison. On her way back, she decided to call Jasmine, and wanted to say that she was coming home, and could they talk. Jasmine's phone went to voicemail, and Olivia left her a brief message. Olivia went back to Emma's to get her things, then headed home, feeling much happier. When she arrived, she called out to Jasmine, but there was no answer. Olivia rang Jasmine's number again, and again it went straight to voicemail.

Jasmine woke up on Saturday morning feeling terrible. Her head was banging, and her mouth was so dry, she thought she must have eaten a bag of sand. She rubbed her eyes, feeling disorientated. Where the hell was she? Under the duvet, she realised that she was only wearing her top and pants. Fuck, whose bed was she in? She didn't recognise the room at all. Jasmine tried to remember what had happened last night, but trying to think just made her head hurt more. She vaguely remembered dancing with a guy, and hands on her hips, and he had wanted to buy her a drink. She was sure that she had said no. But she did remember dancing with a woman, or had she dreamed it? Sitting up, she felt a wave of nausea as the room spun around. She slumped back onto the pillows, as Susan walked into the bedroom. 'Hey, how are you feeling?' she asked, handing Jasmine the glass of water. 'Looking at you, I would say not too good!'

She sat on the edge of the bed, waiting for Jasmine to finish drinking. She took the glass from her, and set it down. Jasmine looked at Susan, 'We didn't, did we?'

'No. You were in no state. I brought you here to sleep off the alcohol, I couldn't let you go home alone.'

'Thank you.'

'Not that I wouldn't have jumped at the chance.' Susan looked intently at Jasmine.

Jasmine got up quickly, excusing herself, and dashed to the bathroom. She emptied the contents of her stomach, which was mainly liquid, into the toilet, and flushed it. Susan followed her to make sure she was okay. Jasmine was sitting on the floor, her head in her hands. Susan stroked Jasmine's shoulder, 'I didn't think the idea of sleeping with me was literally sickening!'

Despite herself, Jasmine smiled weakly. Susan helped Jasmine get freshened up and made her a hot drink. Once she was feeling slightly more human, Susan suggested that she have a shower, then maybe she could manage a bit of breakfast.

It was now quite late on Saturday afternoon, and Olivia was getting concerned that Jasmine hadn't arrived home, or tried to call her. Suddenly, her phone rang, making her jump. She saw Jasmine's number, and was relieved. She held the phone up to her ear, and before she could say anything, she realised that the voice at the other end wasn't Jasmine's. 'Hi, Olivia? It's Susan. Sorry to bother you, but Jasmine's just left, and I've just found her phone on the floor. Can you let her know it's here.'

Olivia hung up, and put her phone down.

About half an hour later, Olivia heard a key in the door, and looked up to see Jasmine, looking tired and dishevelled. 'Olivia, you're home,' Jasmine pulled her shoes off, and started to walk towards Olivia.

'I tried calling you.'

'I lost my phone.'

'Susan just rang. You left your phone at her place.' Olivia looked upset, and Jasmine wasn't sure that she could deal with this right now.

Olivia asked, 'Did you spend the night with Susan?'

Jasmine was exhausted, 'You know, I can't keep doing this. I know I made a mistake not telling you what happened with Phoebe. I tried to apologise. But you fucked off back to Emma's on Tuesday. You've been gone four days. So what if I'd had enough, and went out dancing last night. I got drunk, Susan happened to be at the club, and she took me home because I was in such a state. If you can't trust me, I can't do anything about that. Maybe it's not meant to be for us.'

TWENTY THREE

Over the last few weeks, Jasmine had tried really hard to get on with her life. As before, she threw herself into work. Laura and Jason really felt for her. Still, with Olivia gone, maybe she would start to get back to her old self. Olivia had left for Cornwall over three weeks ago, having given in her notice. They hadn't started looking for a replacement yet, Jasmine just couldn't face it at the moment. Laura said that she was fine on her own for now. Jason didn't want to push anything, as Jasmine was still rather delicate. Jason and Laura really missed Olivia, the office just wasn't the same without her. Neither of them could believe that she was gone. She and Jasmine had had their blips, but they always seemed to work them out.

At home, there were so many reminders of Olivia, particularly the two paintings of St Ives, but Jasmine couldn't bear to put them away. She was still wearing Olivia's ring, too. She wasn't ready to be with anyone else yet, although she knew that she would have to move on eventually. Still, it had only been a few weeks. Jasmine had spent a bit of time hanging out with Fran. She and Phoebe had split up, so Jasmine and Fran were trying to help each other through things. At least they both understood what they were each going through, and they kept telling themselves that it was for the best. Walking through the lounge one day, Jasmine looked at the small lemon tree that she had bought at the Eden Project. In its pot in the sunshine, with its beautiful white flowers blossoming, all the memories of that holiday came flooding back. She remembered Olivia dancing around on the sand, arms outstretched and her face to the sky, and Jasmine sank to the floor, hugging herself, tears flowing down her face.

Olivia was finding it difficult settling back into life in Cornwall. It seemed so quiet after London. She missed Emma, Laura and her job. She missed Jasmine so badly, it was unbearable. She wondered how she had let things get this far. She had gone home to Jasmine to apologise, and had made things worse, like she was on some kind of self-destruct. What was the matter with her. Ella loved having Olivia at home, but she was worried about her. Olivia wasn't eating or sleeping properly. She tried to get Olivia to talk about what had happened, but she would either clam up or cry. Becky was thrilled to have Olivia back home, but after a few days she hated seeing how unhappy she was. This wasn't the Olivia she knew. When they were sitting on the beach one day, chatting, Becky said that she couldn't understand why they couldn't work things out. Olivia started crying again, she felt that crying was about all she did these days. 'I really messed things up. I was selfish and immature.'

Becky said, 'Look, it takes two, you know.'

'Yes, but if anything happened, I just bolted. That business with Phoebe, I didn't give Jasmine a chance, I said that it was just a matter of time before she would be with someone else. I really hurt her.'

'You were upset, she must have known that.'

'I disappeared on her for a few days. Then when I went home to make up, I accused her of sleeping with Susan. It's like I just couldn't stop myself. She deserves someone better than me. I kept hurting her, she'll be better off without me.'

Olivia had been back in Cornwall for over three weeks. It was the day of Ben and Tina's wedding, and Ella was helping Olivia and Becky to get ready. They had their hair done, and Olivia wore hers up. With all the excitement of the day, it helped to take Olivia's mind off of things. She decided that from today, things would be different. She was going to pull herself together, and get on with her life. The sun was shining, and the family were all excited. Ben and Tina were getting married at the local church, and going on to Tina's parents for the reception, with the marquee in the garden. The wedding was taking place at midday. Tina was wearing a stunning white satin dress, with little rose buds embroidered on it. Olivia and Becky wore dresses in a deep claret satin, which matched Ben's tie and waistcoat. The service was beautiful, and

Olivia wiped a tear away as Ben and Tina exchanged their vows. As they walked out of the church, everyone congratulated the happy couple, and some threw confetti. Everyone then made their way to the reception.

The garden was beautiful, with a large lawn and borders full of spring flowers surrounding it. The marquee was white, and decorated with fairy lights and flowers. The tables were set up for lunch, and Olivia was sitting at the head table, along with Becky and Dan. The lunch was lovely, and afterwards there were a few speeches. The band began to play The Way You Look Tonight, and Ben and Tina made their way to the dance floor for the first dance, soon followed by more couples. Liam was there with Lucy, and Becky danced with Dan. Olivia smiled, watching her parents dancing closely. She looked down at her left hand, and the ring that Jasmine had given her. Maybe she should take it off now. Her heart ached so much, she didn't think she could stand it. The band began the next song, Just the Way You Are, and immediately Olivia was transported back to her first date with Jasmine. Feeling that she couldn't breathe, Olivia stood up to go and get some fresh air.

'Dance with me.' Jasmine was looking longingly at Olivia.

'Wh, what are you doing here?' Olivia couldn't believe her eyes.

'I was right, you do look gorgeous in your dress. I want to dance with you. Please.'

Jasmine's heart was beating so fast. She took Olivia's hand, and they both felt that familiar electric connection, as she led Olivia to the dance floor. They danced, letting the music wash over them. 'I can't believe you're here.'

'I can't believe I let you go,' Jasmine said as she looked into Olivia's eyes.

Ella, Steve and Becky couldn't help watching to see what was going to happen. After seeing Olivia miserable for these last few weeks, they really wanted her to be happy. As the song came to an end, the next one began, Gershwin's They Can't Take That Away From Me. Jasmine sighed, she loved this song, she found it achingly romantic. She softly sang along in Olivia's ear, 'The way you changed my life, they can't take that away from me...'

Feeling Jasmine's body close against hers sent Olivia's mind and body whirling. It felt as though every cell of her being yearned for Jasmine. As the song finished, Olivia wanted to get some fresh air. It was early evening now, and the May air was fresh and cool against her skin. Jasmine followed her out. Olivia stopped, and turned towards Jasmine. 'I'm sorry about what I said, I didn't mean it. The thing is, the feelings that I had for you were so overwhelming, they scared me. When I thought I'd missed my chance with you, it hurt so much, I'd never known anything like it. And when Fran said those things, my world came crashing down around me. I couldn't believe it was happening...' Olivia paused, and a tear escaped from the corner of her eye.

Jasmine wiped it away, 'Hey, it's okay.'

Olivia's tears began to fall freely, and she continued, '...and a part of me thought it was inevitable, like I knew that something would happen, and you would meet the person that you're really meant to be with.' Now that Olivia had admitted her feelings out loud, she couldn't control the sobbing.

Jasmine was astounded. 'You're the person I'm meant to be with. Since the moment I first saw you and wanted to kiss you, I've never wanted anyone else.'

She was also feeling very heavy hearted, Olivia was talking in the past tense. Did that mean she no longer felt the same way. Olivia said, 'Feelings do change, though. Once upon a time, I thought that I might marry Liam. You were in love with Phoebe. Fran and Phoebe were committed. None of us can know what's going to happen.'

Jasmine was feeling scared now, fuck, maybe Olivia was over her now. She looked directly into Olivia's eyes, 'When you stop thinking for a moment, how do you feel, in here?' she asked, placing her hand over Olivia's heart.

'When we were together, I never felt happier or more alive in my life,' she said with certainty.

Jasmine looked wide eyed at Olivia, feeling so much love for her. 'You're right, we don't know what's going to happen. All I do know is that in this moment, I want to spend the rest of my life with you. Also, I desperately want to kiss you,' and Jasmine's mouth was on Olivia's, and she held her tightly. Feeling Jasmine's lips on her, being held like this, Olivia knew that in this moment, there was nothing else that she wanted more.

They made their way back to the marquee, and danced together for the rest of the evening. They were dancing to a slow song, and Jasmine said, 'I love you so much. I've missed you, my life is empty without you. Please come home with me.'

Olivia pulled back to look at Jasmine, into her soft, dark eyes. 'Yes. I've been so miserable, I can't believe we let things get so out of hand. I love you. Ever since that first kiss, when you turned my world upside down, I've only ever wanted you.'

They kissed, not caring if anyone was watching. By this point, most people had heard about Jasmine, the woman who had stolen Olivia's heart. Ella watched them dancing and laughing together. She was delighted to see her daughter looking so happy again.

After the wedding, Jasmine went back home with Olivia. They had got changed out of their wedding outfits, and into pyjamas. Sitting in the lounge, drinking hot drinks, Olivia was asking Jasmine how she knew where to find her. Jasmine reminded Olivia that they had the wedding invitation at home with the address was on.

Ella said, 'I want to thank you Jasmine, this is the first day that Olivia's laughed since she's been home.'

Olivia and Jasmine exchanged a look, and Ella decided that it was time for them to go to bed, and she and Steve said goodnight. It had been a very busy and emotional day, and she was thrilled that both of her children were so happy. Once her parents had gone upstairs, they were at last alone, and Olivia pulled Jasmine towards her, kissing her tenderly. 'You are the most romantic, spontaneous and sexy person that I've ever met.'

Jasmine looked cheekily at Olivia, 'I think I'm going to burst if I don't fuck you right now.'

Olivia laughed, 'And you certainly have the filthiest mouth of anyone I know!'

She stopped talking as she felt Jasmine's hand slide under her top, and felt that familiar, delicious tingle over her skin, as her stomach did its familiar twist of anticipation...

THE END

Thank you for reading my book. I hope you enjoyed reading it as much as I enjoyed writing it. If you would like a sneak peek of my next book, please continue reading below. I would also like to thank my family and friends for their support, particularly when I disappeared for hours at a time to write!

About the author

Citrus Blossom is Sarah's first novel. She had the inspiration for it whilst sitting in the garden. Once she started writing, she couldn't stop! She likes palm trees and pina coladas, but not getting caught in the rain

Visit her website at www.sarahpond.co.uk

or follow her on twitter @palmtreesarah

Other books by Sarah Pond

Hibiscus

When Rachel has her first holiday in years after starting her art gallery, she was expecting some time to herself to relax. She didn't expect to have a passionate affair, and would never have dreamed it would have been with a woman.

Lea loves living in her quiet coastal village. When she meets the woman staying at a nearby cottage, she thinks she's met the love of her life.

Despite their connection, Rachel thinks it's just a holiday fling. Thinking that they'll never see each other again, fate has other ideas. But with such different outlooks and lifestyles, not to mention the distance between them, could a relationship ever work?

Here's a sneak peak of my second novel...

HIBISCUS

Rachel was looking forward to her holiday. Work had been really busy recently, and this was her first holiday away in over three years. After everything that had happened with her ex, she knew that the break would be good for her, and she didn't remember the last time she had been out of London. Rachel's life and soul had gone into the art gallery that she and Tom had set up. If she was being really honest with herself, Rachel hadn't wanted to take any time away. If she kept busy, then she didn't have to think too much about other things. This probably wasn't a conscious awareness on her part. After three years of very hard work, business was doing well, and Tom insisted that she go away to unwind. He knew that Rachel needed it, even if she couldn't see it for herself. They both had personal assistants who would help out, and Tom assured her that everything would be in good hands.

It was a Friday morning, and Rachel finished up the last bit of work, and ran through with Lisa what needed doing while she was away. Lisa assured her that they were all up to date with everything. Tom walked into Rachel's office, 'Will you just go already, we'll be fine!' Tom hugged Rachel, her head barely reaching his shoulder. Tom was tall and slim, with prematurely grey, close cropped hair. He bent down to kiss Rachel on the cheek, and released her. After hugging Lisa and

Eric goodbye, they managed to get Rachel out of the door, and send her on her way.

Rachel left the gallery, and headed to Paddington, to catch the train to the South West. It was a warm June day, and the sun was shining. Rachel let out a deep breath, and decided that she wasn't going to think about work for the next two weeks. This was a tall order, but she was determined to do it, if for no other reason than to prove that she could. The train was quiet, and Rachel found a seat easily, and settled down for the long journey. As her mind wandered, she realised that this was the first time that she had been away on her own. She was thirty now, and previous holidays had always been with her parents, or friends. Her last holiday had been with her then boyfriend Mark, in Corfu. It had been a great holiday, just before she started up the gallery. It was setting up the gallery that had ultimately ended their relationship.

Rachel had met Mark at a party, when they were both twenty three. They had a lot of fun together, and three years later, Mark asked Rachel to move in with him. They settled in well, and were very happy to begin with. Things started to change when Rachel got involved with setting up the gallery with Tom. Mark thought that all she ever did was work. It was true, she was so passionate about the gallery, and there was so much to do. Everything else in her life took second place. Mark felt like he was single again, and started going out on his own with his friends more and more.

He met a lovely woman one evening, and they chatted for hours. He really enjoyed her company. Over the next couple of weeks, he decided it was time to move on with his life, and had a talk with Rachel. He wanted to be with someone he would get to spend time with. Although Rachel was upset, she completely understood, she never had time for anything or anyone if it wasn't connected with the gallery. They parted on good terms, and Rachel hoped that Mark would be happy. Sometimes Rachel would get lonely, but most of the time she was too busy with work to think about it. She did miss having someone to go home to at the end of the day, and just chat with. Still, she had become used to spending a lot of time on her own.

As the train rattled along, Rachel thought about the little cottage that she was going to be staying in. It was in a small village called Kingsand, a tiny one bedroom place, at the top of a hill. It had a view of the sea, and it sounded perfect for a place to unwind. Rachel could relax, read, go for walks, lay on the beach and swim. She had purposely booked somewhere which, although quiet, had the essentials. There were local shops, cafes and pubs. This would mean that Rachel didn't need to go out of town if she didn't want to. She hadn't learned to drive, as around London she didn't think there seemed much point. Public transport was easy and convenient for her. Rachel could listen to music whilst she was travelling, which she found a more relaxing prospect than battling traffic.

The train arrived late afternoon, and Rachel checked the address. Walking along Market Street, she put her case down by one of the benches, taking in the quaint surroundings, and the view of the sea. Rachel took a deep breath, feeling her lungs filling with air, and then let her breath out slowly. The sun was warm on her upturned face, and she smiled to herself. After a few minutes soaking up the view, she decided to get on and find the cottage. There would be plenty of time for exploring over the next two weeks.

The owner had emailed Rachel to say that as she was going to be away, a woman called Lea would be looking after the cottage. In the meantime, the door would be unlocked so she could let herself in, and get settled. Rachel found the road, and climbed the hill to the top. There was a row of quaint little cottages, and number five, Rachel's home for the next two weeks, was in the middle. Each of the cottages was painted in a different pastel colour, and number five was pink. Rachel opened the door, which led straight into the lounge. There was a sofa, an armchair, and a small fireplace. The walls were whitewashed, there were blue curtains, and a big beige shaggy rug on the floor. There was a small television and dvd player in the corner, and no phone line or wifi. Perfect for getting away from everything. It was Tom who suggested that she book somewhere without a phone or internet connection, probably because he knew that Rachel would be too temped to keep contacting the gallery. Rachel had promised Tom and, more importantly, herself, that this holiday was strictly relaxation. Deep down, Rachel knew that she had begun to lose herself, and these next two weeks would give her the time to reconnect.

Rachel put her case down, and explored. It wouldn't take long, as the cottage was two up, two down. The kitchen led off of the lounge, and had a small pine table in it. On it, was a welcome note, and some homemade scones. The note said that there was also some clotted cream in the fridge, along with some milk and jam. Rachel smiled as she read it, thinking how thoughtful it was. She walked back through the lounge, and up the stairs. There was a small bathroom, and the bedroom was quite a good size for such a small cottage. It had blue gingham curtains and duvet cover, and was whitewashed, just like downstairs. She lay down on the bed, and it felt very soft and comfortable. On the wall opposite the bed, there was a painting of a beautiful pink hibiscus. The cottage was perfect, and Rachel could already feel herself beginning to relax.

Rachel went back downstairs, her rumbling stomach telling her that she was hungry. Lunch been some hours ago, a sandwich and a drink on the train journey. She filled the kettle with water to make herself a cup of tea, and went to fetch the milk and cream from the fridge. After preparing the scones, Rachel sat down at the little table with her cup of tea. She could never quite remember whether it was cream or jam on top, depending on whether you were in Devon or Cornwall. She put a big dollop of each on both halves of the scones, and bit into one of them. Where Rachel had rather overloaded the scones with both cream and jam, they overflowed and covered her top lip. Licking it off, she smiled to herself, feeling like a child again as she remembered a long ago holiday in Cornwall with her parents, and her first cream tea. These scones were delicious, so light and fluffy, with a slightly crisp edge, where they had obviously been freshly baked. Once she had finished her tea, Rachel decided to unpack her case. She carried it up the narrow stairway, and lay it on the bed. It didn't take long, as she hadn't packed that much, just jeans, shorts, t shirts and sweatshirts. It would make a nice change from the smart blouses, skirts and trousers that she wore for work. Then she went back downstairs, and turned the radio on. Bruno Mars was singing 'Locked out of Heaven'. Rachel loved that song, and she turned the volume up, and began to sing along and dance, letting the music take her away. She had a sense of freedom that she hadn't felt for a long time.

Lea lived along the road, at the end cottage. She had been asked by Sue, the owner of the cottage, to make sure that Rachel was settled in and had everything she needed. She walked up to the door and knocked, then waited. Lea could hear music coming from inside. Perhaps the woman couldn't hear her knocking. Lea gently opened the door, to see a woman in jeans and a t shirt, dancing bare foot, her long golden brown hair flying around her face. She was completely lost in the music, singing along with all her heart. Lea actually felt her knees weaken. Wow, so that was a real thing, then. She watched her, completely captivated.

Lost in the music, Rachel spun around and caught sight of a woman watching her, smiling. She stopped short, blushing profusely. Lea said, 'Sorry, I did knock, but I don't think you heard me,' as she ran her hand through her short, blond wavy hair. The woman had the bluest eyes that Rachel had ever seen, and it felt to Rachel that they were looking right into her very being. She suddenly felt very self conscious, and didn't notice that the woman was blushing. Feeling flustered, Rachel turned the radio down, trying to compose herself. She pushed her hair away from her face. 'Sorry. Have you been there long?'

'No, I just got here. I'm Lea, I think Sue mentioned that I was helping out?' she said as she walked forward to shake hands with Rachel. She didn't say that she had actually been there a little while, watching Rachel dance. She could see that Rachel was already embarrassed enough.

'Oh, yes, of course. Hi, I'm Rachel.' As they shook hands, Lea was thinking how soft Rachel's were. She wished she had put hand lotion on.

'Lovely to meet you, Rachel. Are you settling in okay?'

'Yes, thank you. It's a very quaint cottage.'

'There's a folder which has info such as local shops and restaurants, useful numbers like taxi firms, that kind of thing.'

'Great, thank you. I've just eaten the scones, they were delicious.'

'I'm glad you liked them. I made them this morning, they're always best eaten fresh.' Lea's blue eyes creased at the edges as she smiled at Rachel, and she again had the strangest feeling that Lea could see into her very being.

'You made them? It was very thoughtful, thank you. I couldn't remember whether the cream or the jam went on first!'

'Here in Cornwall, we put the jam on first, with cream on top. Although, going back a couple of hundred years, this would have been Devon, and Cawsand, next door, was in Cornwall. The main thing is that you enjoyed them.'

'I think I tried it both ways. I have to admit that I did get in a bit of a sticky mess!' Rachel laughed, and Lea thought that for a moment, she looked playful, like a child.

Rachel noticed Lea looking at her, as if she was trying to work something out. As soon as the thought had come into her mind, it was gone again. 'Well, I'll leave you to carry on getting settled in. If there's anything that you need, just give me a call. I live at the end of the road.' Lea wrote her mobile number on a piece of paper, and handed it to Rachel. 'It was lovely to meet you, Rachel. Bye!'

'Bye. And thank you.'

Lea let herself out, closing the door gently behind her. As she walked home, she thought about the girl with the grey eyes, dancing so freely, and smiled to herself.

Rachel awoke late the next morning. She idly stretched and yawned, then sat up in bed. The sun was shining through the curtains, and Rachel felt relaxed and refreshed after such a good night's sleep. She realised that she would need to go shopping for some cereal, bread and a few other essentials. Having a lay-in was a rare luxury for Rachel, and by the time she had dragged herself out of bed and had a shower, it was late morning. Maybe today she would go and find a cafe for some brunch. She rummaged around in the little chest of drawers for a pair of shorts and a t shirt, and decided to take a sweatshirt in case it was breezy. After getting dressed, Rachel made her way downstairs, slipped her bare feet into her flip flops, and picked up the key. Locking the door behind her, she made her way past the other cottages. It was a quiet morning, the only sound coming from some distant squawking seagulls, and the sound of Rachel's flip flops, flip-flopping on the soles of her feet as she walked down the hill. It was a beautiful day, the sky a clear blue, like a canvas waiting for an artist's brush. As Rachel walked, she could see the bay spreading out before her. The sun twinkled on the surface of the water as the sea rippled. Rachel stopped by the low wall, taking in the beach, the water, the sky and the space around her, and felt that she could breathe. Really breathe. Just like yesterday, she let her lungs fill with air, and slowly released it. Rachel realised again how little she was used to relaxing. In London, her head never really switched off from work. If she wasn't at the gallery, she was usually thinking about it.

Rachel spotted a cosy looking cafe, with a blackboard outside advertising breakfasts, lunch, cakes and hot drinks. Perfect. She walked in and found a small table, deciding that she would have a cooked breakfast and a cup of tea. She looked out at the view as she waited, then became aware of movement beside her. As she looked up, she saw Lea walking towards her, smiling. 'Oh, hi. It's good to see you again. Did you sleep well?' Lea asked.

'Yes, thank you. Do you work everywhere here!'

'I work here part time. I usually do more hours in the summer months, when it gets really busy.'

Lea took Rachel's order, and disappeared again. Rachel liked having a familiar face to talk to. Lea brought the breakfast over, and Rachel tucked into it. It was delicious, and Rachel hadn't realised just how hungry she was until she started eating. Once she had finished, she sat back, sipping at her cup of tea. Lea came over to collect her empty plate, and asked what she was going to do that day. 'I think I'll have a wander around the villages and the beach, to familiarise myself with things.

The image of Rachel dancing yesterday popped into Lea's mind, and almost without realising it, she heard herself saying, 'Maybe you'll listen to the radio?' Rachel looked at Lea with wide eyes, and blushed.

Immediately Lea felt terrible for embarrassing Rachel, 'I'm so sorry. I mean, you're a very good dancer, it would be a shame not to make the most of it.' Shit, what am I saying. Stop talking.

Suddenly Rachel smiled, and Lea was relieved. 'Thank you.'

Lea decided she had better go before she made a complete fool of herself. 'Remember, if you need any help, or want a tour guide, I'd be happy to help.'

Thank you, but I don't want to put you to any trouble.'

'It really wouldn't be any trouble at all, I'd be happy to.

Rachel really appreciated how thoughtful Lea was, and after thanking her again, she said goodbye, and Lea disappeared to the back of the cafe.

Lea was thrilled to see Rachel in the cafe. There was something about her. Although it was only the second time that she had met Rachel, Lea had the feeling that she had known her all her life. She really hoped that

Rachel would take her up on her offer of showing her around. She also hoped that she hadn't come across as too keen, and why did she have to mention the dancing? Still, Lea knew that Rachel was at the cottage for a fortnight, then chances were, she would never see her again. Sometimes, she thought to herself, you just have to put yourself out there.

Rachel really liked Lea. People had told her how much friendlier people were in this part of the country. London was packed full of people, but everyone was so busy, rushing from place to place, caught up in their own world. Here, people seemed to take a more leisurely pace. Of course, it was still early in the summer season, and not too busy, as the schools hadn't finished for the summer yet.

It was quite cool today, and the village was not too busy. There were still people on the beach, some parents making sandcastles with their toddlers. As Rachel stood looking at the sea, she could hear the call of the seagulls as they flew above, some of them swooping down to scrabble for scraps of food that had been dropped by the children. The children were far more interested in playing with the sand than eating their lunch. Rachel spent a very relaxing day wandering around, looking at craft shops and the local art gallery. When she first saw the gallery, she momentarily thought of work. Then she remembered her promise to herself, that this holiday was relaxation and enjoyment only, strictly no work. She wouldn't think about work, and wouldn't talk about work. Not that there was anyone to talk to, anyway. Except Lea, of course. This morning had just been a quick chat over breakfast, and Rachel was sure that Lea would be friendly towards all of her customers. Still, she felt very comfortable with Lea, as if she had known her a long time.

Lea was leaving the cafe, and as she walked along the street, she saw a familiar figure sitting on the wall. Again, as she looked at Rachel, Lea noticed a childlike quality about her. So many adults lost this quality, and the fact that Lea could see it in Rachel made her smile to herself. She was going to walk on by and head home, but she felt compelled to stop.

That afternoon, Rachel was sitting on the wall by the beach, letting her feet dangle down as she did when she was a child. She was feeling very relaxed, sitting there with a gentle breeze on her face. She became aware of movement beside her, and turned to see Lea, who was on her way home after finishing work. 'Mind if I join you?'

Rachel shielded her eyes from the sun with her hand as she looked up at Lea, and smiled. 'Not at all.'

Lea sat down beside Rachel, and they both looked at the sea in companionable silence. Lea wanted to chat with Rachel, but didn't want to disturb her if she wanted peace and quiet. She was just thinking about leaving, when Rachel turned to look at her, and asked, 'How long have you lived here?'

'All my life. I love it here.' Rachel slid her sunglasses onto her head, and turned to look at Lea, smiling.

Lea looked at Rachel. She had quite a long oval face, accentuated by her straight hair. Her eyes were quite an unusual colour, a soft pale grey in this light. Last night at the cottage they had looked darker, more like charcoal. 'Where do you live?'

'London. It's so different to here, noisy and busy. But fun and vibrant too. I don't think I've relaxed hardly at all at home, compared to how I feel since I arrived here yesterday.'

'It does have that effect on people. I'm not sure if I could live somewhere like London.' She paused for a moment. 'Still, each to their own.'

Lea smiled at Rachel, and Rachel had a feeling that she couldn't explain. It was comfortable and familiar, and at the same time she couldn't place the feeling. After chatting for a while longer, Rachel said that she needed to buy some food before the shops closed. Lea offered to help her, but Rachel said that she would be fine, and thanked her for the offer. As she left the beach and headed for the small supermarket, she wished she had asked Lea to help after all, the company would have been nice. She enjoyed chatting with Lea. Never mind, she would buy some food to cook herself a meal, then watch a film. There were a few films at the cottage that she hadn't seen before.

Actually, probably all of them, as she rarely had time to go to the cinema or even watch a film at home.

Rachel bought some fresh pasta and a jar of pesto, perfect for a quick and easy meal. She ambled back to the cottage, loving that she was able to take as long as she liked. At home, she felt that she was always rushing around, chasing one deadline or another. She thought how Mark would have liked it here. He would have appreciated her relaxed pace, and she smiled to herself. Then the thought made her sad. She wondered whether she shouldn't have worked harder on their relationship. Starting and building up the gallery had taken so much time and hard work, though. Well, what could she do, it was a long time ago now. Mark was happy with his girlfriend, and she was pleased for him. Maybe it was time that she thought about dating again, she had been on her own for a long time now.

Lea would have liked to have helped Rachel with her shopping. She really wanted to spend some time with her. You've only just met Rachel, she told herself. For goodness sake, you're a grown woman of thirty, not a teenager with a crush. She gave herself a mental kick, and told herself to get over it.

Rachel found that Sunday was a similarly relaxing day to Saturday. She explored the neighbouring village of Cawsand. She felt as though she had gone back in time, it was so quiet and relaxing here. Rachel was realising how different she felt having so much space to think and breathe, and she revelled in the feeling.

As she was heading back to the cottage that evening, she saw Lea leaving the cafe, her blond hair lightened by the sunshine and sea air, shining in the sunlight.

As Lea left the cafe, she saw Rachel walking along, looking very relaxed. Her heart started to beat faster, and she felt her face flush. What is going on with me, she thought to herself. Get it together. Still, Rachel kept being put right under her nose, was she just going to ignore that?

'Hi. How's your day been?' Lea asked.

'Very chilled, lovely thanks. Have you had a good day?'

'Pretty good. Busy.' Lea was just thinking that now it was hopefully going to get a lot better. Okay then, carpe diem. 'Um, I was wondering, I'm just going home for dinner. Would you like to eat with me this evening?'

Rachel thought for a moment. As she cocked her head to one side, some strands of hair fell across her face, and she pushed them away, 'Actually, that would be really nice, thank you.'

Lea smiled, and they walked along the road together. When they arrived at Lea's home, she unlocked the door to the pale blue cottage, and welcomed Rachel in. They took their shoes off, and Rachel noticed sand on the floor under Lea's canvas shoes. Lea invited Rachel to sit down. Inside, the cottage was quite similar to the one that Rachel was staying in. The lounge was a bit bigger though, with a table and chairs at one end, and a sofa, and a couple of armchairs, in front of an open fireplace. Lea offered Rachel a drink, and then said that she would start making dinner. They chatted whilst Lea prepared dinner. She was making a mushroom risotto, and sliced up onions and garlic to put into the pan, where she had already heated the olive oil. While Lea worked, Rachel watched her. 'You're a very accomplished cook,' she said.

'I'm used to getting on with things quickly, having worked in the cafe for so long. What do you do in London?'

Rachel laughed, and Lea looked quizzical. 'My partner said this holiday is strictly no business. I'm not allowed to talk or even think about it! This is my first holiday for over three years.'

Lea's face had dropped, 'Oh. How come your partner isn't here with you?' Her voice was flat now.

Rachel looked confused for a moment. 'Sorry? Oh, I see what you mean. No, Tom is my business partner. I don't have a partner at the moment. I just don't seem to have the time for a relationship. That's why I've been sent on holiday, to relax!'

Lea had stirred in the arborio rice, and had begun adding the stock to the pan. 'Well, this is the perfect place for it. Lots of open spaces, sea air and beautiful scenery.' She turned and smiled at Rachel, her blue eyes bright and dancing in her suntanned face. Rachel noticed pale freckles around Lea's nose.

'So, what would you recommend for me to see while I'm here?'

'There are so many places to explore. Personally, I think the best way is on foot or by boat.' Lea's heart started beating rapidly, 'If you would like to, it's my day off on Friday, we could take a boat trip together. I'll pack us a picnic, it'll be fun.'

'That sounds great, thank you.'

They chatted about it animatedly whilst the risotto simmered on the hob. 'That smells delicious. I can't wait to taste it.'

Lea scooped up a mouthful of risotto on a spoon. She let it cool slightly, then held the spoon towards Rachel.

Lea was now standing so close to Rachel, and for a moment, holding the spoon mid air between them, she looked right into Rachel's eyes, holding her gaze. 'Here, taste it.'

Rachel closed her mouth over the spoon, then drew back, closing her eyes, 'Ooh, that is delicious.'

Lea couldn't speak for a moment. She watched Rachel lick her lips, and so desperately wanted to kiss them. She suddenly remembered herself, and turned back to the pan, clearing her throat.

As Rachel opened her eyes after tasting the risotto, she had the strangest feeling. For a fleeting moment, she had thought that Lea was going to kiss her. As soon as the thought had touched her consciousness, it was gone again, like a feather in the wind.

Thank you for reading

If you'd like to find out more, please visit
www.sarahpond.co.uk

Printed in Great Britain
by Amazon

23981339R00196